T0120987

EVOLUTION

Book One of the Cell Series

MARK LE LERRE

authorHOUSE®

AuthorHouse™ UK
1663 Liberty Drive
Bloomington, IN 47403 USA
www.authorhouse.co.uk
Phone: UK TFN: 0800 0148641 (Toll Free inside the UK)
UK Local: (02) 0369 56322 (+44 20 3695 6322 from outside the UK)

Published by AuthorHouse 11/02/2022

ISBN: 978-1-7283-7622-6 (sc)
ISBN: 978-1-7283-7621-9 (e)

Print information available on the last page.

CONTENTS

Before 1
Now 6
John And His Torture 11
A Nostalgic Movie Called Saw 13
Lucy And Fucking Wendy 19
A Wolf Among The Sheep 24
Diplomacy And Fried Chicken 29
Lunch With Fucking Wendy 33
Heather The Housewife 34
Espionage 37
Jake's Story 39
Charlie Confesses To Anna 44
The Sheep Teaching The Wolf 46
Chicken Korma With A Side Of Deception 50
Heather And Lucy On A Memorable Date Night 53
A Spy Makes Her Choice 56
The Wolf Saves A Sheep 58
Freya And Charlie 64
We're Going To Have A Baby 67
Anna, Reflections Of A Revolutionary 71
The Establishment 76
The Wolf Guards The Sheep 79
A Present For Heather 83
Amber Gets A Phone Call Before Her Afternoon Run 84

Anna's Meeting Went Just As Expected ... 87
The Wolf Needs To Hunt ... 90
Three's Company ... 94
Lucy's Introduced To A Wolf ... 101
John's Anguish ... 103
A First Date And A First Experience ... 108
The Shepherdess Needs To Avenge Her Sheep ... 113
Jake Makes A Discovery ... 117
The Investigation Draws A Blank ... 120
John's Reluctantly Taken Out Stalking ... 125
A Movie To Forget ... 128
Back To Work ... 131
The Wolf Has A New Plan ... 139
A New Turn In The Investigation ... 142
An Interesting Night ... 146
John And The Wolf Go Swimming ... 150
An Investigation Stalled ... 155
Two Wolves Meet ... 158
Cheryl Is Being Hunted ... 161
Jake And The Gang Cheer On A Savage Tanya ... 163
Hangover Sex Is The Best ... 167
Lucy Needs To Protect Her Sheep ... 170
The Fragility Of Jake's New Life ... 172
How To Trap A Wolf ... 176
The Wolf Swim's ... 180
Tanya See's Jakes Other Side ... 183
Who's Watching Who? ... 185
Revelation ... 196

Before

In a squalid residence in a poor area in a city that knew better times a boy is hiding underneath his bed. It's a common occurrence for this child. So much so that he's created a nest of sorts with teddy bears and various books to both comfort and take his attention away from the familiar noises which are still reaching his senses.

There's a muffled sound of his mother crying battling with the sounds of punches for the privilege of corrupting a twelve year old mind. The boy shakes uncontrollably and tears run down his face as he contemplates the worst that the night will throw at him. He hates listening to his mother sobbing, until she slips into a merciful albeit troubled sleep.

As if to accompany the poor woman on the other side of the wall the boy's sobs are steady and eventually his sleep will be equally troubled.

He'll be tired at school tomorrow again probably falling asleep and he knew that his teacher had reported it several times to the authorities but there was no evidence of physical abuse so nothing was done.

But then an unusual sound breaks the misery, the doorbell rings once then again. The boy looks at his watch and sees that it's past two o'clock he wonders who could be calling so late as the sound of his father now snoring is interrupted by the disturbance. The boy holds his breath fearfully until the rhythmic snoring picks up it's usual tempo, the drunken bastard could sleep through anything after spending most of the day in bars drinking with his buddies.

Footsteps now as the doorbell rings again and desperate pleas as a soft voice begs for patience while she hurries to get to the door knowing fully that if he wakes up her miserable night will reach a new level of torture.

"What is it? Why are you here?"

says the soft whispering voice.

"I haven't called you."

Now a stern man's voice full of confidence and authority "Ma'am you don't have to call us any more. The country's changed and we've been monitoring your home for weeks now."

He changes his tone now, less authority and more sensitive.

"This is Marie she's a social worker who's been assigned to your family. We're taking you to a safe place where he can't hurt you."

Now the boy hears the lady called Marie speak with a Hispanic accent.

"You're safe now Jane, we're able to help you. Where's the boys room? He'll be looked after in a foster home pending an investigation. There's an officer here who'll take him now."

She persisted.

"Best for him if you don't make a fuss and you'll see him under supervision soon I promise."

Now heavy footsteps outside his bedroom and the boy shakes uncontrollably as his door opens gently. There's a shocked intake of breath as the policeman and social worker take in the scene. Then his mother bursts into uncontrollable tears at the realization that her son's been sleeping under the bed trying to hide from a world of violence. As Marie kneels down on the floor and encourages the boy to leave his refuge he picks up one thing that he knows he can't lose, a shiny silver dollar.

The events that led to such a bold action to be taken by the police and social services to force the boy and his family to get the help they desperately needed had begun a year ago.

The final straw was the futility of yet another election between two candidates who were both in their seventies and the only possible appeal they could have for the voters was their charm and the appearance of that dependable uncle. These two characters must be described together because they are simply clones of a political system that desperately wants to maintain the status quo. These men were groomed throughout their political careers as the rare individuals that can give the allusion of free thinking men while all the time bowing down to the corporate masters who really ran the world.

It was obvious that nothing was going to change yet again, either vote for one or the other who cares anyway.

Then it happened, the spark that ignited the tinder that started the blaze.

A relatively small scale walkout in a distribution center by the predominantly young workforce. These people mostly in their 20s were sick of seeing the rich get fatter while they struggled to meet increasing costs like rents, groceries and even healthcare. They just couldn't understand why on TV they kept hearing that the billionaires was doing so well yet they couldn't afford even the most basic human rights.

Anna was a young single mum who it transpired had a hidden talent to whip up a crowd into a force to be feared. Who would have realized that the somewhat petite and shy girl whose sole purpose to the billionaire owners of the company was to collect products from the vast shelves and take them to the packaging center, was a threat.

But she was and others too. Too long had these people put up with being constantly timed to perform whatever mundane task they each fulfilled in this money making machine that rewarded them so pitifully.

When a popular worker was dismissed for taking too long on a toilet break something snapped in the huge warehouse.

Tension was as always running high anyway and the sight of the poor man who was far too old to be treated so disrespectfully was just too much. The poor guy begged, he actually begged the supervisor who was less than half his age.

Anna would always remember the voice of the supervisor as he said.

"Sorry Sam but if you've got a health issue you should be off sick."

Sam was crying now and replied meekly that the company didn't give sick pay. Anna actually heard a mature man announce to all the world that he had hemorrhoids through sobs. Everyone knew that the company didn't sway on its three strikes and out policy so they all knew that Sam was history.

Anna as she was stood watching the miserable scene unfold held a box in her arms. Eyes watering for her friends plight she meekly, quietly said "no."

The supervisor was calling for security now as Anna said more confidently "no"

Other staff had stopped their tasks to stare at one defiant young girl who dared to stop work as she said again **"NO"**

More defiance in her voice now as the supervisor turned to look where the single, basic word was coming from.

The next time the girl shouted the single syllable others were joining in and realizing that she was gaining attention Anna dropped the fragile box.

As it hit the floor the contents smashed loudly and Anna now with a scream shouted **"NOOOO"**

She was shocked to realize that all over the huge warehouse people were shouting 'no'. As well as this things were being smashed as if in respect for the box at Anna's feet.

She was storming across the warehouse now and gaining a wake of brown overalled workers as security turned up to evict poor Sam.

Sam just stood alongside his supervisor both dumbstruck by the unfolding break to the humdrum everyday routine. Sam looked at his tormentor and burst out laughing.

"Fuck you."

He said as he rushed to catch up with Anna as quick as his hemorrhoids would allow.

Security was useless against sheer weight of numbers and soon the whole workforce was outside in the parking lot listening to Anna as she stood on a pallet board platform that had been forklifted as high as possible.

Management turned up to try to diffuse the situation but as the men in their expensive suits told their subordinates to get back to work the crowd started to get ugly. It took all Anna's newfound oratory skills to save the situation and the arrogant men hastily retreated.

Eventually the police arrived to try to pacify the situation but they made it clear to those who were once in charge that there's nothing they can do. After all they'd been being underfunded for years now and felt more affiliation to the protesters than the pompous men in ludicrously expensive suits the cops could never afford.

The local press were on the scene soon enough eager to scoop the big story before god forbid the dispute was resolved but resolution never happened.

The next day national media were there with their vans and technicians all trying to get that interview with the now famous Anna.

The small industrial dispute was becoming national news and in a society that had had decades of erosion of workers rights the inevitable happened. Within two days the whole nation it seemed was on strike and they all wanted to hear Anna. A revolution had begun and a General chosen to lead it.

Eventually Anna was called to Washington to meet with politicians and even the president. As the young girl was led by Whitehouse aids she took in the opulence and was awestruck until she suddenly realized that this didn't represent her or millions like her. This magnificence represented just a small minority of Americans.

Eventually she met her president and would never forget the arrogant old man ignoring her but tolerating her presence long enough to get a publicity photo before quickly rushing off.

She wondered if like Sam he too had hemorrhoids troubling him.

Anna decided that day in that place of power that she'd never give up until there was real change and her generation had to force it. Anna was soon supported by like minded young people who were energetic and full of radical ideas about how the country should evolve.

They called themselves Cell and grew in numbers drawing not just workers but lawyers too who gave their advice.

In a lesser state maybe Anna would have been snatched in the night to end up in some government dungeon destined to suffer before disappearing. But this was a democracy and didn't do that kind of thing besides the dye was well and truly cast and the riots that would result would be catastrophic.

Instead the establishment allowed Cell to grow and accepted their right to become a political party and when they demanded fresh elections there would be elections. It was arrogantly assumed those young people would embarrass themselves but instead they won by a landslide.

The evolution was about to begin.

Now

"Shit bollocks and fuck it"

Heather left a trail of profanities behind her as she rushed through her chaotically disorganized flat. Heather lived in a standard ground floor flat. All over the country accommodations comprised mainly of houses split into two flats one up one down.

She'd stayed up late last night with her girlfriend Lucy who'd left early to get back to her district ready for work, bitch, how did she do it? They'd been up half the night fucking like a couple of teenagers and that bitch just gets up at stupid o'clock and swans off. Un fucking believable.

Heather was hooked though and as the young girl hastily sipped a scolding hot cup of coffee she smiled at the thought that she might have actually fallen in love. They had clicked straight away and seemed made for each other but my god the sex was enough to make a nun love her.

Heather was twenty four years old and a small girl but with a confident big personality.

As the TV played in her living room Heather pulled on her knickers and carried on rushing. But not before she had a chance to check out her beautifully created tattoos and several piercings which in a past era would have labelled her but not in this new world. She had short purple hair that showed off the artwork on her neck of a strikingly beautiful dragon tattoo with purple scales that seemed to shimmer in the light.

As she dressed the TV showed yet another montage of state awards that were given out as an incentive for conscientious hard work. Soon after the evolution there was a fear that a lack of monetary reward would lead to laziness but it hadn't and these gimmicky shows of state love made no difference.

Currently there was a man in overalls who Heather recognized instantly as the man who works at her central support building.

"Congratulations Wilbur on your achievement."

The well known interviewer obviously had a heavy workload to get through as she went through the formalities handing over the glass trophy in the hexagonal shape that represented Cell the government. Heather mouthed the next sentence which she'd heard a thousand times.

"Your country loves you."

And quickly Wilbur was replaced by another worker.

Heather looked at her trophy and smiled remembering the day she received it but she quickly snapped herself out of her daydream.

She was late and still had one thing to do and stepped onto the scales gripping the handles of the scanner, it automatically checked her health in respect of body mass as a laser scan ran up and down her slender frame. Satisfied that it had all the data it required the machine bleeped and flashed green.

If she was adequately fit and healthy she'd be free to order whatever she wants in her shopping. Heather ignored the printout and slipped on her yoga pants, shirt and sneakers then ran out into the bright sunshine and down to the bus stop just in time .

The familiar face of the driver smiled as he scanned her wrist barcode, everyone had one tattooed permanently from age 16 which was the age of independent adulthood.

The driver joked with her that one day she'd miss the bus but Heather knew he'd wait, the old fella had an obvious soft spot for her. Heather was a likeable and very attractive girl in a tomboyish way and really didn't show her twenty four years. She could easily pass for a teenager which was one of the things Lucy found attractive about her apparently.

The driver programmed the next stop in and sat back to relax with his paper while the bus pulled gently away.

The bus didn't actually need a driver with the current technology easily capable of creating automation that made human intervention superfluous. But society needed purpose and long ago now it was realized that automation had as many drawbacks as benefits. The 'driver' didn't drive at all but the social interaction he provided was essential and now that cost efficiency was just a dark history this took priority.

Heather had sat down in her usual seat and nodded to the familiar man opposite her, he was wearing a green short skirt that showed off perfectly waxed legs and ankle boots which Heather thought was a mistake in this heat. Finishing his look was a white string vest and prompted by his choice of clothing Heather smiled and enquired.

"Your day off Steve? Going anywhere nice?"

Steve smiled and took a bottle of sun cream out of his bag saying.

"It has to be the beach today Heather."

The girl just smiled and blew him a kiss before taking her book out. Steve picked out his e-book too and smiled at the prospect of a relaxing day.

Heather was reading a classic by George Orwell called 1984 and she looked out of the window as she wondered how Orwell could have imagined such a horrible world.

Life had always been good for her as she was so young during the evolution she couldn't remember anything before but she'd heard so much she kinda knew. As she looked out the window at the residential district that was her home Heather thought about the insanity called money. Clearly this was a stupid idea as in the end only a few people had an insane amount of it while the vast majority had barely any. People worked two or even three jobs just to survive because of a concept called debt, unbelievably they had to give up the money to pay for everything. This seemed to unsurprisingly lead to the rich people eventually acquiring all the money and living extravagant lives. Fucking hilarious when you think about it, the rich were like farmers and people were livestock constantly consuming unaware that they're ultimately being used.

No wonder people snapped and forced the evolution.

People still worked obviously but that was to provide for society and not to earn money. Money had been eradicated and people were clearly better off without it. As Heather daydreamed the TV screen on the bus continued showing the awards and now one was being handed to a beaming police officer resplendent in a rather fetching uniform of shorts and sleeveless top with the Cell logo on it, a matching baseball cap finished the look. Thankfully the volume was turned down to give the passengers a bit of peace.

Heather worked in the care state known fondly as Floricare where every aspect of the societies vulnerable lived from the disabled to the old and infirm. It was a beautiful place to work as there was everything there within that district from cinemas to restaurants and every accessory to make lives as independent as possible.

The care state was situated on the south eastern coast and had beautiful beeches as well as a very pleasant climate which made it a lovely place to be cared for and in turn those caring enjoyed an enviable lifestyle.

The bus pulled up to Heather's stop outside the big central support building for the care district, she nodded to Steve who would get out at the next stop which was the waterfront.

For Steve that ultimately meant a day relaxing on a sun lounger sipping drinks that would be bought by waiters. As Heather walked past the driver joked that tomorrow she'd miss the bus prompting Heather to say "You'd never leave me hanging like that Bill"

Heather stuck her tongue out at him showing a silver stud as was customary these days then blew a kiss.

She headed towards the staff building just stopping to pick up a latte from the Starbucks before she scanned in at the walk through sensor. The sensor glowed green indicating that her temperature and oxygen levels were in a zone that indicated good health, clearly she was fit and good to work today.

The building was clean and clinical with magnolia walls and black and white tiled floors, since the evolution a big effort had been made to avoid this kind of mundanity but somehow this building had slipped through the net. Heather sipped her coffee as she walked through the changing rooms. She put her bag in the usual place next to a sparkling sequined purple bag that indicated her friend was already showering.

Heather put her latte down and stripped off putting her clothes in the locker then grabbing a towel off a constantly replenished stack she walked through to the shower room where she was greeted by a friendly smile.

Heather's friend Tanya had an amazingly lean muscular physique which made her a formidable looking girl. Tanya was born male but as with everyone at fourteen years old had a genetic test to ascertain her true gender which was female. Every child at that age was given the option of changing gender regardless of the test results which were just to help them make the choice. Tanya had chosen to be female but also wanted to keep her penis which wasn't in the least unusual for either gender swap as many men these days had vaginas and even breasts.

The two girls showered in the large busy room. The shift was about to change and this was a busy time, people of all ages and genders were chatting as they went about the compulsory duty of minimizing any chance of taking any viruses into their workplace. Through the usual bustling shower facilities they noticed that a young man was transfixed on the two girls and instinctively they both hugged and stuck their tongues out at him and for the young man the spell was broken. He laughed and blew a kiss before grabbing his towel and exiting.

It was perfectly normal for Tanya to attract attention from either sex as she had what Heather described as a humongous cock. Both girls always joked about Tanya scaring guys off with her remnant of masculinity.

Laughing both girls walked to their bags. As they passed they both picked up sealed packs of scrubs in their sizes from a bench that was being stocked up by a familiar guy for the shift change. Heather slapped Wilbur on the shoulder and smiled saying.

"Congratulations on the award mate."

Wilbur grinned and thanked the girl as Tanya who was still as naked as the day she was born put her arms out indicating that a hug was in order. Wilbur looked genuinely terrified at the prospect which made both girls laugh but Heather jumped in to save any humiliation.

"She's just messing with you mate. Well done."

As they walked to their bags Wilbur heard the little girl chastising the muscular one.

As they dressed Heather finished her coffee in one gulp while Tanya talked about her client Katie. Katie was rich before the evolution and had been obviously against losing her luxury and status. She'd fought every inch of the way into her new life and eventually had been placed into the care state for her own safety. There were rumors that she'd once been suicidal but Tanya would never say and Heather wouldn't ask.

All Katie's energy was now spent moaning and giving Tanya a hard time. Yet they seemed to have built quite a bond amazingly and underneath the insults they were inseparable. Tanya was especially bubbly today as she'd found an old movie she thought Katie would like called Saw. It was in a blank case and Tanya had found it at a Bringy which was the nickname for the local opportunity to exchange tat. It was a popular venue for a day off and often people came away with vintage watches boasting names like Omega or Rolex or gold jewelry that someone had grown bored of. You could find just about anything there on the tables that were intended for picnics in the local park and Tanya loved going to them although she rarely understood what she was looking at.

Once she'd found a box with 'make up' the concept of which was lost on Tanya who'd never seen such items as blusher, eyeliner or lipstick but she'd liked the colors so she took it.

The result after Katie had explained what it was had been hilarious and when Tanya showed Heather the photos of her 'made up' Heather almost wet herself laughing until Tanya gave her a dark look.

"Apparently I'd put too much on"

Tanya said and explained that it was popular before the evolution. Heather just thought it was insane to paint your face and had wondered what purpose it had. But on occasion Tanya found an old DVD which was only useful as Katie who clung to the past like a drunk hanging onto their bottle had refused to get rid of the antiquated machine. Tanya always grabbed anything that she thought would make Katie smile and help her to reminisce about her lost life.

As both girls hugged and kissed on the lips at the station where Heather caught her bus they heard a sigh. The guy from the showers just looked at them both and smiled sadly.

John And His Torture

The place Heather worked if you could call it that was a small bungalow and like all the care state had been built from scratch so it had every modern aid they needed but most importantly it was very open plan with spacious rooms. This was essential due to the network of tracking on the ceilings for hoisting kit which every cottage was equipped with. As John was in need of full care this was well used.

Heather gently opened the front door after ringing the doorbell so as not to disturb anyone. She entered a large room that accommodated living space and a kitchen area so John could be left to relax while his carer got on with normal chores like cooking.

The room was painted in colorful pastel shades as was the fashion, green and lilac and various pictures adorned the walls. Facing a comfortable sofa a TV screen built into the wall was on and Heather was relieved to see that the awards were over and now an astronaut was being interviewed and quizzed about her upcoming mission.

"Of course since the evolution the environmental crisis as we all know has eased considerably. But this mission to Mars is still as important as ever as, if we've learned anything from those insane days before, it's got to be that our society is fragile."

She looked at the picture of the orange planet then back into the camera and said.

"We need to explore and find alternative habitats in case that madness ever gets a grip on our lives again."

Heather's interest waned as the familiar face came on to say.

"Cell better for you, better for me and better for everyone."

Heather heard the splashing in the bathroom now which like all other rooms was accessed directly from the living area. She knocked on the bathroom door and came in, John was being hoisted out the special bath by Jeff a very kind night worker who Heather liked.

"fucking hell Jeff you know you didn't have to do this"

She half heartedly berated her colleague but secretly she was glad he had.

"I'm good Hev and I know you're going to give our guy a great day so thought I'd give you a head start."

At this Jeff winked at John as if there was a lads conspiracy somehow. This sadly could never happen as John had been completely paralyzed for twenty years now effectively he was imprisoned in a shell of a body.

John heard Heather's voice before he saw her and as his limp body swung into position over his wheelchair he thanked whatever God had sent her. John took in the beautiful girl whom he'd become attached to over the last years and noticed that somehow the impish Heather actually managed to make her scrubs look sexy.

John had long ago given up feeling guilty about the fantasies he had for women he knew, especially this one who gave him so much.

John wished to himself that he'd never had that accident and in turn wasn't fucked up. But fucked up he was and that was his daily torture for that's how he considered his life having given up long since wishing for a chance to die.

It's not that John was a particularly bleak man and before the accident with that drunk driver he'd been very happy and active but that's probably the point, he'd had everything stolen from him. Nowadays he only looked forward to ridiculous highlights in his imprisoned life like the taste of a delicious meal, the feel of the sea air on his face or of course best of all a chance to ejaculate when Heather washed his penis in the bath. He always wanted to say sorry but that would be lying blatantly as when he got to the point he always willingly surrendered to his carnal desire.

Even that simple pleasure had been stolen from him today, fucking typical. Still upwards and onwards thought John and pondered on what they were going to do today no doubt lunch on the seafront which was always Heather's choice on a nice day. Then a thought hit John, if they go swimming she'll have to dry him and that meant another chance of a sneaky ejaculation.

"We're going to the cinema this morning"

John overheard Heather telling Jeff. Fucking bollocking wanking assholes.

Breakfast had been mundane as always and John was hypnotized by Heather's firm round breasts through her loose top as she secured him into his wheelchair, Heather obviously never wore a bra under her scrubs.

Oh god he'd have to snap out of this, an erection in public was always an embarrassment. Just think of something else like what movie will be showing yes that's what John will fixate on. Fuck she's bending over now.

A Nostalgic Movie Called Saw

The cinema was an ornate building designed in a 1930s style which depicted the golden age of film.

It was normal in the post evolution world to design public buildings in a way that made them stand out and this was no different. The elegant façade loomed as Heather walked alongside John who's wheelchair had been set to automatically track her movement and stay three feet away.

Once inside Heather smiled at the usher who always had that effect in a uniform that belonged to an Agatha Christie novel. He scanned them in and led them through the vintage foyer with it's plush red carpet and gold leaf everywhere. Ornate statues of famous stars like Humphrey Bogart, Charlton Hesston and Jackie Chan drifted past as they headed through to see what was showing today.

They walked up to a counter and another member of staff took over from the usher and greeted them.

"Hi you guys it's lovely to see you two back again."

The rather attractive girl was wearing a striped apron that matched her cap which in turn covered a clipped haircut. Heather and John being regular patrons knew the girl well and Heather always felt a pang of regret as the girl had once given Heather a card which was the common practice to indicate that you're attracted to someone and want to take it further.

Heather remembered the card as describing her as fun, bisexual and adventurous but never remembered her name.

John was automatically elevated to the height of the two ladies as his wheelchair correctly assumed that a conversation was beginning, it was one of many technological advances that were made possible without financial constraints. The girl waved a hand over the counter which prompted a holographic display that appeared alongside her showing the Cell logo.

"Now what genre are you interested in today? Children's, comedy or horror?"

She smiled and winked.

"We've got vintage pornography showing on screen six if you'd like?"

As she suggested each genre the holographic display changed from scene to scene representing each one and at the mention of the pornography the scene showed a couple making love but in a very functional way Heather thought. She laughed and said.

"Oh god no thanks. We don't need that today."

Then Heather looked at John's face that was at her level and as if reading his mind she reached a decision.

"Let's see what's on the horror screen please. I just can't stop laughing at those pornographic movies."

At this the girl behind the counter smiled and leaned into Heather as if sharing a secret.

"Do you think that that's actually how people had sex before the evolution?"

Heather remembered watching the last one they'd seen about a stepdaughter who'd seduced her mother's new husband. In the end he'd ejaculated over both the daughter and mother's faces as they looked up from their subservient kneeling position with pleading eyes. She answered.

"God I really hope not."

Then they both snapped out of their reverie with Heather quickly saying.

"Horror please."

And instantly the sex scene vanished to make way for a trailer of a gruesome montage of gore and utter fear inducing carnage. But at the end of the trailer the title came up 'Saw' To the girl's surprise Heather burst into hysterical laughter and had to explain herself telling the usher about her friend with the angry old lady who were both watching the same film today.

"Yes please we'll have to watch that one definitely."

Heather said and asked for two cola's one in a beaker and thickened for John. As the hologram disappeared the usher turned around to get their drinks and John noticed that she was wearing a thong bikini bottom under her apron just as his chair started to lower.

As his wheelchair followed the automated tracking system that guided him through the automatic doors and into one of the specially designed bays for wheelchairs John thought of Katie and wondered. How bad could this movie be and soon enough he found out.

The film was brutal and in-between the scenes of gore and horror John who'd been keen on cinema before his accident was having hysterics, more the pity that he could never share this hilarity with anyone. John looked out the corner of his eyes and saw Heather's distorted face and realized she was obviously more sensitive to this kind of movie than him. Heather was clutching her knees to her chin and her uniform shorts which were designed for hot weather were showing more than a bit of bare hip. John's mind wandered from the movie into one of his reveries and he suddenly was transformed to another scene entirely.

Instead of the cinema with people enjoying a rare adult movie instead of the usual stomach churning scenes of animation John and Heather we're watching the film on their own in an empty auditorium. Sat back in the Comfortable velvet seat John put his arm around the girl who was dwarfed by him and as he looked into her beautiful eyes she winked at him.

The next second small but nimble fingers undid John's trousers and his penis sprung out of its fabric prison as if desperate to escape. They kissed passionately as her hand skillfully massaged John's manhood but before too long he was feeling the grip of his climax approaching. Then Heather broke away from kissing him and as he felt soft lips engulf his penis John couldn't hold back anymore. His hands held her head as she gulped down his semen.

Then there was a light disturbing his daydream and suddenly John was imprisoned in his useless body again but the dream as it drifted into memory had been a heavenly reprieve. Like a prisoner returning from a good parole John was content to return to reality, his moment of ecstasy and the sensation of having bones and flesh that actually worked had been a rare break.

John noticed Heather unfolding oblivious to the erotic part she'd just played in his mind, Heather just looked at John and said "I need an ice cream" then she winked and said "First let's get you freshened up."

John just thought 'Fuck'

After the movie they walked as usual side by side and John daydreamed that they were in fact both walking and holding hands, in John's dream world Heather reached behind him and squeezed his buttock. Well no harm in dreaming is there.

John knew that what was coming up was possibly the worst aspect of his cruel life. There were regular public toilets in this district and each one had a room that in spite of it's pleasant décor and the nice music that could be requested on the wall monitor was John's most dreaded place.

Having entered the spacious and colorful environment Heather used vocal commands to set some relaxing music and set the lighting to purple which she really liked and had to hope John did too. The music was a chilled song about the seaside and it always relaxed Heather when she played it with Lucy. The lyrics gently played as John sensed the sling straps being placed ready for the hoist "If you're fond of sand dunes and salty air" sang the gentle female voice. Then the mechanical sound as the hoist moved along the ceiling track and out of the corner of his eye he could see Heather ready with the straps and verbally commanding the hoist "Stop. Lower"

Then that song again in the background "Quaint little villages here and there."

A little bit of tugging and then Heather's voice instructed John to be lifted gently up and out of his chair.

In John's mind the mundane and very grotesque necessity that he hated transformed and the room expanded to reveal an audience all transfixed on the center stage where Heather now dressed in a top hat and tails was the magician. She waved a wand and John levitated off the wheelchair to rapturous applause from an imaginary crowd and John floated through the air. He was rudely awoken from his imagination as he landed rather heavily on the platform with it's soft padding and rails and then after much manhandling to release the hoist he could feel himself going downwards as Heather adjusted the height then the dream of magic was totally destroyed as he felt the inevitable degradation of her pulling down his trousers and ripping his nappy or as they say pad.

John knew it was soiled by the smell and he'd been on one of his long periods of constipation until the moment when he'd heard about the movie that grumpy Kate is watching today. Somehow his body had relaxed and well this is the result. Heather cleaned John's embarrassment using the wipes from the dispenser and disposing them into the toilet which fed into a storage tank to be removed and composted. Everything was recycled.

The music stubbornly played on with it's relaxing tempo as Heather ever sensitive remained undisturbed by her unenviable task. Heather had the hose now which on her instructions omitted a gentle spray to clean John's personal area before on demand being replaced by a flow of warm air then the finishing touch was the application of nappy rash cream.

Heather had as always been really gentle with him from the beginning rolling John from side to side to remove the sling right up to sliding his trousers up but it was an embarrassment for John and he hated it. Heather as always had respected John's dignity throughout the process and unlike others didn't show any reaction which would embarrass him cruelly. As if she had read his mind she said "Ta da and as if by magic my gorgeous man's ready for lunch."

As the hoist on Heather's command did it's job and he gently settled into his wheelchair.

As they left the station they heard the self cleaning system start on closing the door as John's wheelchair moved into formation next to his carer.

Next on the itinerary was lunch and as always he hoped it'd be Italian, namely carbonara, how she knew he'd liked it he had no idea but miraculously she did and those days were special.

John would drift back in time to evenings out with his girlfriend before the accident. John was snapped out of his daydream by Heather softly announcing they were going for seafood, fuck, shit, assholes and bollocks.

Still at least the seafood restaurant had that sexy brunette John liked, she always wore a hilarious uniform that brightened up John's day and John was especially infatuated with her breasts. When your life is as mundane as John's it's amazing what'll cause excitement and the times when he felt guilty of his perverted obsessions had long passed.

They walked the short pleasant journey to the restaurant and as they passed between two giant sized statues of lobsters John cringed inside at the crassness.

He'd forgotten how hilariously tacky this restaurant was but that thought evaporated as they entered.

His favorite waitress greeted them, she was wearing a tight blue and white striped blouse and tight black trousers with brown knee length boots, a pirate hat finished the whole look.

"Hi Heather, hi John do you guys want to sit in or out today?"

said the waitress but all John noticed was her breasts bursting underneath her straining blouse. Oh God thank you for that.

Heather chose inside and they sat under an overhanging lobster pot with it's catch of plastic crustaceans inside. Heather ordered him bream mash and mushy peas off the soft menu and ordered herself a Cesar salad which made John realize that Lucy was coming around tonight. Heather was such a creature of habit.

In the background a TV played in the corner and John could just about make out a familiar documentary about the evolution. He knew it well by now as it played often and he could put the words in place as the volume was turned down to allow the sea shanty music that finished the whole restaurant ambiance fiasco.

The presenter a handsome middle aged man obviously picked for his maturity and reassuring grey hair was talking as the screen moved on to images familiar to John.

Various scenes flashed slowly in a montage showing insanely massive warships and nuclear weapons then next scenes of slums that were prominent before the evolution. John knew well that the presenter would be emphasizing the madness of capitalism and how lucky we all were to have survived it. It played out like a communist propaganda film from the cold war but this time it was truthful as John knew from his own cruel life experience.

Now there was footage of people in the present going about their days with Pan Am smiles almost battling to see who could radiate happiness the most. The scene was a park and people played ballgames in their summer clothes, all had firm and slender bodies as obesity had been eradicated through the state run dietary program based on exercise and health.

Basically if you kept fit and exercised you chose whatever you wanted but if your weekly scan showed any issues indicating anything but a fit healthy body inevitably when you tried to order shopping restrictions were placed.

John barely noticed the waitress taking the order as he concentrated on remembering the rhetoric of the program.

There was a map of the country now showing how it had been re arranged since the evolution, basically there were pockets of humanity in individual city states that had their individual purposes.

John knew that he lived in the care state known as Floricare and there were functional states like the engineering state where pretty much everything was built. But there was also the creativity state where every aspect of design happens. Everything from architecture to the design of the next generation phone that everyone will have is designed there as well as art's like paintings or ornaments, even children's toys and books.

Also the technology state that was currently busy with the Mars mission but also housed every aspect of scientific advancements including medical. There were other states and of course and they all had one thing in common, nothing had a monetary value attached to what they produced. The documentary showed different states each time so this time might be technology but the next time might be one of the holiday states on the west coast or in Alascation.

John noticed it never showed the administration state where the government was housed as well as the armed forces.

After emphasizing the benefits of living in a productive group of city states the documentary showed what filled the other eighty percent of the country, nature. The lack of humanity was daunting and miles upon miles of country were just not allowed to be influenced by mankind at all. This played a significant part in reversing the carbon footprint of Murca through defeating it's capitalism led desire to consume.

The only sign that humanity even still existed in areas that ranged from forests to deserts were the monorail lines that linked the states and remnants of towns and cities being rapidly reclaimed by nature. But even the monorails were built on concrete pylons and the trains ran thirty feet above ground and had little impact on those natural havens.

As the busty piratical waitress served their lunches John saw the familiar face on the screen and he just thought 'Cell better for you, better for me and better for everyone'

Lucy And Fucking Wendy

Lucy woke up early as normal and stretched out in her extra large bed, as a six foot tall lady she qualified for it. She slipped her legs out of the covers and stretched again.

Her body ached from the strenuous activity she'd had with Heather the night before. Lucy took a moment to acclimatize herself to consciousness and not for the first time reminded herself that her flat desperately needed decorating. As Lucy considered her tired flat décor she remembered that she had a busy day today and decided that a good run would be in order to set her up.

As Lucy stepped out from the communal hallway into the brilliant sunshine she immediately brightened up. As always she took time to warm up slowly before clicking her watch timer and kicking into her stride at her designated spot.

Today was going to be the day she broke forty minutes for her route that measured just over ten kilometers.

Forty one minutes and twenty four seconds later she clicked her watch as she reached the corner shop and pulled a face acknowledging that she hadn't hit her time but jogged slowly across the road to her flat.

Traffic was a thing of the past in this world as most people used the bus's.

Lucy noticed the unusual sight of grey clouds in the sky as she opened her door to the hallway then she just shrugged and bounded up the steps to her upstairs flat.

Lucy had opted for an upstairs flat as it was known as she wanted privacy as well as a bit of a view and as she walked into her living room the brightness hit her. She walked across to the kitchenette and made herself a coffee which she sipped as she texted Heather.

"Hi gorgeous I've just got back from a run and need to hear your voice. Can I call you after my shower?"

Lucy put the mobile phone down on the counter which she'd chosen in blue simply because the other option was pink and she couldn't bear to think of her having a Barbie phone as people called them. She laughed as she remembered that Heather had a pink phone.

Lucy stepped out of her Lycra shorts and pulled off her sports bra as she walked through to shower.

Lucy thought of Heather while the Luke warm water cascaded down her firm body. She masturbated eventually screaming Heather's name as she reached a climax her body quivering with pleasure and her knees giving way.

When Lucy had dried off she went through to the kitchen and made herself a fresh coffee as she looked at her phone. She couldn't stop a smile as she saw the message agreeing to her request, Lucy told her flat system to phone Heather and felt a pang of anticipation as it rang.

"Well hello you fucking sexy bitch."

Heather's impish voice echoed around the spacious apartment.

"I've just been thinking about you."

Lucy replied. Heather somehow read Lucy's mind and in a soft voice just said.

"Did I make you climax?"

"Oh yes you did"

"Good because I want nothing more than to do that for you, you know that I'm yours."

Heather said in a more serious tone.

Lucy found herself smiling manically at the effect the conversation was having on her and carried on sipping her coffee. But she felt the need to ground things a bit and drew the subject onto something slightly less provocative.

"Am I coming to yours this weekend babe?"

The reply retorted back instantly.

"Oh fuck yes please."

Lucy looked at the time which bought her crashing down to earth and told her lover that she really had to go.

She dressed in her trouser suit that she felt was more appropriate for the day ahead, it was acceptable to wear official looking shorts with her blouse and jacket for work but she felt that the last thing her day needed was her legs and bum on display. She remembered the grey clouds that she'd seen and decided that trousers and jacket were definitely called for.

As the now suited Lucy walked across the road to the corner shop she couldn't stop a spring in her stride and her smile was evident.

Mr Patel was as always at his shop that never seemed to close and had her paper ready as she entered.

"Here you are Lucy now you have a safe day and catch lots of baddies."

He knew her profession and as many of his generation had allusions of an exciting life for her that only belonged in movies nowadays.

Lucy as always humored the man and winked as she said.

"Officer Lucy's going to clean up this here town."

She made a pistol with her fingers and imitated blowing gun smoke away from the barrel. The older man smiled at the joke and hoped for her safety inwardly as Lucy walked out the shop thinking that a bit of excitement in her work-life would be a fucking miracle.

Lucy liked to walk into her work and enjoyed the stretch after a strenuous run, she stopped at a Starbucks outside her work and had time to skip through the paper while slowly eating a croissant and sipping her coffee.

There was friction apparently in the government in the capitol but that was normal, this time over the death penalty that had been the one and only dictated act from Anna who everyone knew was in charge in spite of the allusion of democracy. There was a strong feeling after the evolution that it had to go but Anna was adamant and being the hero of the time she wasn't crossed.

As Lucy looked up from her paper she saw a familiar guy walking towards her, the barista smiled at her and somewhat nervously said.

"Do you want a top up? Or another croissant?"

Lucy had suspected that he was keen on her for a while now and braced herself for the inevitable card but none came and she just declined and thanked the young guy. As he tactfully retreated she went back to her paper.

There was an article about the coming state national games which filled Lucy with pride as she knew Tanya through Heather and Tanya was favorite for gold in the MMA event.

But then a headline caught her eye "Cop brutally murdered in the engineering district"

It said that police were heading up a manhunt and appealed to the public for information. Wow that's dreadful she thought but silently suppressed the feeling of jealousy that they had a real crime to investigate. Lucy shrugged the guilty thought off then picked up her coffee and left the busy coffee shop heading to her office.

Lucy walked up the stairs as usual and strolled through the large open plan room that housed the different departments of local police.

As Lucy passed domestic incidents she saw a middle aged man being interviewed and just made out the gist of the conversation. Lucy couldn't help exchanging a stare with the man she now knew assaulted his wife. He really didn't look the type and had an officious looking moustache and wore a smart outfit of short skirt and a button up shirt. Lucy couldn't help but look at him with disdain making him guiltily avert his gaze.

Her interference in the interview won her a glare from the officer investigating making Lucy pick up pace.

When she got into her section she was accosted by Wendy who as usual was stressed.

"Fucking hell Luce that wanker Channing has been fighting again"

Lucy held a hand up to stop her partner and reminded her of their agreement "No grief till I've had my coffee Wendy you know that" Lucy and Wendy were in sole charge of social violence which basically involved any incident that took place between strangers. It was a shit job and unlike Wendy who was old enough to remember the time before the evolution when crime was out of control Lucy hated the mundanity. To say it was a bit dull was a huge understatement and again the guilty thought about that murder and the thrill of a proper investigation jumped to mind. Lucy slumped into her chair and picked up the recently added picture of her and Heather.

Ten minutes later a slightly mollified Wendy was explaining that the miscreant in question had got hold of some hard liquor and tried to leave the uncompliant district which was forbidden on account of his history of violence.

His district was home to those criminals and people who could not or more often would not adhere to society life and was to a degree the unspoken threat that encouraged people to comply. Not that much encouragement was needed as nowadays life was good and there was an abundance of what was once considered luxuries.

For example mobile phones that had once been a cause of competition and jealousy with so many being developed in competition to each other were now just one model. The best model in fact that technology was capable of producing.

T only competition was between the designers in the tech district to get their work approved. In order to appeal to the government assessor's that design had to be totally up to date with as long a lifespan as possible, No more built in obsolescence with it's insane wastefulness.

But regardless of the progress society had made there were still some who didn't accept it. There were no children in the unaffiliated district as the concept of reproduction was a matter for official consent and like elsewhere it was easy to enforce through an additive in the food and water.

This was an unspoken aspect of modern life but everyone accepted it as necessary. Many applied for parenthood and we're assessed based on psychological and intellectual viability, eugenics was just another accepted part of life in this new society.

Most of the uncompliant district were likely to stay there for their pitiful unproductive lives but some did eventually integrate into society and this potential was seen via constant monitoring from drones and cctv. The system constantly monitored and would flag up antisocial behavior to the relative department of compliance like Lucy and Wendy who were assigned to police cases of social violence. Out of all their charges the most unlikely partnership knew Channing very well and had to see him just about every week.

As they watched the drone footage of the miscreant assaulting the border control officer both Lucy and Wendy tensed up knowing that they would have to yet again travel to his cesspit of an apartment but at least mostly thanks to Lucy's kind nature it never resorted to violence.

Wendy had reluctantly accepted her partners sensitive approach and it proved perfect.

As the two officers gathered their things and got ready to head out to work Lucy noticed that the domestic violence suspect had broken down in tears. She was slightly ashamed to realize that she felt absolutely no sympathy for the man.

"Oi you soppy fucker get a move on."

Her partner widely known as 'fucking Wendy' broke her thoughts and they both left.

On their way to Channing's district they picked up the customary latte that always appeased Channing and by the time they got to his flat both women were a little tense but as usual the 'posh wankers coffee' put a smile on his face as it was a luxury that would never be accessible for him normally. Lucy opened up the conversation.

"What have you gone and done this time Ian?"

As usual Channing tried to justify his aggression by implying the border guard had "looked at him as if he was a queer!"

Wendy stood in the doorway registered the chaotic mess and filth that always left her feeling in need of a shower. She could smell the sweet odor of marijuana but that wouldn't be a problem these days, her mind wandered back to the old days when drugs were illegal but alcohol and obesity killed people in huge numbers. She felt the inkling of a headache coming on as the nice copper talked to the thug.

A Wolf Among The Sheep

John was dozing in bed that afternoon, the lights were a dull green and gentle music played on the house system when he heard the doorbell.

He could just about make out the soft voice of Caroline the manager and strained to listen to the words but to no avail as currently whale sounds which had been put on to relax him were frustrating him by drowning out the voices.

"Hi Heather I've just come to let you know that I'm bringing a new guy to introduce to John later, he's from the engineering state and his name's Jake. He's applied for a transfer I think he'll be great for John."

Immediately Heather felt a tension building up in her shoulders and reprimanded herself mentally then said "but John's so complex to look after do you think a newbie will cope?"

Heather had a very close attachment to John that bordered on unprofessional which Caroline was very worried about and the kindhearted softie of a manager persisted.

"He'll be great Hev just you see and I'm putting him on to shadow you for a week so you can mold him into shape."

Caroline let out a sigh and decided to come clean with her subordinate.

"Heather I'm going to be honest with you, I'm getting pressured to split you and John up."

As she said it she saw a visible change in the young girl, but before she could say anything Caroline jumped in "I'd never take you away from him you know that surely, but I thought that if I could introduce a guy to John the brain brigade might ease off"

She was referring to the psychology team who assessed John and his life regularly. Heather hated them as she felt they assumed too much without actually knowing him. She recovered her emotional slip and conceded saying "Well I guess John is a bit crowded with us girls and he could do with the male company"

It's a fact that even now with gender not being restrictive in any aspect of society, care workers were predominantly women. Caroline gave Heather a huge hug and left after reassuring her that her security as John's guardian angel was not in threat.

Heather slumped into the soft sofa and wondered what this new guy would bring to there lives. Inevitably Heather's mind wandered off to Lucy and how she'd surprised her with an aggressive sensual nature amazingly as she had such a gentle character in every other situation.

Heather's mind drifted back to that first night together when they went silently up to Heather's bedroom. They kissed passionately until Lucy thrust her onto the bed and hungrily undressed the younger girl who was feeling a degree of shock but that emotion was dwarfed by her arousal as Lucy held her buttocks and her tongue explored Heather's body. Lucy was sending her into spasms of ecstasy until Heather unable to hold off any more climaxed violently holding her lovers head firmly in the position she desperately needed. As Heather was lying back trying to recover herself she sensed the now naked Lucy moving up her body until Lucy tantalizingly kneeled over Heather's face. To both of their surprise Heather was greedily stretching her neck in order to reach that beautiful source of pleasure. Lucy proceeded to tease her lover for what seemed an eternity and after climaxing on her they both collapsed into each other's arms to fall asleep.

Heather was snapped out of her daydream by a soft voice from the living room monitor that informed her that John was waking up, it always amazed Heather and someone once explained how it works off the activity in his brain but Heather was unable to understand the science.

She didn't finish till six officially but Tracy on the evening shift had kindly said she'd come in at five knowing how eager her friend would be to get home and start her three day weekend.

Shifts of work were based on age so Heather being young did four eight hour days a week and Tracy being over fifty only did four hours of four days. Work in this world nowadays was about productivity and the need to fulfill a role as opposed to the need to earn hourly pay. This meant that people worked hours that fitted into their ability and lifestyle not the constant need to earn money to meet the constantly increasing costs.

They'd both liked their different shifts for Heather liked evenings off to go out with her friends and Tracy who's husband had passed away some years ago enjoyed sitting with John in the evenings.

Heather noticed the TV was on a familiar program, it was a soap opera and unlike the vintage stuff she'd seen when Tanya got a DVD from a Bringy the storyline was generally positive. Heather often wondered how people had expected society to function in the before but then again it didn't really.

She looked at the TV show and smiled at the scene that depicted a pretty girl and her boyfriend in Alascation which was one of the most popular holiday states.

The setting was a beautiful lodge and Heather recalled that the storyline was a love triangle among staff but she knew from experience that they'd end up finding a solution, probably a three way relationship.

The scene between the lovers was broken as the actors playing guests marched in after a hike.

The carer told the TV to pause while she attended to John not wanting to miss any of one of her favorite programs. Heather knocked on John's bedroom door and asked the voice recognition for gentle pink lighting and their wake up mix which played while she controlled the ceiling hoist with voice commands. As she hooked the straps into place and said "up" Heather wondered when technology would totally replace her but she knew that was pointless nowadays as there's no longer financial incentive to cut costs that had caused such suffering in the past.

All the time music played in the background at a gentle volume and John's angel wondered what he was thinking.

John was wondering if there was a God interestingly because before the accident he'd been a fairly good catholic but since the disaster that stole his freedom he couldn't accept any deity that'd be so cruel to him.

Anyway his thoughts were disturbed by the doorbell sounding which sent John's mind off in a frenzy of activity, too early for Tracy and no normal visits on a Friday. Heather shouted that they'd be out soon and Caroline's voice acknowledged.

John was intrigued by this turn of events and wondered what caused two visits in one day as his wheelchair silently conveyed him into the living room which was the default after a nap. Behind he could hear Heather straightening the bed.

The excitement of a break in routine was gripping John right up to him seeing that face.

How could they allow this person into John's world?

John had always been a good judge of character and somehow his disability had enhanced that sense although he had no idea how. Maybe it was an evolutionary survival trait but John was convinced that he was confronted with evil as he saw that face for the first time. As the ever attentive Caroline introduced John to the man called Jake the crippled helpless man's mind was running wild trying to catch up with the new twist in his personal horror story. Heather told the TV to change channel and the lodge scene disappeared.

As the news played Heather asked what drinks everyone wanted, having taken the requests John's favorite carer retreated to the kitchenette. John was in his usual spot next to the sofa and thankfully Caroline was next to him but on her other side was that man who was triggering all John's alarms. Eventually Heather returned with the drinks.

As the others chatted over tea and biscuits John's mind drifted back to a different time, before he'd come to this place when he'd lived in New York. In the background the TV reported the latest successful stage of the Evolution space mission that was a first step on the road towards colonization of Mars. That inhospitable planet was deemed to be mankind's best hope if the evolution experiment failed and we resorted back to the self destructive path of capitalism.

But John's perception of the TV was subconscious as his mind took him to a living room that was sparse with magnolia colored walls and special furniture that appealed only for it's ability to be wiped clean. Nevertheless there were two dominant smells that John's sinuses always picked up and they were urine and disinfectant.

John was in a very crude wheelchair compared to the technological miracle he has now but others around him sat in armchairs and followed their normal routines from rocking to muttering nonsense. At least no one was masturbating today, that always caused chaos if the staff saw it which wasn't often, normally John had to just sit and watch someone enjoy yet another pleasure that was significantly absent in his own life .

But today no such torture was evident only an old style TV showed footage of national strikes that were crippling the country.

"They could fucking complain" thought John "Try a day in my fucking life" Just then John's thoughts were interrupted by two staff entering the room to take him away for pad changing torture.

They ignored him as they pushed his chair towards his bedroom which wasn't big enough to accommodate the equipment needed to deal with a body that had absolutely no independence.

Both girls were just that, young girls who barely had the skills needed for independence from their mothers. The criminally low pay their demanding job rewarded the staff with meant that anyone who wanted to start to build a life for themselves and start a family had to seek better pay or end up working a ridiculous amount of hours. So John's world was maintained by people who either didn't have the skills, aptitude or physical ability to do a better job.

Today both teenagers were chatting about the scandal that had unfolded that involved John directly.

"Well I always knew that Jen was a nasty bitch, it was obvious wasn't it. I mean she was always fucking horrible to you."

Her colleague just looked across John as they were attaching the sling to a questionable ceiling hoist and tilted her head and smiled a rather deceptive smile. All she could say was "Yes I know."

John was floating jerkily through the air now and he wished he could have more confidence in their ability to execute this hazardous maneuver safety but he didn't. The less talkative girl flicked the TV maybe to divert the subject away from her failure to stand up to a monster. But there was no escaping the source of recent excitement in their mundane jobs.

"Well I'm just glad that she's gone and what she did to this one."

She looked down at John now lying on his bed impotent as always.

"Well what did he ever do to deserve that?"

As she said the words they pulled John's pants down to reveal bruises that were multi colored and might even have been beautiful but for the means of their creation. John would never forget her eyes as she hit him with her fists challenging his body to react in any way but he didn't and couldn't.

The other staff had been terrified of Jen but then eventually Lee had plucked up the courage to go to the manager who reluctantly had no choice but to act.

Jen had been encouraged to resign and John gathered was working in another care home now a fact which added to John's already significant misery.

The real travesty though was the fact that Lee had never been seen since as she was a bank staff due to family commitments and as such she had no contract that guaranteed her hours of employment. She had been the real victim and John felt for her particularly strongly as she'd been a ray of sunshine in John's stormy life.

Apparently Lee was now working in a Walmart stocking shelves insanely in John's mind but this was a cruel world.

As the two girls went about their task in John's reverie he saw the TV showing scenes of rioters including police officers clashing with the military, the TV scene was suddenly one of far away inside a space ship that was speeding on to it's destination, the astronauts were in great spirits as their leader announced that solar panels had unfolded and were fully functional. He emphasized that this mission had only been made possible by scientific advancements unhindered by financial restraints.

John suspected the guy was reading a well learned speech meant to push a political point. Then suddenly a familiar young girls face saying "Cell good for you, good for me and good for everyone."

John was suddenly not interested in the TV anymore and there was a more pressing matter that required his attention, one of survival that had been triggered by another menacing person entering his world. It was standing right over him now and he could hear the words it used to win over those John needed to protect him. Just another kick in the teeth for a guy who's had to live through every misery life could throw at him. As the two people who John knew were devoted to his safety and happiness chatted happily to a monster who John instinctively knew to be malevolent, John's mind that was trapped in a prison of flesh and bone wondered what shape his next torment would take? Would this guy actually be John's next torturer or worse would he bring an end to John's torture in some murderous way. Inside his cell John suddenly smiled at the thought that a monster might inadvertently be an angel of mercy.

Diplomacy And Fried Chicken

The airport was a quiet and bleak building in spite of the best efforts of those who were tasked with designing the countries link with the rest of the world.

All the décor was a throwback to the 1970s and the flower power movement with beautiful and vibrant colors everywhere.

But Anna just sighed at the fact that the warmth of buildings like this came from people not paint or funky wallpaper and people were missing. Well hopefully soon she could fix that she thought to herself as she patiently awaited the one flight due in today.

Anna and her equally bored security guard sat and drank coffee in the Starbucks which with the whole airport had opened for this flight.

"The problem Charlie is that we need to be a part of the global community"

Charlie was a broad and strong woman with fiery red hair in a ponytail and had a selection of tattoos on her neck, face and hands, Anna never saw anymore of her as she always dressed unusually formally.

Anna had been reluctant to bring Charlie along but her confidant Paul had insisted and anyway Anna liked Charlie who always spoke openly. In a rather too masculine voice the security professional just said.

"Well boss I don't know why we need them. I mean they must hate us surely as we've achieved something that the whole world said was impossible."

Anna smiled at her friend and shrugged.

"We won the war against money but we still can't keep people imprisoned in this country. People are free to leave if they want and we need agreements in place to make it possible."

Anna remembered the people who were concerned about loved ones who lived abroad and the opportunity of family contact. Anna was determined that her country would never be a prison like communist nations of the past.

So they built airports in key States so people could come over from abroad which had satisfied those naysayers. But it was obvious now that trade needed to be rebuilt with the international community.

The barista interrupted their conversation and cleared away the now empty cups.

"Do you want another Anna?"

Anna smiled at the unknown server who like everyone recognized the country's leader. Anna declined but Charlie asked for another latte and Anna noticed a look in her guards eye she recognized. Charlie was infamous as a womanizer.

As the barista went off they re opened their conversation.

"We've got one commodity they desperately need Charlie. Lifestyle."

Charlie just looked incredulously at her boss and was rewarded with an explanation.

"Our holiday States are on the table as a holiday destination for other countries Charlie. They are considering it as a sort of detox from the stress of a life dependent on economy. People can fly from France or Britain to Alascatia or the other holiday states and have a few weeks when they don't have to worry about money."

The barista put the latte in front of Charlie and gave the muscular lady a smile that said "Yes"

As soon as they were alone again Anna gave her companion a stern look and Charlie shrugged and said as she picked up the card the barista had placed by her cup.

"Sorry boss but I just like sex."

Then quickly changing the subject back to politics said.

"Okay then Anna that makes sense but what do we get out of this deal? I mean their money is useless to us now."

Anna knew she had a valid point and many in the government felt that way too, but Anna was ambitious and was convinced that she could eventually spread her beautiful country's philosophy into other parts of the world.

She knew that if people came and saw that life could easily exist without the enslavement of money they'd return to their homes changed.

Before she could explain further they heard on the PA system that the international flight was landing, interrupting the sounds of the coffee machine that was gurgling away as a member of ground crew was obviously getting the drinks for colleagues.

The flight today was running on aviation fuel and that saddened Anna who knew that her scientists had perfected electric powered aviation years ago and she'd offered the tech globally but had received a cold reception. She had realized then that she mustn't allow her country to become exiled from the world, education was the key but not educating the rich governments but the proletariat.

Anna and her friend and bodyguard finished their drinks as the ground crewman was now loading the tray of cups on an airport vehicle. He saw the two getting up and quickly interjected offering them a lift to the single flight. They both accepted gratefully and sat opposite each other behind the driver.

The first impression that hit Anna as Johansson stepped off the Norwegian aircraft that had been acquired for this diplomatic mission was excess. Walking down the stairwell from the plane was an army of diplomats and bodyguards, it made Anna and Charlie seem insignificant in comparison.

In the beautiful sunshine Anna felt overdressed in her suit but this was another thing that Paul had insisted on and seeing all the entourage in fine clothes she was glad he had. Charlie however as always dressed in a suit fitted in perfectly, which seemed her one concession to professionalism but Anna knew she'd protect her defiantly.

The Norwegian prime minister was all smiles as his disheveled blonde hair blew in the breeze and reached out to shake Anna's hand as an official photographer took a picture. Anna was taken by surprise and took a step back glaring at her counterpart.

"I thought we agreed that this would be low key Boris?"

The man just frowned and said "Sorry Anna but it was out of my hands. The press office are in charge I think."

Johansson's English was impeccable but now and then his Scandinavian accent broke through. Anna just smiled and said "I understand that Boris. Paul even talked me into wearing this suit on such a beautiful day."

As they walked towards the waiting cars Charlie fell in line with her numerous opposite numbers in the foreign security detail and smiled her dirtiest smile at a rather pretty lady with braided blonde hair. As the Scandinavian professional protector smiled back Charlie decided that this might be a good gig after all.

The Norwegian party was completely prepared for what to expect as the cars moved through streets that were practically empty compared to their bustling capital Oslo.

It's a fact that all the world had watched in horror as the events leading to the evolution unfolded, everyone expected bloodshed but those in charge had more to fear than lost lives. The global status quo of hierarchy was being threatened but arrogance runs through those in power like the blood in their veins.

Eventually when the realization sank in that this once leader of the capitalist societies was lost forever, the modern aristocracy of the world started to fight a war on information. It had been easy as they controlled the media and there was no counter information offered to the bleak picture that the capitalist world fed to it's public.

Spies were recruited who travelled to Murca to get information on this rogue state so Johansson like his fellow national leaders knew exactly what was happening.

As they headed through the administration state Johansson thought on the fact that he actually liked Anna and really couldn't believe the amazing opportunity she had thrown his way. The car had a driver but Johansson noticed that she just monitored her passengers instead of the road, he marveled at the driverless technology that this alien place had created.

Then he thought about the shares he and his cabinet ministers had bought up in anticipation of the travel boom that the revelation of holidays in Murca would create. There was no downside at all as far as he could see, people would get holidays and him and his cronies would get rich. To Johansson's delight the fleet of cars pulled up at a KFC and he looked at Anna beside him saying.

"You read my mind I'm starving Anna."

Then he sighed and said in an altogether less enthusiastic voice.

"Of course you know my security will need to sweep the building."

Anna just laughed and nodded towards Charlie sat in the front next to the driver.

"So will mine Boris, so will mine."

Lunch With Fucking Wendy

Lucy and Wendy had had a very normal morning for them with interviewing Channing then on to speak to the officer he'd assaulted. When finally they'd done as much as they could on this case they went for lunch.

As the sombrero clad waiter complete with checkered shirt and cowboy chaps walked up to take their order Wendy's voice suddenly broke through the murmuring of discreet customers.

"Of course she fucking won't have a baby with you, you fucking twat. What do you think?"

The waiter knowing his customers well turned back to walk away and Lucy looked at the older couple on the next table and said.

"I'm really sorry but I'm going to ask my girlfriend to have a baby with me tonight and my buddy here is trying to Tell me to stop worrying."

To her surprise the man looked straight at Lucy and said.

"When I was going to ask Frances I almost fucking shit myself but here we are now two adult daughters and a grandchild on the way."

At this all four diners burst into laughter until the lady called Frances just said.

"Do it, you won't regret it."

The mood became light-hearted and after the waiter bravely took their orders the two police officers joked with each other until the faux bandito returned with Lucy's light salad and Wendy's usual burger and chips.

"I'm just bored to death Wendy."

Lucy confessed.

"We go around telling people off for being rowdy and nothing ever changes. They still keep on drinking and kicking off."

Wendy sighed and went into her usual diatribe that she saved for Lucy's moments.

"You're just young babe and you don't have my perspective. Back before the evolution it was fucking insane with druggies and muggers every fucking where. No Lucy I fucking love the boredom."

Lucy just smiled and confessed.

"I just wish one day we'd have a real crime to investigate."

Heather The Housewife

Heather had got home in time to clean her flat and put on her most fuck me now outfit. It was leather shorts and a tight top that clung to her small breasts and also showed her sexy flat stomach. If Lucy didn't drag her to bed and fuck her senseless as soon as she walked in the door she'd have to take the lead and that wasn't the outlook that was driving Heather into a frenzy of lustfulness.

Heather loved being submissive to Lucy's dominant character and they just seemed to fit together perfectly but she'd just have to get a grip cause her lover and mistress wouldn't be there for an hour yet.

She decided to catch up on the TV show that had been interrupted by the introduction to the new guy.

"Play 'Alascation nights' ."

Heather ordered her home system and it immediately started the TV show from where she'd left off as the hikers continued to invade the moment that the two key characters had been having. Heather sat down and watched as the actor who played a ranger and was the third party in the love triangle entered the scene.

Meanwhile Lucy was stressing about the question she wanted to ask soon.

As she so wanted a baby and it was a worry that the younger Heather wouldn't.

As the monorail train silently glided to Heather's district it was all that she could think about.

On a screen at the end of the train was a familiar information clip about the decadent transport before the evolution burning fossil fuels. Now it said that with our windfarms and new technology harnessing energy from the sea electricity was abundant, the documentary ended with the slogan "Cell, better for you, better for me, and better for the future."

Lucy barely registered the screen as she was anxious, so much so that she had a rum and cola from the refreshments car to calm her nerves.

As she scanned her arm in the station it was all she thought about and also during the twenty minute walk to Heather's flat.

In fact right up to the moment she saw that beautiful body in those shorts and those breasts. Fuck, those breasts were too perfect to resist. Lucy grabbed Heather and pulled her straight into her. Then forcefully kissed her young lover exploring her tongue with her own as if making sure it was capable of the satisfaction she would demand soon. They stumbled into the bedroom and onto the bed hands holding the parts of each other's body's that both girls adored all the time tongues seemed to be battling for superiority. Inevitably Lucy ended up on top and lifted Heather's top off to reveal perfectly formed and firm breasts nipples that were small and erect, Lucy gorged herself on Heather before sitting up and grabbing Heather by the waist.

Heather was in a state of ecstasy and was on the brink of orgasm when she felt strong hands on her waist forcefully twisting her body until she was face down on the bed. As she lay there dazed, hands were nimbly undoing her buttons and then sliding her shorts and panties down her thighs and ankles before she heard the clothes being thrown to the floor. Now hands strong and at the same time soft and gentle caressed Heather's pert buttocks.

Heather had a firm bum that she knew people often stared at.

Then Heather felt her body quivering as her buttocks were eased apart and as she felt the warm moistness of Lucy's tongue invading the part of her body that for most girls was too private she screamed in a mind-blowing orgasm.

Afterwards they enjoyed a take away then cuddled on the sofa with a movie and shared a marijuana cigarette that Lucy had bought.

Drugs were legalized soon after the evolution and marijuana was grown as freely as any crop in the agricultural state.

The thing that had been torturing Lucy had been shadowed by the feeling that she felt for the first time in her life, she might be actually in love. Lucy had been in relationships before but somehow Heather was different, maybe it was her youth yes that was likely it.

Lucy thought of the extensive sex education at school when Lucy had learned about girls and boys and discovered her sexuality. Apparently in the days before the change there were labels for different preferences and Lucy would have been called a lesbian.

But that thought seemed too ridiculous now like the concept of labeling different races, after all everyone's the same deep down.

Heather had been telling Lucy about her day at work and the movie that Katie must have watched.

Lucy had her legs wrapped around Heather's waist and was stroking her lovers hair when the conversation caught her attention.

"Then there's the new guy at work who freaked me out hun. He seems weird but I can't think why"

Heather said then she quickly added.

"Maybe I'm just being over protective of John."

Heather unlocked Lucy's long legs and went to the kitchenette to get the bottle of wine while Lucy admired her naked bum. They rarely dressed at either of their flats and there was no false modesty or prudishness, both girls were fully aware that the other was as infatuated as herself.

As Heather poured the wine and settled back into the embrace of those thighs Lucy aired her concern.

"Maybe you are overreacting but me and Wendy could do a bit of quiet digging if you like. You know people should trust their gut feelings more, they're normally right."

Heather was laughing now uncontrollably but when she recovered she said.

"Sorry Lucy but the thought of Wendy and quiet just set me off."

Both girls appreciated the improbability and as they shared the humor Heather twisted around and nuzzled up to Lucy's chest which was always comforting.

At this point Lucy remembered the question and while stroking Heather's cheek and feeling her lover in her embrace felt confident enough to ask.

Espionage

It had been a fucking long day and Charlie needed a drink badly. She never drank on duty but now at the end of such a full and stressful day she knew she had to have something to dull her senses or she'd never get to sleep.

Anna was at home in her modest house and Charlie's relief had taken over at nine o'clock to stay up all night on vigil and the exhausted bodyguard was crossing the street from her charge's residence.

She looked across the road to the guest residence which had been built to accommodate many more people acknowledging the need for many bedrooms to cater for diplomats and staff.

Charlie laughed at the ridiculous level of security and wondered what they were so scared of as she walked past the modernist building with it's square features.

There was a bar in the grounds and Charlie often went there for a drink before returning to her flat in the staff section, it wasn't her ideal choice of venue but she was way too tired to head into town.

When she entered the poorly lit bar Charlie acknowledged the barman who once had been foolish enough to hit on her but that was history.

"Hi Brad, save my life and pour me a large one would ya."

Brad grabbed the scotch bottle and a glass and looked into her eyes as he poured. As the measure slowly reached the top of the glass he stopped just in time. His customer just blew him a kiss then mouthed.

"Thank you"

"Anyone would think you'd had a busy day?"

The words came out of the background of the otherwise empty bar and Charlie felt a tingle as she recognized the Scandinavian accent. Turning away from the bar she saw the blonde security agent she'd noticed earlier.

"We're on different sides but both having the same thoughts."

Then Charlie raised her full glass and asked.

"Do you want some company for a nightcap?"

Her opposite number just smiled and led the way to a booth where a single tall glass of beer betrayed her solitude.

"It's not exactly buzzing in here but I think things are looking up."

After sitting down the girl introduced herself as Freya and laughed when Charlie told her her own name.

"I thought that was a boys name?"

Freya explained holding her hand up in apology but Charlie had heard it all before and just scowled.

"Charlene"

"But that's a nice name."

came the silk smooth reply.

Charlie just pointed into her throat and mimicked vomiting. Both girls laughed and soon the conversation flowed, they talked about their countries, their families and all sorts but there was a distinct line they both didn't cross.

Several drinks later a somewhat worse for wear Charlie offered to walk Freya home but the Norwegian just frowned and said.

"please not there I'm off work and want to be somewhere nicer than that shit house."

Charlie never missing an opportunity suggested her place and to her delight Freya accepted.

The next morning Charlie felt the full effect of way too much scotch and turned onto her back in her bed pinching the covers. Then she noticed the exposed naked body of Freya lying face down next to her and it all came back, they'd kissed and undressed but the rest was a blur. Charlie couldn't resist kissing the firm muscular buttock before getting up to make coffee, Freya just moaned in joy and said.

"Don't go."

As she looked around she just made out the tattoo "kiss this" on Charlie's left buttock as she left the bedroom saying.

"Just getting coffee babe, I'm coming straight back."

Jake's Story

In his modern flat Jake pondered his situation while watching a news program on the built in tv. Jake was out of his depth and boy did he know it. He cursed that cop again for the millionth time as it'd been no big thing until he'd turned up.

Jake had been a sexual predator all his adult life and didn't see what was wrong with it, probably because he'd grown up watching his father abusing his mother as a matter of routine. In spite of his mother's attempts to shelter him by sending him to bed when his dad's drinking started Jake still heard everything from the muffled punching to the animalistic grunting then worst of all his mother's sobbing coming from her bedroom.

Those days ended abruptly after the evolution when his father was deemed unable to adapt to society and his mother was given help to adjust to normal life. But Jake at the age of twelve went to a foster family and lay awake most nights waiting to hear the familiar sounds which never came.

In the background the news anchor droned on about the inter state games due for next year and showed a picture of a beautiful black haired girl in MMA regalia which caught Jakes eye for a moment but it wasn't what he was looking for.

Jake was interested in the national news. He toyed with a dollar coin in his hand as he watched and drifted into a memory of his father giving him the soon to be useless dollar the last time he had tried to be sober. The memory was the only real positive one he had to do with his dad and the coin was precious beyond it's once monetary value. Jake had kept it all these years and normally toyed with it when he was anxious and he was anxious now as the news reader talked on about trivial stuff that meant nothing to Jake.

All seemed good for the young man who trained as an engineer and been working on a production line making kitchen appliances most of his adult life.

To all those involved Jake was a success story but in the privacy of his flat that story ended as relationship after relationship failed due to his aggressive nature.

In the end he gave up and instead settled for one night stands picking up girls in bars which was quite easy due to his stunningly handsome features.

Then one day he'd discovered a new sexual adventure, when he was walking home one night after a few drinks in a bar Jake found himself following a pretty young blond girl in a sexy mini dress. It was easy to get her attention by asking her for directions then he grabbed her by her waist with one hand the other covering her mouth while he dragged her into an alley.

A simple threat of violence silenced the girl and he got to work pushing her against the wall telling her not to look around while he reached under her dress and tore her knickers so he could force his way into her.

She was trying to keep the noise of her crying down to a quiet sob which turned him on intensely until he ejaculated inside her with one hand around her waist and another pushing her face against the wall.

The next day Jake was terrified and called in sick at work spending the day waiting for the cops to come and arrest him but nothing happened and to Jakes surprise there was no mention on the news or anywhere come to that.

Could she really have not reported him? Jake swore to never put himself through that anguish again but a demon had been released that night and it had to be appeased.

So eventually he went out again this time though he planned it well. Jake was if nothing else a meticulous man and the next day when the tv announced a manhunt Jake was confident of his safety.

Jake took his old clothes and the condom he'd worn around the city in a bag disposing them in various bins no two items together. And just like that any link was gone, perfect.

Jake got away with it twice more until the end of his run of luck.

The cop had tried to apprehend him alone foolishly and didn't notice Jake pulling his knife out until too late as the blade slipped into the poor guys abdomen and thrust upwards by chance hitting something fatal.

Jake saw the life slowly ebb away in his eyes as his mouth opened and closed several times until the body slumped to the gutter lifeless. Jake just stared at the poor guy feeling in awe at the power he had displayed turning a once human being with life into the pile of flesh and bones at his feet.

He snapped out of his daydream and walked away leaving the girl staring at him dumbstruck at the horror that had just played out.

Jake dumped his mask that night in a hiding place he was confident with then went about changing clothes and walked home.

The next day he found out the body had been discovered hours later as someone heard the girl crying. She'd been too scared to move.

Jake thanked his luck but knew there and then he had to escape the engineering state as he was now a murderer and the law was clear that taking a life meant losing your life.

Jake had applied to transfer to the caring state three weeks later on the grounds that his mother was there. It was a brilliant excuse although Jake had cut all ties with her and had no intention of ever seeing the pathetic bitch again.

But now here he was a self diagnosed sociopath about to take care of a cripple which freaked him out but on the plus side that slut training him was fucking hot.

His relief was physically visible when Jake saw on the national news that police were still searching his old home state for him and Jake turned his attention to getting ready for his first day in his new job. He put on jeans and a t shirt and went through the weekly process of health scan on the system that in his new flat was in the bathroom, the light flashed green and Jake took the printout to check the figures. He knew that he'd gained weight since leaving his old State but wasn't worried to see the confirmation on paper, it's easily fixed he thought as he dressed.

Jake took a car from the carpool near his flat and scanning his barcode at the office he'd felt slightly awkward as the guy pointed towards a small blue vehicle that a colleague was readying. As the attendant offered him his card Jake politely declined but the guy instead of being offended just smiled and said.

"Well if you change your mind I'm here."

Jake was inwardly feeling disgusted as the guy in denim hot pants and a crop top winked but managed a smile as he walked away from the office towards his car. He programmed the address for the central support building and sat back to enjoy the journey.

At central support Caroline was waiting for him as he walked up from the carpool and on seeing her newest staff member she beamed a beautiful smile.

"Welcome Jake to your new career. I thought I'd meet you here as it can be a bit daunting at first."

Jake felt himself tensing up as nerves that had been unrealized started to become apparent. Caroline immediately recognized this in the man and with an almost maternal instinct she said.

"I've got you starting after the shift change as the showers are hectic and I wanted to give you a couple of weeks to get used to it."

Jake was aghast and just said.

"Shower?"

But Caroline remained confident as ever and led him through.

To Jakes surprise the more mature but still attractive woman led him into a locker area and started to undress, when he stood still she smiled and said.

"Sorry Jake but everybody showers before work here. Absolutely everyone with no exceptions."

At this he made a decision that he had clearly no choice so he rapidly and rather shyly started to strip off the clothes he'd only just put on an hour ago. The totally naked Caroline waited patiently and Jake noticed that she stole a glance at him in spite of generally facing away. Jake had no issues with his body but this was a completely alien lifestyle to the man who'd always lived in the more conservative engineering state.

The showers were empty when they entered although Caroline as she lathered herself with soap assured him that an hour ago they'd have been full of staff getting ready for their shift.

As they walked out the building both in scrubs that felt very comfortable to the newbie Caroline stopped him and gave Jake a hug.

"I know it's scary at first but believe me you'll get used to it."

She stepped back to size up the man and with genuine concern said.

"I moved here six years ago and if I'm honest it terrified me but I love it here now."

Jake was reeling from the rare show of concern expressed towards him but then their bus arrived breaking the moment.

Jake stepped aside to let Caroline go in first after a somewhat cautious Heather had opened the door. She'd been there for an hour and had only done the basics saving as much care routine as possible for Jake to watch.

Caroline stayed for a cup of coffee and it seemed to Heather was a bit keen on the new man that had gatecrashed their lives. Heather made the coffees while Caroline went through the safety protocol explaining the fire safety equipment which can cover the whole place in foam in a few seconds if it detected that calamity. Then there was the defibrillator in the hall fully automated and it talked you through the procedure. Right down to the first aid kit in the kitchen but Jake was most surprised that there was a panic command for the house system that constantly monitored every room. It was simply "help help help" presumably three times to avoid accidentally setting it off.

Jake played the shy nervous part brilliantly and knew he had won over the maternal instinct of Caroline but felt a coldness from Heather. He'd just have to play that one carefully.

"Here we are the coffees."

Said Heather disturbing the small talk as she joined them at John's coffee table.

"So Jake what made you decide to relocate then?"

Heather was determined to try and like the man so led the conversation to a personal level.

"That's a bit of a sore point."

Said Jake remembering a well planned story he'd created on the journey from his old state.

"My wife passed away a year ago and I guess there were just too many memories to stay. I've always wanted to try something different to engineering so here I am."

In the silence that followed Heather felt a pang of guilt at her judgement of the poor guy and Caroline broke the thought as she said.

"Well Jake we're glad to have you here but I've got to be going so I'll pop by later to see how things are going."

With that she got up and Heather felt lingered on a handshake with the handsome young man a bit too long. Flirting with a guy half her age really the sly old vixen, Heather had never seen her like that before.

John had watched the trio go through an introductory process and was aware that the kind natured Caroline was completely taken in by the man who'd entered their lives. Somehow though John was getting the impression that Heather was instinctively suspicious of Jake and John wondered if she'd realize what the crippled John already knew.

On the TV the morning national news was playing and an attractive young news anchor was reporting on the manhunt in the manufacturing state. The serial rapist that John had heard about before had eventually murdered a cop and John felt a pang of sorrow at the thought of a life lost.

And just like that the wolf was among the sheep.

Charlie Confesses To Anna

Anna was preparing breakfast in her modest house the same time as Charlie was having sex with her Scandinavian security agent. As she poured her bran cereal into the bowl Anna considered her day ahead and smiled while her cat elegantly strolled up and down the kitchen counter. Anna wondered if Charlie had actually managed to hook up with the foreign official that she'd told her boss about.

Anna had classical music playing on the house system and took a moment to wonder which composer had written this piece of artistic genius, she'd encouraged the arts in her Murca but as yet the interest in creating this genre of music had been disappointing.

There was no actual protocol that forbade the liaison of the security agents and in Murca with it's naïve attitude towards espionage Anna had no hesitation to give Charlie permission to go for it if she wanted, not that she ever needed it before.

Anna gave Donald his bowl of cat food on the counter but the cat was still obsessed with Anna's cereal and she had to elbow him away as she poured the almond milk.

In the background the TV was on the news and Anna frowned at the police chief from the engineering state. Even though it was muted Anna knew that he was confessing that there was no immediate likelihood of an arrest of the murderer and rapist at large. Anna knew that she'd have to bring this up at the coming meeting with her regional representatives but hoped she could add good news after this coming meeting.

Johansson had been as friendly as ever and she'd gone through the motions of entertaining the Norwegian leader but the negotiations were scheduled for today.

She took her bowl through to the living area and sat down to watch the TV as the music played on.

Then her official assistant but actual second in command Paul came downstairs in his dressing gown. There was much speculation about their relationship but it was never confirmed that they were an item which wasn't exactly dishonest as they only slept together occasionally.

He walked through and kissed Anna on the lips before telling her off.

"You didn't put the coffee on."

"Sorry I didn't think you'd be up already Paul."

Anna confessed as her friend went through to get his caffeine fix. Donald was still ignoring his food and started pestering Paul now. Paul was tolerant of most creatures but never liked Anna's cat much from the first day she'd found him, he just frowned at Anna as he gingerly lifted the errant feline of the counter.

"It's bloody unhygienic, animals in kitchens."

But as he'd turned to look at Anna the cat had jumped back up.

Eventually Paul was sat next to her on the sofa watching TV, he just said.

"So do you think Charlie would have got her girl then?"

Anna smiled and said.

"If I know my favorite security agent they're probably together as we speak."

The Sheep Teaching The Wolf

Jake was surprised to find that he was nervous but Heather was bristling with confidence as always.

When they'd finished with the mundane process of bathing their charge and he'd had his breakfast Heather addressed the issue of what to do today and asked if Jake was ok with a swim, at his acceptance she was visibly excited.

Jake explained that he didn't have trunks but Heather was having no excuses and soon enough found a pair of John's which would suffice. Jake was entering a whole new world and to his surprise found himself enjoying it.

He'd felt a sense of empathy towards John who had no control over his life as Jake remembered a troubling childhood.

Jake had slowly put the thickened gloopy coffee onto John's tongue as instructed by Heather and he'd been happy to learn that his natural swallowing response took over.

But soon they were ready to go and they left the bungalow into a gloriously beautiful day.

As Heather and Jake walked along either side of John Jake noticed how attentive she was to the cripple, it was like he was actually participating in their conversation. Jake found himself talking to him too although he'd never reply and it's not a given that he's even listening.

"We're a bit early for the pool John."

Said Heather looking straight at him. She turned to Jake and smiled then explained.

"Too soon after breakfast for him mate. Possible choke risk."

Heather just smiled and looking behind John so he couldn't see she mimicked choking with her hand to her throat and a fearful look.

"Don't worry Jake you'll get used to it."

Then Heather said.

"We'll go to the kiosk, that's always fun and it's a beautiful day."

They carried on walking till they eventually got to a spectacular waterfront and Jake as a former engineering state citizen marveled at the thousands of wind turbines out to sea.

But then as his gaze came back to land he realized that the beach was inhabited by naked sunbathers all relaxing on sun loungers. He found himself staring when Heather interrupted his fascination.

"Buddy we don't have any hang ups about our bodies here."

And for the second time today someone assured him he'd get used to it but he wondered if he ever could.

On arriving at the kiosk Jake was impressed with it and realized that if you didn't know it was there you'd never see it. It was sheltered by a row of trees from the waterfront and backed onto a woods so had a cozy feel and there was plenty of shade to be had which was a blessing most days.

Heather guided John's wheelchair into position at a wooden table off to the side which had an adjustable height setting so he was able to fit with his legs under in spite of the cumbersome wheelchair.

Heather saw a friend across the way from them and looked at Jake smiling.

"That's Canavachat she's awesome and the guy with her is Mathew. She's been looking after him for ages."

Heather called them over and true to her nickname Canavachat started a line of conversation which had to be interrupted as Heather excused herself to go to the bathroom and get the coffees. Jake found himself listening to a conversation about boots that was going over his head and he secretly wished for Heather to return.

Mathew in a muffled voice that came out almost as a whisper said.

"John poorly."

Both carer's looked at John and to Jakes horror he was convulsing, the poor man was shaking jerkily and his eyes seemed to convey panic. Jake just froze as the glamorous lady known to him as Canavachat pounced and went around to the back of John's chair to retrieve his recovery meds from his bag. Jake looked on as she took out a large blunt syringe and carefully checked the label before with her free hand she pulled aside John's lower lip to squeeze some syringe contents behind. Jake saw that his teeth were clenched as the silent carer moved her hands around to repeat the action on the other side of his mouth and as suddenly as they'd started the convulsions eased off.

Finished now Canavachat looked at the watch on John's wrist and calmly said to Jake.

"Three minutes and thirty four seconds. Try and remember that."

Heather was back with the coffees now and saw immediately what had happened.

"Fuuuuuuuck that's annoying. I wanted to show Jake for his training."

Jake just stared in awe of a woman who was nothing to him but had through sheer professionalism become an angel on demand and saved the day.

They spent an hour in that beautiful place and the three carer's and their charges sipped their coffees while Mathew did a puzzle and talked to John in a gentle and caring voice.

The two ladies had no idea that Jake was shaking after the emotion of John's seizure had hit him. He really didn't understand why after the violence he'd seen all his life but somehow seeing this harmless and reliant person going through that had an emotional effect on the sociopath.

Heather saw a tearful look on the man and felt that a distraction was needed so cutting Canavachat off she made excuses and they left the other two to head for the pool.

John meanwhile was having the usual intoxicating aftereffect of his seizure or more honestly the medication that always alleviated it.

He had been slowly getting more anxious all morning instinctively knowing that he was in the presence of evil. John knew that he would inevitably need rescuing and was glad that Heather's crazy friend had been there at hand but he knew he wouldn't be left alone with the wolf.

Yet.

The pool was a magnificent building built to an ancient Greek style with pillars and statues of gods in the entrance hall and soon they were walking through the main changing rooms with both male and female patrons in various states of changing.

Jake felt a panic rising in him at the thought of undressing in front of strangers again but to his relief Heather showed him the private room where a hoist and table were available for carer's. Jake turned to the bench to put their bags down and when he turned around he was shocked to see Heather had taken her top off and was about to slip out of her shorts. She realized his embarrassment and just smiled and said.

"Don't be a prude buddy we've got no secrets here."

Winking she pulled her shorts down to reveal a perfectly shaven pubic area and Jake noticed her serpent tattoo that wrapped around her left leg with it's head finishing at her groin, the forked tongue stretched out to Heather's vagina. Jake laughed and said.

"You're a bit of a firecracker Heather aren't you? But I'm not going to bite babe I'm here to work and learn."

On that note Jake started to undress and Heather was impressed at both his physique and his self control, normally guys were shocked by her favorite piece of body art.

John was still feeling the effects of his epilepsy medication as he felt the warm water envelope his body which was always a very pleasant sensation and his mind started to wander, John was unsure about Jake, yes his senses were setting off all kinds of alarms in his head but he'd seen Heather test the guy and he'd been fine. More than fine he'd been a perfect gentleman and hadn't even stared at Heather's breasts with their pierced nipples.

Strange things were going on but not enough to stop John from daydreaming about his favorite lifeguard who was on duty in her red swimming costume that showed just enough buttock and accentuated her breasts. She had blond hair braided that ran half way down her bare back.

In John's mind she ran over and performed a perfect dive into the pool then swam up to rescue him. In John's daydream the rest of the pool was empty and the beautiful lifeguard had dived into the pool perfectly and creating barely a ripple, as she broke surface her long hair framed a beautiful face with perfect cheekbones and piercing blue eyes.

John felt her hands on his body as she swam backwards supporting John with strong arms.

Then suddenly he was lying on his back at the poolside and she was kissing him passionately while her hands undid his shorts and freed his penis. Next her head started to move down his body and her lips were just about to take him in when.

"Uh oh it looks like we're staying in the pool for a bit longer."

Said Heather looking down through the water.

"Fuck right off."

John thought and the moment was lost as he saw the blond lifeguard leaving the pool area, ending her shift.

Chicken Korma With A Side Of Deception

Johansson was pacing up and down in the modest house. The Norwegian government wasn't prone to extravagance by modern standards but Johansson was still used to more luxury than this and it made him wonder about the type of residence that Anna lived in.

Still he paced up and down as was his habit when he was anxious and he was certainly anxious now. The whole idea of his public being able to holiday in Murca was brilliant and it really didn't take long for him and his ministers to see opportunity to make a nice profit.

The Norwegian travel industry could capitalize on these insane people and just because the Murcans didn't want money it didn't mean his people shouldn't.

There was really no downside, that seemed apparent, his people could get a holiday and the travel industry could create package trips at reasonable cost but not free though as in Johansson's world profit was paramount.

He poured himself another healthy measure of brandy from the decanter on its tray and after taking a good gulp he continued his pacing. He always hoped that a stiff drink would stop his stutter but it never did.

The politician looked at a picture for a moment that showed the Alascation countryside and wondered what was keeping his head of security.

Then at last his reverie was interrupted by a firm knock on the door, Johansson immediately said.

"Enter."

And chastised himself for the poor impression that he'd given of his current temperament. The man that entered was very well presented and wore an Armani suit that fitted his muscular frame perfectly, not for the first time on this trip Johansson thought that his spy chief hadn't hidden his status very well.

"Well Jan, did our girl make contact?"

Jan Olafsson was head of the Norwegian intelligence service and actually had no particular function on the security detail other than information gathering. The spy chief had been quick to pounce on the opportunity that presented when Charlie had flirted with one of his agents, Freya and he'd immediately told her to get into a position to advance.

The rather too enthusiastic Freya had decided that there was a chance that the lone security agent Charlie would need a drink after such a long shift and her hunch played out beautifully, the rest was just excellent.

Olafsson felt a pang of smugness as he shared the news that Freya had learned, apparently after several hours of energetic lovemaking the otherwise careful security agent had allowed her guard to slip and confessed that the Murcan people were far from happy with their little utopia.

He helped himself to a glass of whiskey from the drinks tray and filled his commander in on what his agent had learned. The only possible flaw in the plan that could make Johansson and his government richer still was eliminated.

The capitalist leaders in Europe had made it very clear that the public would never be allowed to visit Murca if they got too much positive feedback from the Murcans. The information that the two reveled in over their rather good drinks all pointed to unrest in this rogue state.

In a more modest setting still Anna shared a marijuana cigarette with Charlie while Paul cooked them dinner in the kitchenette. The smell of chicken korma battled with that of smoke for the two ladies attention and Charlie was always happy to be invited to her bosses for dinner when the former chef Paul was cooking.

Anna sat back and laughed at the revelation that the Scandinavians actually thought they'd got one over on her.

"So Charlie you're honestly saying that she thought she'd fucked you into such a state that you'd dropped your guard?"

Charlie smiled at her friend and winked before confessing.

"Three hours Anna, I'm telling you if fucking was a sport that girl would win medals."

Anna said.

"Not gold though."

Charlie just frowned.

"True enough boss I'm still the champ but she certainly gave me a run."

Paul intervened.

"Enough smut Charlie. Did she take the bait or not?"

Charlie took a long relaxing draw on her cigarette and smiled then said.

"Just like you told me Paul, I refused to share anything last night and only after the three hours of sweat then I relaxed and gave in. She said she wanted to know how life was without money and I really think she was genuinely curious."

Anna then added.

"They all are Charlie, that's the whole point. If we're going to get the world to demand to follow our lead we need them to see how life could be without money."

Paul interjected.

"The establishment have to think that people aren't happy and it's failing Charlie. Otherwise they'll never let their people come here and mix with our public."

Charlie was out of her depth and knew it but she'd played her part as dictated by Paul who had a flair for subterfuge.

"Well if you really think that they'll believe our security is that lax and I can spare a whole morning to play bed gymnastics with their security agent, then we've nailed it. I guess it's all a question of whether they're that gullible?"

Anna who had learned a thing or two about human nature during her tenure just took Charlie's hands in hers and said.

"Trust me honey they will believe anything that supports their plan to make money from their public. It's their big weakness and our strength."

The conversation ended as Paul bought two plates of pilau rice and chicken korma to them and as he went back to get his he said.

"Well we'll find out tomorrow one way or another. If Boris signs the agreement they must have fallen for our little bit of espionage."

Nothing else was said during dinner which was normal with Paul's cooking but afterwards the three of them enjoyed an evening of music and marijuana watched by Donald the cat.

Heather And Lucy On A Memorable Date Night

Oh Fuck this was a mistake, why had she agreed to it? But then Heather had never been so aroused in her life and it was obvious that Lucy was in a state of ecstasy with the control over her slavish partner at her fingertips.

As Heather looked into her mistresses eyes across the table she felt another spasm of pleasure running through her body and Lucy licked her ruby red lips and slowly winked.

It was unsurprisingly Lucy's idea and she'd reveled in fitting the small discreet device into Heather's vagina tightening the straps just tight enough to hold it in place.

Lucy had the remote control in her pocket and had been expertly keeping her lover on the brink of orgasm all night.

On the bus Heather had almost felt her knees give way when the gentle vibration hit. But in busy restaurant Lucy was having a ball with her toy as their waitress was sexy as hell and she knew Heather would be aroused already.

The restaurant was in the style of the orient and the décor was as is the way lavish to the point of crassness but that was the norm nowadays.

The two girls sat at a quiet table overlooked by a life-size Buddha which made Heather even more self conscious. Low lighting and a huge indoor water fountain set the scene as well as oriental style lantern's hanging from the ceiling, it was all very nice although Heather suspected there were different cultures clashing here.

It suddenly struck Heather that actually she was the toy that Lucy was playing with and that thought made her even more turned on. Fuck this is awesome.

Lucy was exactly where she wanted to be, in control of her lover. She had lovers before who had been submissive but it was obvious that they didn't love it. Not like Heather who clearly found this kind of relationship exhilarating and all evening had been so obviously aroused by their little toy.

The thought of it inserted into her girlfriends intimate area just served to add to the excitement and Lucy pondered on what she'd do to her later.

The two girls shared a sizzling platter of garlic king prawns then enjoyed a crispy duck with spring onion and cucumber on pancakes, but the food no matter how delicious wasn't being fully appreciated tonight.

Adding to the eroticism of the night their waitress was super sexy and had been flirting with the customers all night.

Lucy was taken out of her daydream as the red haired beautiful waitress turned up with the customary satisfaction form.

"I hope you are both satisfied tonight."

She said as she stared into Lucy's eyes and placed the form into her hand. Lucy noticed that their waitress had stunning big blue eyes and returned the stare saying simply.

"Everything was delicious."

Then the waitress was called to another table and the spell was broken. As Lucy filled out the customary satisfaction form excellent on every aspect a naughty thought struck her and almost instinctively she wrote Heather's phone number followed by a little heart. She had no idea what would come of it but the thought of sharing the cute waitress with Heather was irresistible.

As they got their jackets and bags Lucy was sure the waitress stroked her buttocks as she brushed past, maybe the evening was going to lead to another level in their relationship.

As they walked through the deserted street towards the bus stop Heather took Lucy's hand and pulled her into a doorway one arm around Lucy's neck and the other fumbling in her pocket for the control. As Heather thrust the small box in Lucy's hand they kissed passionately while the submissive Heather squeezed her mistresses hand until she trembled in ecstatic orgasm, as her legs gave way her lover caught her holding her tight in those strong arms.

Life's fucking perfect.

Totally satisfied now Heather suggested that they walk home being as it was such a beautiful evening prompting Lucy to take her hand. Soon the subject of conversation was heading towards parenthood.

"I suppose we'll have to be more mature when we're both mum's babe?"

Lucy was testing the ground but was confident what Heather's reaction would be to her question.

"Fuck no. I'm not changing a bit."

Lucy stopped walking and squared up to her partner.

"Thank you darling."

The other girl gave Lucy a quizzical look which inspired an explanation.

"For being you Heather. Thanks for being you."

The two hugged holding each other tightly and Lucy whispered.

"I love you."

Into the petite girls ear. For the rest of the walk they both talked about their baby and pondered every aspect of parenthood agreeing certain parameters like that Heather would have to stop work and in turn would be the one to carry the baby. Modern insemination methods had advanced hugely since the evolution and gestation was only three months now which was a huge relief for many people. Their baby would be every bit genetically theirs as if Lucy had actually impregnated Heather. But for now the two girls were completely unaware of all this and both agreed happily to start the process tomorrow morning by phoning the medical center.

When they got into Heather's flat they both went straight to bed discarding their clothes in a trail from the door to the bedroom. Finally Heather removed the device that had been arousing her all evening which was no longer needed.

A Spy Makes Her Choice

Freya woke up in this strange bedroom disorientated for a while and in her half asleep half awake state wondered where she was. Slowly awareness of the space around her started to make sense and she remembered everything.

Freya's looked around her temporary quarters and not for the first time this trip was impressed, this was the first time she'd been able to fully appreciate her accommodations and it was lovely. Unlike normal functional bedrooms the security agents had been truly spoiled here in Murca and her bedroom resembled that of a luxury hotel.

Freya was however in a state of confusion.

Her mission had gone absolutely perfectly and Olafsson was ecstatic at the news she gave him.

But as she left the warm comfort of the bed to use the bathroom she was uneasy, she'd been disgusted at the knowledge that her government was preparing to capitalize on a financial opportunity.

The Norwegian public will probably never learn the disgraceful corruption behind this agreement but nothing gets past the intelligence service and they all knew that Olafsson was right up front in the queue to profit.

As Freya walked back through in her silk pajama's she tingled when she thought about Charlie who she'd managed to get permission to see tonight and as they were flying back tomorrow morning it was her last chance. Freya had been impressed with the tattooed redhead who amazingly had kept up with Freya's insatiable sexual appetite and Freya would certainly try to manipulate her position to get more time with her.

She'd easily persuaded that idiot Olafsson to allow one last information gathering exercise but Freya who altogether had more aptitude for espionage than her boss had doubts. Yes she had acquired the information everyone seemed hell bent on being the truth and yes it had been hard fought for which had tested even Freya's skills.

The revelation that Charlie eventually shared that there was unease in Murca and the Norwegian people would be spending holidays with very unhappy guests from the other satellite states didn't add up.

The daydreaming agent walked through to the living room in this part of the house still in her PJs, she needed coffee which to her surprise had turned out to be very good.

Scandinavians loved their coffee and considered themselves as somewhat discerning but this blend rivalled anything back home.

She acknowledged Sven another NIS agent masquerading as security but only in passing as he relaxed with his book and as she prepared the coffee machine the reality hit her.

Yes the coffee was superb and so was the beer for that, in fact everything was more than the adequate level of quality that she'd expected. She'd eaten some of the tastiest food she ever had and was assured it was all organic which sat well with her.

"Sven do you want coffee?"

She enquired but the reply was just a gruff disapproval at the interruption.

Freya went back to her bedroom to leave her colleague to his book. Back in bed she understood what was happening and over her superb coffee Freya made a decision

The Wolf Saves A Sheep

Heather was warming to her role as trainer and mentor to this man who'd invaded her world, she had a confidence that applied especially well.

She'd met Jake at the entrance to the central support building and showered with him chatting about John and his history. She enjoyed the time while they went through the motions of safeguarding the reliant residents some of whom were too frail to survive a virus.

Heather was disappointed that Tanya wasn't there as she'd have loved to see Jakes reaction to her naked manhood but was impressed at her new colleagues ability to accept her body without the usual male reaction. The shower room was busy as usual and Heather noticed the guy that had paid her and Tanya attention the week before. She just looked at Jake then to the guy with her impish smile and winked at her him as she grabbed Jakes muscular buttock and squeezed.

Jake was not in the least surprised by Heather's action as he'd got to know her over the week and they'd built a strong friendship already but Jake knew it would only ever be friendship. He saw the object of Heather's little mischief and smiled as the guy doubled over laughing causing stares all around.

Heather shared the news that she was hopefully going to be a mum and Jake was taken aback.

"That's fantastic news Heather. I'm really pleased and from what you say about Lucy she'll make an excellent...."

The sentence hung in the air unfinished and Heather laughed.

"Mum Jake, she'll be a mum and I'll be a mum. Both mum's."

Jake was embarrassed at his ignorance and apologized.

"I'm sorry Hev I'm being ignorant but we're so different in the engineering state."

He looked a bit beaten as he said.

"Very different."

Heather just grabbed her towel and passed Jake his saying.

"You'll get used to it mate."

Those words again. Jake just smiled and assured his colleague that she'd be a great mother.

As they got on the bus that would drop them off at John's house both carer's enjoyed chatting about their charge as the TV showed the next stage of the Mars mission.

A scientist was standing in front of a large chart that showed the enormity of the distance the spaceship had to travel before walking towards a desk. The scientist waved his hand over the desk to cause a three dimensional holographic display of the space craft. Jake found himself distracted by the program as the expert showed each section in greater detail prompting Heather's annoyance.

"Hellooooo Mr spaceman I was asking you a question."

Jake apologized and shrugged prompting his mentor to repeat her enquiry.

"I was asking you how confident you felt Mr spaceman?"

Jake had now administered John's seizure medication twice and reassured Heather he was capable of dealing with that situation on his own. Heather just smiled and excused her concerns putting them down to overprotection.

As the bus slowly went through the district the TV monitor showed a familiar attractive and pristine presenter who said.

"Cell, better for you, better for me and better for everyone."

After the normal mundane activities had been achieved Heather announced a visit to the zoo. She'd asked the staff yesterday to pick up the specially adapted car needed as it was too far to walk and the vehicle sat outside the house on the driveway.

Not for the first time Heather contemplated the madness of ownership and how wasteful it must have been for everyone to individually own a car. The thought of all those vehicles everywhere was too much, for a girl used to a more sane world. It was mind boggling but Heather had seen the films showing people sitting in the torturous traffic jams. Like metal prison cells on an endless conveyer belt of misery.

Heather with Jakes help packed a bag that was essential for the trip and made sure John was prepared properly for the day out.

At the zoo the trio left the car in the parking station on charge after they'd extracted John from the back using the voice controlled winch and ramp that was needed to accommodate the wheelchair.

Jake had never been to a zoo before and had no idea what to expect but this wasn't it at all, he'd expected the exotic animals he remembered seeing in books in his childhood.

But when they'd scanned through the entrance the first section they went into was a vast open area with brick buildings dotted around with open doors and windows.

The first thing that happened took Jake totally by surprise as a long haired cat ran up and jumped onto John's lap much to Heather's pleasure.

"Hello Princey you handsome bugger."

She said as she stroked his long brown fur. Now Jake took in the scene properly and all around were people interacting with cats of all colors and sizes. There was a big lawn where people picnicked and the cats were all around them as much craving the attention as the bits of food that humans shared with their feline companions.

Heather knew this one though and Jake looked at her questioningly.

"Princey was a stray that lived near John's house and he's beautiful aren't you my handsome boy."

Heather had started explaining the situation but got sidetracked by the huge cat's demands of attention.

"Anyway he wasn't doing so well so we reported it and here he is. But he always seems to find us as soon as we arrive."

Jake was enjoying himself now and found himself stroking the cat still rubbing his chin on John's. Heather explained that in her State you had to apply for the right to have a pet but permission was rare and normally only applied to people who were alone or reclusive or both. A compromise was the zoo that had all the once common domesticated pets and it was always a popular place to visit.

Jake noticed that the area was surrounded by trees that seemed to be the only boundary and were adorned with cats in branches.

"But they must breed!"

Jake said with a shocked look but Heather explained that they were all neutered and looked sadly at Princey.

"No more fucky fucky for you my beautiful boy."

She said as she kissed him on the head.

They chatted happily about how different their states were and not just in the climate which was nowhere near as pleasant in the engineering state.

Jake told Heather about his upbringing in the more conservative environment by his foster parents but not about his natural mother and definitely not his father, almost as if he didn't want to tarnish this beautiful place..

They'd seen the farmyard animals and the goats especially had been super attentive to John in the open environment then they'd had lunch in a hilarious barn style restaurant with scarecrows everywhere and straw on the floor.

The waitress was dressed in a checked shirt and dungarees which Heather wholeheartedly approved of as Jake noticed her looking at the waitresses curvy breasts in the tight shirt under the denim. As she walked off Heather couldn't help but look at her arse which made Jake laugh.

"Really Heather you are disgusting."

He chastised. Heather just stuck her studded tongue out at her colleague and said.

"Like you wouldn't?"

Jake just thought how little she knew and smiled. Then after lunch and a chance to see that John wasn't soiled and change his pad in a purpose built restroom that was compulsory everywhere it was likely to be needed then they went to the 'doggy area' as Heather described it.

That's where it happened.

John had had a fantastic day with Heather and the wolf and he was in his prison with a different view today which was always nice. He'd seen Princey as happened every time they came to this strange place which was always nice as he felt an empathy from the cat that also had limited communication skills, not as limited of course. Lunch had gone well and John also liked the look of dungarees on a sexy waitresses body so that was a tick in the excellent box on John's mental satisfaction questionnaire.

Yes all had been going brilliantly then suddenly, well let's just say it all turned weird. The dogs were in a similar enclosure to that of the cats with the same houses scattered to accommodate those animals that were totally adjusted to domestication. There were no pedigrees as that kind of selective breeding had been banned early after the evolution. The last of the poor creatures had been neutered and loved here after being seized from those people who used them for their greed or obsession.

They lived with the maximum care for the genetic flaws that had been ignored for years until one by one they died off and the bad skin of Yorkshire terriers, bad hips Labradors not to mention the myriad of snorting short nosed breeds died off too.

The dogs that inhabited this enclosure were all bred there and had been selected accordingly as there was an acceptance in the government of the human need of animal company.

Which made the incident even more strange.

While Heather fussed over a particularly beautiful and friendly pooch near one of the houses they were taken by surprise to hear a snarling.

This did happen so the handlers who were attending to safeguard the public weren't too concerned, it was probably just a little domestic between two dominant males. A handler in his khaki trousers, matching top and yes actually a baseball cap with dog ears sticking out the top that pointed like those of Alsatians walked past John's group towards the trees from where the snarls emanated.

"Hey there fella what's this all about."

The official gently said but with authority of someone who understood pack mentality. The snarling ceased and all around a tension lifted, that's good it's all sorted people thought as did Heather who'd positioned herself in front of John protectively.

Jake was aware of the lack of dogs near them when suddenly there was an outburst of barking as a large animal that certainly had the remnants of Rottweiler in it burst out of the trees. The poor guy in the baseball cap tried to stop it but the beast was huge and it's mission was paramount as it hit the handler full on, it stopped to snarl a warning at the terrified man but held no malice towards him.

It just looked up and straight at John, it's eyes were fixed and it's muzzle snarled showing yellowing teeth that were capable of causing immense harm.

It jumped off the handlers chest to the poor man's relief but soon relief turned to horror as his vision took in the scene, his arms lowered to show the beast heading straight towards the wheelchair guy.

All that stood between a mouthful of fangs and that poor disabled guy was a small purple haired girl and there was no way that petite young body could resist the huge dog.

John was scared witless as the scene unfolded but he noticed handlers running towards them grimly realizing they'd never be in time to save Heather. In a split second John mentally begged Heather to jump out the way, for fucks sake a young girl dying to save his pathetic life was insane.

As the dog pounced towards the defiant Heather who had her arms around John in a protective stance time seemed to slow, and the third member of the party who had not registered to the animal intercepted the miscreant.

They fell to the floor safely away from both Heather and John and as the dogs snapping jaws tried to reach Jakes face Jake somehow managed to hold it long enough for help to arrive.

Handlers who normally represented the fun aspect of the zoo with their different doggy ears protruding their caps descended onto the melee and soon a quick thinking girl with white West Highland terrier ears had injected a sedative into the struggling dog and it fell limp.

Her eyes wide to the point of comical proportions when seen with those ears immediately looked towards Jake who was now kneeling up, with Heather tears streaming from her eyes looking over him.

When they'd got back to the house Lucy was waiting for them as she'd heard about the incident from a colleague who had been assigned to investigate. Lucy had decided that it was best to wait at John's house as when she phoned the zoo they'd left. Lucy ran over to take Heather in her arms and kissed her all over her face as if trying to kiss away the tears that had flowed so inevitably after such an adrenaline rush.

Eventually Lucy let go and looked at Jake who felt a pang of anxiety as the person he knew was a police officer closed the distance between them, he nervously put a hand out to introduce himself but Lucy wasn't accepting it. She wrapped her arms around him and squeezed so hard he found himself panting for breath. Lucy was crying now that her emotions had won the battle with her clinical policewoman's personality. Jake heard the words.

"Thank you."

Repeated over and again between sobs.

Later Lucy would discover that the dog had been beaten by it's old owner who was wheelchair bound. As soon as the authorities rescued the dog they realized the embittered man only wanted an animal to torment taking out his anger on the poor thing. By the time he'd been taken to the zoo the psychological damage was done and seeing the wheelchair triggered a survival instinct passed down from generations.

Lucy's colleague told her over the phone that the dog would be destroyed and Lucy sensed that he was tormented by this but Lucy could only feel hatred for the beast and was happy to hear it's fate.

She thanked officer Cortez and went back into the busy bar where she'd left Jake and Heather to take the call.

She'd insisted on taking the hero of the day out with Heather for a night of beer. In spite of his modesty she knew from what Cortez had told her before just what he'd done.

Lucy took a draw out of her beer and then began to convey the information that she'd learned.

The trio enjoyed each other's company and were more than a little drunk when they staggered to the car outside (a perk of being a copper) as the car scanned Jakes barcode along with the girls ones Lucy told the car to take them home Jake first. As the soundless vehicle conveyed them the trio continued their conversation oblivious of the fact that two of them were soon going to be adversaries.

Freya And Charlie

It had been a dull day for the two security guards and they both had been professional throughout. Charlie had stood by her boss all day and the only concession to her own needs was the lunch at the western restaurant where Charlie had enjoyed a steak with peppercorn sauce while Anna had a Cesar salad.

Freya in the entourage had grabbed a bite but envied the simplicity of her counterparts life, all day had been a testament to the different nations and their opposite ideologies.

The Norwegians had used high tech equipment to sweep every venue for weapons or bombs in a well rehearsed operation whereas Charlie had just walked into the venue like the restaurant where she acknowledged the staff by name then shouted to Anna.

"All clear boss."

Everyone got the joke and even the Norwegians found it amusing, except for Olafsson of course who just frowned until Johansson nudged him and whispered something that invoked a smile.

Freya loved the fact that everything here was over exaggerated and sniggered at the waitress dressed as an Indian squaw.

Now though after a takeaway pizza at Charlie's place which had been unsurprisingly delicious both girls were naked on the bed and Charlie stroked Freya's long blonde hair as the Norwegian snuggled up to her.

Freya looked around and felt a pang of jealousy towards her counterpart. The upstairs flat was surprisingly effeminate considering the occupant whom Freya had got to know over the last few days. There was an oak wardrobe and matching furniture all oak which Freya knew must be sourced from Murca, normally this quality in the rest of the world would be out of reach of someone of Charlie's status.

Freya had assumed that her modest quality lifestyle was sensible but looking around now it made no sense to her, there seemed to be simply no waste here. Charlie's bed was equally robust naturally and her duvet cover was pink? Freya looked at the mural on her lover's wall and laughed causing an inquisitive look from Charlie. Freya felt inclined to defend her outburst and looked up at Charlie saying.

"I'm just wondering if I'll ever understand you Charlie."

She looked at the mural that covered a whole wall and said.

"I'd never have you down for cartoon bunnies and pink?"

Charlie lay back and burst into laughter now as Freya straddled her leg over the muscular body putting herself into a commanding position looking down questioningly. Charlie felt an explanation was in order though and told her counterpart that her ex girlfriend had chosen it which explained everything.

"Believe me I'm entitled to a re decoration in two years and those fucking bunnies are going to be gone babe."

As they both laughed Freya turned serious now and decided to tackle something that she'd been pondering all day. She didn't know how else to say it so she just came straight out with it.

"I know you know."

The mood changed abruptly to a kind of the awkwardness that was descending on the couple.

"What do you know Freya?"

Came the reply.

"People aren't unhappy here Charlie. It's obvious and I can't understand why those arrogant morons can't see it."

Charlie just said.

"I've got no idea what you're talking about babe."

Freya smiled at her friend and said.

"You're beautiful and a great bodyguard my sweet but you are not a spy."

She leaned over and kissed Charlie on the lips saying after.

"Trust me Charlie I know espionage and this is probably the worst false information operation ever."

Charlie breathed out a sigh of relief and just gave Freya a crooked smile by way of apology which the Scandinavian found amazingly sexy and unexpected.

"I've hated this fucking lying Freya honestly. But I'm totally loyal to Anna."

Now both girls were disturbed by an unusual downpour against the bedroom window which added to the ambiance in the pink room. Freya as the rain subsided reassured her saying.

"It's really okay darling, I'm a spy anyway and the idiots who give me my orders are stupid. You have no idea how lucky you are protecting someone like Anna."

Freya just laughed and when Charlie tried to interject she silenced her by putting a hand up.

"My world is consumed with greed Charlie and the people who are in charge think only of money. I want to come here and live with you."

Then they hugged and now that the tension between their affair was lifted they made love for nearly two hours before they collapsed onto either side of the bed. Charlie said looking into those big blue eyes.

"What happens now?"

Freya smiled at her and simply said.

"Nothing, I'm certainly not going to say anything and my ignorant bosses think they're always right."

Freya sat up and suddenly looked seriously at her lover.

"I want asylum Charlie, I want to live here with you and guard Anna like you do. I don't want to protect people I don't respect anymore."

The revelation hit Charlie like a sledge hammer and she stared into those deep blue eyes before saying.

"I really don't think Anna will have a problem with you staying but you realize that you can't now."

Freya had already worked that out and just pulled a sad face before laying out her idea.

"I go home and will continue your deception perfectly. You're no spy Charlie but I am and I can persuade the assholes who will debrief me that people are miserable here then they'll allow our people to visit. They like me will see the truth and eventually you never know the world might change."

Charlie felt a pang of relief and was ecstatic that the subterfuge was over between them. Charlie who had a reputation for sleeping with every good looking girl she met was actually in love and wanted no more lies in their relationship. She looked across at those fucking frolicking bunnies and felt jealous of those little pointy eared bastards who will get to stay together in their permanent state of bliss on her bedroom wall.

"But how about us Freya? I want us to be together."

Freya smiled and reached over to kiss Charlie passionately before saying.

"That's the thing, if your plan will work you'll need at least a year before I can defect. Then people will be used to coming here and it will be impossible for our establishment to close the link. You're part of the deal is for Anna to invite Johansson for some diplomatic reason and she has to insist that I'm on the security detail for her favorite bodyguard. Then and only then I can come over."

Freya smiled and said.

"Meantime we can continue our relationship as my people are obsessed with getting information on your country. They'll love to have me in the loop as it were but all along I'll be working for your boss."

Charlie just lay back and cursed those lucky fucking bunnies.

We're Going To Have A Baby

Heather couldn't control her excitement on the way to the birthing clinic and it was getting on Lucy's nerves.

They'd got the bus to the hospital and we're currently walking through the maze of corridors all clinically clean. The hospital housed every department of medical requirements from dentistry to gynecology and this was the pediatrics wing.

The corridors were decorated with murals of cartoon figures in scenes varying from underwater with Comical crabs and sharks and every creature in-between to the moonscape with funny aliens. The expectant mum's were rushing past a scene with every kind of aircraft from balloons with their wicker baskets full of excited characters to old fashioned biplanes with mustachioed warriors hanging out the open cockpits.

They noticed none of this though as Lucy rushed her bubbly girlfriend along. 'She's fucking skipping now, she's actually fucking skipping.' Thought Lucy but she bit her lip and just smiled at Heather as she shimmied her along.

Lucy in reality was absolutely ecstatic with Heather's reaction to the prospect of starting a family but just at that moment she really wished the annoying bitch would get a move on.

At last they arrived at the birth planning clinic and they were greeted by a waiting room with five people in it, two couples and a single lady. Two guys who were obviously together were talking to the single lady and opposite the other couple were whispering quietly.

Lucy took in the scene with a police woman's analytical eye. She'd noticed the anxiety evident in the quiet couple and presumed that like herself and Heather it was their first time. The two guys were being reassured by the single lady who was evidently a seasoned veteran of parenting.

Lucy noticed the walls adorned very pleasant pictures of stalks flying along with babies hanging from their beaks in colorful hammocks. In the middle of the room was a table with electronic tablets on for reading but no one was interested in them.

The girls went up to the reception desk which had been designed to lighten the mood from one of tension. The lilac desk was curved and adorned with cartoon squirrels gathering nuts and the receptionist looked up from a computer screen to greet them both with a warm smile.

"And you must be Heather and Lucy."

He said pleasantly the familiarity helping the girls to feel at ease.

"You're booked in to see Mr Davies, he won't be long."

The man who Lucy guessed was in his fifties gestured to a coffee machine behind him and asked if they wanted a drink? Both girls declined and after thanking him went to wait.

As Heather sat down with Lucy she suddenly realized that her girlfriend's hand was hot and clammy in hers and the usually calm Lucy was squeezing the hell out of Heather's hand. She turned to face her partner and smiled before kissing her and then said reassuringly "It's okay Lucy."

Before long they were called to follow a rather attractive nurse who's pink scrubs framed a perfect long tall body.

In the consultation room Heather took the lead which somewhat shocked Lucy but as she was unusually out of her comfort zone she didn't mind at all.

In the bright and colorful room the consultant stood out in an old fashioned brown three piece suit and bow tie which was something neither girl had ever seen before. He was a very mature man who Lucy suspected was a bit old for that position but she wasn't about to imply anything derogatory about Mr Davies as he introduced himself. He was actually very warm and friendly and as he sat on the edge of his desk Mr Davies opened up the conversation.

"This ladies is by the best and worst job I've ever had."

He paused to look the girls in the eyes before continuing.

"I'm sure you can understand that being a part of the decision to bring a child into our world is joyous. But equally having to inform couples that they aren't approved to have a baby is a great burden."

The pleasant man seemed to drift away slightly before snapping himself back into concentration.

"I'm obviously optimistic for you both but I must implore you to both keep your feet firmly on the ground as the process is intense and the vetting can be brutal."

Both girls looked thoroughly beaten by the opening speech but Mr Davies quickly interjected.

"But let's for the sake of our spirits be optimistic here. So there's a process that follows your application and we need to take it in steps, firstly the hardest part is the application to the government which is a simple form but has caused my need for a plentiful supply of tissues in my consultation room."

Heather who had been somewhat intimidated so far put her hand up causing a rogue laugh to escape the surgeons professional guard. He suddenly looked more relaxed.

"I'm sorry my dear if I've given the wrong impression but this is absolutely not a formal process. You don't need permission to ask me anything."

Heather blushed slightly but said in a placid voice.

"Sorry doctor but what's the likelihood of us getting our baby?"

Clearly this was a question the professional dreaded and unusually for him he let Heather's use of the inappropriate term doctor slide. As a surgeon it was officially Mr Davies.

"Well it gets adjusted to meet the projected needs of society but currently there's roughly a sixty percent chance of refusal. But please don't be dismayed by this."

Lucy noticed the picture on his desk now of Mr Davies and a lady of similar age. But there were no children. The surgeon noticed her attention and explained.

"Mrs Davies and I were never able to have children unfortunately."

He smiled a rather melancholy smile and clarified that after medical advances since the evolution fifteen or so years ago it was likely that they eventually could have but they were never approved.

The rest of the consultation went off without much emotion as the now slightly distant Mr Davies explained the medical procedure of creating the sperm that one of the girls would have produced had she been male. The sperm was administered to the other girl in a surprisingly unscientific process and Lucy considered the fact that it would be the closest she'd ever come to having heterosexual sex if she was to be mum. Eventually he explained about the birthing process which seemed brutal to both girls but he assured them that it was a painless process thanks to modern unaesthetic. Both girls took in all the information methodically and Heather, Lucy noticed had lost her enthusiasm significantly, Lucy just hoped it didn't signify a change of heart.

After his consultations Mr Davies thought of the two girls who'd been to see him earlier and he took a rare moment in his professional life to think about something that is very much a tender subject.

As he walked past the receptionist Mr Davies gave his usual farewell but the guy thought that the surgeon he admired was rarely distant and almost aloof but it was quickly dismissed, he knew how much the mature medical professional got emotionally involved in his job.

Mr Davies as normal got the bus back to the flat he shared with his wife but unusually he stopped to pick up flowers from a street vendor and as he walked in and handed them to the woman he loved she was surprised at the show of affection.

As Mrs Davies held the bouquet he flung his arms around her and soon she realized that her husband was sobbing for the first time in years.

Meanwhile Heather was having dinner out with Lucy at a French brasserie but there was an awkward uneasiness about the normally happy couple.

Accordion music played in the background as the waitress took their order.

They both enjoyed the food here and the fact that the waitress was wearing a striped top, short skirt with fishnet tights and a beret didn't register with either patron. Even her ridiculous false moustache went unnoticed to the two who were avoiding a question that was hanging in both their minds waiting to be broached.

Lucy ordered the escargots to start and a rare steak with a side salad for main but Heather who couldn't imagine eating snails had salad to start and fish pie to follow. The waitress said "Merci Madame's."

And beat a hasty retreat realizing the tension.

Heather looked Lucy in the eyes and said to her lover.

"Go on then, it's on your mind so just come out with it."

Lucy just smiled and confessed.

"Yes but we're both thinking it. Don't you dare pretend you don't want to ask your mother to help us out."

Heather took Lucy's hands in hers and smiled as she said.

"Of course I will ask mum you nutter. I want a baby with you and will do anything to get there."

Just then the waitress returned with their starters and as she put the plates down Lucy looked up and choked. The false moustache had come loose and was flapping in the servers breathe.

The faux Frenchwoman just couldn't stop herself from laughing and as she saw the two girls had obviously resolved the previous tension she ripped off the offending hairpiece.

To Heather's and Lucy's surprise she said in her native tongue.

"Pardon moi mesdames, je suis desole."

Then realizing her lingual slip she said quickly.

"Merde."

Then.

"I'm so sorry but this ridiculous thing keeps doing this."

As she walked off Lucy looked at Heather and said almost in a whisper.

"Ooh LA LA."

Anna, Reflections Of A Revolutionary

Anna sat back at her desk in the government buildings in the administration state. Her office was very basic for a person in such a position of power and Anna liked it that way. Her surroundings were very minimalist and she lived a simple lifestyle, the only concession to the demands of her job was her house which accommodated several rooms for political demands like a press room.

The country had changed so much since her and her friends had whipped up a frenzy of anger and resentment at the ruling class and Anna was proud of all of it.

Well almost all but you can't change people who felt they had the right to privalege she had found out the hard way but the few pathetic attempts to change the nations direction back to capitalism had failed.

Stupid and arrogant to think that anybody would support them, even the military after the documents were publicized that had been found which had shed considerable light on the real motive behind just about every conflict since world war two.

It seemed the country's troops had been sacrificed at the alter to the corporate Gods. The true motivation for endless wars had been money, namely the arms industry that had supported a multitude of governments.

So the revolution won and slowly dismantled the very beast that had devoured countless lives throughout history. From a pharmaceutical industry that had no interest in cures but instead churned out medicines that treated symptoms. Pointless except that is to keep the money flowing into the bank accounts of the few.

Then there was the food industry with it's cruel treatment of livestock all the time creating bigger more efficient farms that had endless diseases. The solution to keeping animals healthy in such a cruel environment was to fill them with drugs that created an opportunity to force rapid growth using more drugs.

Of course this was really harmful to the consumers but that was no problem as the industry also paid millions of dollars to lobbyists who kept the government on side, nobody ever held them accountable.

Every part of life had become poisoned by one common evil that had to be eradicated if the country was ever to recover.

Money had to go and the process had been amazingly simple, through showing the corruption in the now state run media the masses took little persuading.

Of course a long time ago people may have had savings or holiday homes and such but by then capitalism had stolen that prospect from all but the very few who lived in massive mansions and had property everywhere it seemed.

Yes the revolution had been relatively simple really but not what came after which was a transition of gargantuan proportions. But the transition happened and with relatively little complaint, such was the devastation that the elitists had created that people just accepted any change to their lives had to be good.

However when the jackboots started kicking down doors as does happen in times of revolution it wasn't to drag away frightened enemies of the state.

The new authorities under Anna's leadership sought to seize only information because Anna's genius was to not imprison her enemies initially but to discredit them.

And that was the end of any doubts about the future as they uncovered a myriad of conspiracies from addictive chemicals in soft drinks to the truth behind the mass sickness caused by modern farming.

The final nail in capitalisms coffin however was the discovery that a prevention for cancer had been discovered years ago and suppressed, profits from treatments were deemed too valuable for pharmaceutical companies to risk.

Anna felt physically sick when she read the minutes of the meeting between the CEOs, what disgusted her was the way those bastards talked about profit projections comparing the cure to treatment.

Anna did have a villain to throw to the masses however and that villain had much blood to it's name. The mob got to see public executions which were ingeniously staged, like the Nazi book burning from another time this regime executed paper. Not valuable paper carrying the means of learning but pointless money.

People were encouraged to bring out their cash and throw it on the fires all over the country to the speech playing on big screens where Anna explained the evidence found of inhumanity. Anna made sure to emphasize that the evil that enslaved humanity wasn't a person or people but simple greed which everyone succumbed to on some level. The only way to beat this enemy was to abolish it's manifestation.

So began an exciting new social experiment. Could society survive without money or more to the point the need to earn money mostly to pay it back into the system that required the labor that earned it?

The many naysayers determined that masses would stop work and people would empty supermarket shelves as all produce was effectively free. In rare cases that did happen but not for long and not much and eventually that was resolved by a clever system of online shopping that controlled consumption.

Society proved more resilient than to just rely on a financial system to function and people carried on. Unencumbered by the depressing thought that their jobs were essential to survive, mechanics, police officers, teachers and everyone carried on.

Every productive member of society was awarded a holiday twice a year and didn't have to save up for it in any sense. When that holiday came it wasn't overshadowed by the fact that others could afford a better resort or first class travel and everyone enjoyed either active skiing holidays or relaxing cruises or many other ways to have a break. In fact holidaying became the savior of Cell the new government as many people needed work due to a massively less wasteful society. So every kind of holiday state emerged.

Work for everyone became more of a social interaction mainly due to the lack of cost efficiency and work became a necessity to fulfill a need in society.

Every societal function that once needed a minimal amount of people to fulfill it was now unencumbered by the need for profit and efficiency. A warehouse like the one Anna used to toil in because it was staffed to a minimal level to maximize profits no longer had such restrictions.

Society was actually focused on needs based production as opposed to wasteful consumerism driven by jealousy and greed. The factories now produced to give society what it needed and not what consumerism said it wanted. Everybody had computers, smart watches and just about every luxury that they once desired but also had time to enjoy them. Also the need for new versions of everything was no longer prevalent as that too had been driven by consumerism and it's constant brainwashing through the media. A phone was just a phone and because it needed no other function than to serve it's owner it could be allowed to last longer and not be superseded by a new must have model.

Anna snapped out of her daydream and remembered that she had a council meeting this morning to talk about this months problems and the unfortunate topic that she dreaded.

The sad truth that human nature kept showing its ugly side was always undeniable and no level of spin could sugar coat it. Anna knew people would try to persuade her to end the death penalty for the capital crime as always but she never would support them.

Society had to function in a safe and secure environment so the life for a life policy had been implemented, not the cruel and abhorrent death row of the past that kept people waiting for years to pay the ultimate price for crimes. Cell insisted that a person was tried quickly and humanely, the case was assessed at a council meeting like the one Anna would attend today and the person would be humanely dispatched through a simple series of injections.

While waiting they were in a secure yet comfortable prison which was the norm now, no more brutal profit orientated detention centers. Anna had been shocked to realize that even crime punishment had been corrupted by the desire to creare a profit.

On an altogether more positive note however Anna was excited about the progression of her idea to spread her country's ideology which had turned out better than expected.

The revelation that the Norwegian security agent had worked out the truth had shocked her at first but she soon realized that the situation actually presented a fantastic opportunity. Through Charlie who's loyalty was beyond doubt this operative could serve Cell brilliantly.

The leader walked over to her coffee machine and made a latte before walking over towards the window. Anna looked across at the guest house and smiled at the lavish security detail strolling around outside the building. There was a light drizzle now and along with the moderate climate in the administration state it would make those guards miserable.

She wouldn't dream of leaving Charlie outside like that but that's the difference between Murcan ideology and capitalism. Insecurity would destroy them and their insistence on creating massive social imbalance as if to put a barrier between the elitists and the proletariat would lead to their ruin.

Anna thought about the prospect of having a defector in her security detail and smiled as she noticed an attractive figured girl pacing in front of Johansson's temporary quarters, her blonde hair was plaited again and flowed under the NIS baseball cap.

Anna smiled and walked over to call her aide making a mental decision on the way, she asked for coffee's to be taken out to the Norwegian security agents and as the assistant confirmed Anna allowed herself a moment of smugness before thinking about politics again.

She pondered how to deal with the coming meeting as she looked at her security guard carrying a tray of steaming hot coffee's across.

Anna's council consisted of 100 people overall representing fifty city states, they were drawn by lottery and replaced every five years at intervals. The hundred were drawn evenly from the States and comprised of a naturally random reflection of society between genders and races. The only discrimination was that they had to be aged between sixteen and thirty years old. No longer would the fate of everyone be decided by people with no understanding of ever day life for Anna's council could accommodate anyone from a surgeon to a lumberjack and due to the city State system that diversity was guaranteed. They worked in their local governments addressing all issues of their State through an online information platform that was open for anyone to refer to. Health, exercise, dietary consumption and everything was recorded and monitored but not privately and never in any interests accept those of the collective society.

Any issues would be addressed at a monthly meeting at the administration state but a special meeting could be called anytime as was the case today. The engineering State had a killer on the loose and it's representatives a young girl called Lisbeth who had various tattoos and piercings and Anna considered as very level headed for her seventeen years. And Jeremy who had descended from one of the wealthy families before the evolution but Jeremy held no grudge and he'd become a doctor as he grew up into a far more modest environment than his parents had known. Jeremy was twenty nine years old so coming to the end of any public role he could play.

Anna liked Jeremy but was always conscious that had things been different Jeremy could've been lording over the likes of Lisbeth as opposed to governing alongside her.

The meeting today had been called by Anna to find out what was being done to address the spate of sexual assaults in that state, the latest one had left a police officer dead which obviously escalated the issue considerably. Anna sighed as she reproached herself thinking that she was starting to behave as emotionally barren as the filth who'd governed before her. She reminded herself that these were young girls who were as this meeting would take place being helped to deal with their traumatic experience by psychologists and family. They would undoubtedly be scarred for life no matter how much society tried and then there was the police officer who'd tried to apprehend the monster, he left a widow and young child.

This meeting would involve other issues but all overshadowed by this horror story. It's hard to concentrate on a drainage problem or spike in lethargy in some State after you'd heard about a life prematurely ended but society must go on.

Anna sighed and looked up at the photo of her and her young daughter that was taken when they were last together in Alascatia.

They'd had a fantastic holiday and hiked in the county every day before spending evenings in a lodge style hotel talking to other vacationers each sharing their experiences of that particular day. Anna fondly remembered telling everyone about the time her and her beautiful daughter had seen a brown bear on the path.

Some of the guests were drinking the syrupy drink that people favored in that chilly area and some were sipping rich hot chocolates as they sat by a roaring huge fire in the beautiful lounge area, but Anna and her daughter preferred marijuana and smoked their drug of choice. She remembered the relaxed feeling, safe in the hotel after an enjoyable evening with guests from every corner of Murca. As Anna shared the details people gasped in awe and Anna's young daughter Heather looked at her through admiring eyes.

The leader snapped out of her reverie and walked downstairs to wait for her car to take her to the meeting and especially to spend time with Charlie who hopefully appreciated the opportunity to take her lover a well deserved coffee.

The Establishment

In an oak paneled office in an elaborate country estate Taylor-Smith pondered his computer and sighed. He was about to have an online meeting with the world's most clandestine group.

It's safe to say that the likes of Mossad and the CIA would have envied the security of this select group of elites, especially as director's in both those intelligence agencies belonged to this little club. In fact it's been a practice of this group to ensure a member placed high up in every intelligence agency in what they consider to be countries of relevance i.e. capitalist pseudo democracies.

Rarely has a political leader been elected in one of these countries without their approval and if that terrible event occurs that person is quickly destroyed through the media that the Establishment own.

Taylor-Smith gazed out the window and daydreamed of going out in his Ferrari although he really didn't look likely to be a sports car driver. The old man was the epitome of someone in denial of his age and he needed a member of his staff to hold the car door so he could ease his failing body into the magnificent vehicle. Taylor-Smith owned eighteen sports cars most of which were classics but only one was suitable for him to drive with his weak strength and it was a modern model with power assisted steering and other driver aids.

That aside the local villagers knew to keep clear of that particular car which had more than once grazed another car. It would be funny if it wasn't for the fact that as was often said in the village pub he'd kill someone one day.

But not today clearly as the impatient old man sits in a slowly deteriorating mood while watching the boxes on his computer screens light up showing members. The meeting wasn't able to start until the relevant parties were present and inevitably the same bastards were late.

Eventually his screen's went green indicating time to start the meeting and first to speak was a famous or rather infamous media tycoon known to Taylor-Smith and most of the world.

"Before we entertain this madness I'd like to say I'm against it completely."

Taylor-Smith grimaced at the coarse Australian accent of the man who'd only ever been accepted for his media control. The man continued.

"We just need to separate Murca from the rest of the world. I've spent years feeding the moronic public bullshit about the country and now you want to let them back in?"

Taylor-Smith had personally lost a significant amount of money due to the Murcan political upheaval and even though he was still well established in the Forbes rich list with billion's in assets he always felt a grievance towards them.

He however kept quiet as he was confident that the option of Murcan holidays would be approved to allow government Minister's to have their legal albeit dubious profiteering. The Establishment was always keen to allow a little corruption here and there to keep political leaders happy.

Now Olafssons window highlighted and he assured his skeptical colleague that all the conditions that the Establishment had demanded before allowing Murca to connect with the world had been met.

"In short ladies and gentlemen the colonialists aren't in the least happy with their society and if anything we might even be able to force them back into the global community."

The Australian media giant was absolutely disgusted at this and looked like a spoilt child who'd been chastised in his box on the computer screen but before he could cut in another media entrepreneur spoke up.

She had created a social media platform being among the first to realize the evolving market for that type of communication. Social media had been welcomed into society as a way to connect with friends both currently and from the past but of course it was a way of gathering information on its users just like search engines but on a more advanced level. She'd been quick to use her money to buy up any new competition to her own platform therefore ensuring her relevance.

"I'm equally dubious as our colleague and want to echo his concerns."

However Taylor-Smith could see that the two media billionaires one from selling newspapers and TV stations none of which interested Taylor-Smith and the other from social media which was definitely not in his world were holding no sway. The aristocrat himself coming from a long heritage of influential family knew only too well that these people like many others were accepted purely for their usefulness to the Establishment, not their opinion.

The last 'tycoon' that pushed his influence too far and tried to step above his station accidentally drowned in a very well publicized incident off his luxury yacht in the Mediterranean. Taylor-Smith knew that the opportunity to profit from a possible opening up of the Murcan market was too much a temptation to miss for the old established members so this enterprise would be approved.

The ageing billionaire looked out his window at the beautiful clear blue sky as the discussion droned on and he thought of a coming business deal to buy up a popular department store which had been struggling for years. He smiled at the thought of acquiring it's assets under the guise of a rescue plan but knew all along he'd sell everything off to increase his wealth. Thousands would lose their jobs but never mind.

Finally there was the vote and the old man accidentally pressed the wrong key but it really didn't matter as it was approved by a landslide.

The Wolf Guards The Sheep

They were on the seafront and Jake walked alongside John's wheelchair as usual. The device was covered in hundreds of sensors like cars and the technology was amazing to John.

They walked along the promenade and Jake paid little attention to the naked sunbathers lying on the beach, in this state of beautiful sunshine and good weather swimming costumes were rare and normally only used if you needed to walk somewhere. Nudity was acceptable horizontally but not vertically.

The wolf seemed pre occupied and eventually found something he seemed to be looking for, in a country themed restaurant a TV could be seen at the back. The restaurant was open to the waterfront on one side, country music was playing in the background and the furniture was rustic wooden.

After scanning them in Jake guided John's chair into position and an awfully dressed waitress came to take their order, she had a denim mini skirt, checked shirt with waistcoat and a gun belt holding two plastic colts. Her long blonde hair streamed out of a cowboy hat and to John's amusement the hat actually had a sheriff badge on.

She took the order while eyeing up the wolf but he didn't notice and was obsessed with the TV as he gave the order.

When you're deprived of your abilities your mind automatically steps up a gear as a self preservation mechanism but even taking this into account John's ability to sense other people's emotions was uncanny, not that anyone will ever know. But this strong empathetic skill told John that the wolf was getting anxious while watching the TV. As the world's most fake sheriff bought the food John could just see the headline on the news program "Cop killer still not found" John instinctively knew it involved Jake.

As each mouth full of food was placed on John's tongue waiting for his body to naturally swallow it, all John could think about was Heather and the way the wolf had taken her in. As Jake relaxed a little bit and started to be more attentive to John he wondered what the future held for him.

Out the corner of his eye John could make out the TV showing an episode of the popular sitcom about a group of girls living in an apartment block in New York and their friends. John couldn't quite remember the name of it but he'd enjoyed it before his accident, reruns were common but obviously vetted carefully by the authorities for their impact on society. It was obvious when you saw the constant flow of mindless drudgery that flowed out of the screen designed purely as light entertainment.

Eventually lunch was over and they left the burger bar with it's poor attempt to create a western ambiance and on the tv a familiar voice was saying.

"Cell better for you, better for me and better for everyone."

As they left the restaurant and went into the beautiful sunlight Jake kept them on the waterfront, John could smell the sea air mingling with the familiar smell of sun cream and food from various restaurants.

He listened to various conversations as they slowly ambled onwards with the background drone of the massive offshore windfarm continuous. Two girls walking in front of them talked about the coming election lottery for new leaders in another State but John couldn't make out where.

"Are you going to watch it then?"

One girl asked and was assured the other wouldn't ever miss one. The TV coverage of the surprised new politicians was always a highlight and few missed it.

When they eventually sat together on the promenade John was deep in his thoughts. John wondered if the wolf would say anything to him but he wasn't interested in John at all but constantly checked out the young girls who were dressed for summer as always in this State. As an exceptionally attractive girl with red hair in a ponytail jogged past in a graceful motion John had an epiphany. To his embarrassment they were clearly both mentally undressing her, John was horrified to think that his mind could be at the same level as the wolf.

Jake's mind was instinctively going in the direction that John suspected but on a level John would never have the imagination to comprehend. Jake had seen the girl jogging and was feeling an urge that could not be suppressed for long, the urge to force her to submit to him, for him to have absolute control over that beautiful and virile young girl. Maybe he'd make her his, yes that's exactly what he'd do but first he'd have to plan it. Runners followed the same routes he knew so he'd have to find out if she did this run every day then maybe he could follow her home then just a bit of surveillance and after a bit of good honest work he would get to have her.

Eventually they left the waterfront and it's familiar sounds and smell's and walked back to John's house. When they got back Jake noticed that the TV was showing a video of the coming Mars mission and the space craft was on the platform ready to shuttle the astronauts to their actual mission transport. A scientist was explaining the technology involved as pictures of the vessel that Jake felt was pure science fiction flashed on the screen. John was positioned able to watch the program while Jake busied himself in the kitchen.

"Of course the ship was built in space as the logistics of getting such a huge craft out of our atmosphere is overwhelming, especially the solar panels."

The scientist said as the video showed the test of the panels unfolding which made the habitat capsule look tiny in comparison in spite of the fact that it can sustain eight people complete with all provisions for over two years. As the scientist described the physics of how the solar energy could propel the craft over a hundred and seventy million kilometers John considered how the craft made him think of a butterfly with it's beautiful wings elegantly stretching away from it's body. Jake returned into John's line of sight and lifted a familiar beaker of coffee that was thickened to make it safe to drink, if that was an accurate description of the process of consumption. As the gloopy mixture settled on his tongue John noticed the attractive sight of the mission leader who'd become somewhat of a celebrity in Murca, she was explaining about the mental and physical preparation her and her seven crew mates had gone through. The program ended on a clock counting down to the estimated launch time showing seven days fifteen hours and twenty four minutes before the ever familiar girl saying.

"Cell better for you, better for me and better for everyone."

As John finished his coffee he was relieved to hear Jake announce time for a nap just as the theme tune for the afternoon episode of 'Alascation nights'

So after his three days on shift Jake found himself using a community bike that he'd found in one of the many stations and sat on the waterfront where the girl had been discovered.

His effort was soon rewarded and this was going to be so easy as she'd ran past this exact time a few days ago when Jake had been looking after the cripple. It was easy to follow her on his bike from a distance so as not to arouse suspicion and when he saw her going into a modest ground floor flat Jake's excitement jumped to a new level. Jake was confident that like many people these days she was single and he loved to see her perfect muscular body glide along as he watched the beautiful red haired girl go about her daily routine.

He saw her in her local Starbucks having coffee before work in her casual clothes and he'd had a dinner at the restaurant where she worked one night as a type of sick minded courtship.

He considered the fact that he could get some cards printed and give her one inviting her to an intimacy in the way people do so casually here but he didn't want that level of familiarity. So far two women one who was old enough to be Jake's mother and one boy who had made Jake laugh later as he was in a G string and string vest at the time had given Jake cards. But it seemed weird to him after his life in the more conservative engineering state.

Still slowly the killer was changing and he was being off balanced by his transformation. The friends he'd made here we're amazing and the fact that he'd been able to socialize at all shocked him but he put that down to the environment and this states' liberalism.

Jake went back to work after his busy four days off and was confident that he'd planned his coming hunt well, so he'd spend a nice three days working with John before he'd enjoy his next conquest.

In the showers he barely noticed his surroundings and the various bodies on display as he went through the compulsory ablutions, and all he could think about was the red haired girl all day until he got back to his flat and opened a beer to sit and watch TV.

A Present For Heather

Lucy was cooking risotto in the kitchenette and Heather was indulged in George Orwell's masterpiece when Heather's phone showed a text from an unknown number.

"Who the fucks this now?"

She said as she opened the message and read out loud.

"I don't know if you remember me but my name's Amber and I served you and your friend in the restaurant the other night. If you're still interested call me♥"

Heather straight away glared at Lucy who winked and said.

"Don't pretend you didn't want her. You were eyeing her tits up all night."

Heather was taken completely by surprise and didn't know how to react but rallied with a great reply.

"Well in my defense I did have your fucking remote control vibrator up my snatch."

They both enjoyed the rather crass humor but eventually Lucy admitted to her indiscrepancy confessing that she quite fancied the redhead too.

"Amber is a sexy bitch, let's see if she wants a threesome?"

This was a revelation for Heather who'd never even considered this before but she found herself saying shyly.

"Ok"

After dinner as usual they were cuddled up on the sofa Heather with her head resting on Lucy's breasts when Lucy remembered her lovers old concern.

"Did you still want us to check out Jake at your work?"

Heather shook her head and said.

"Nah it was just me being overprotective, the guy seems to be fine. I'm more worried about phoning Amber. I mean what shall I say?"

Lucy caressed Heather's cheek and suggested.

"Oh just say hi I'm Heather and I'd like to sit on your face while my girlfriend eats out your pussy, Duh obviously."

Then Lucy remembered her intention.

"Unless you want her to yourself I mean that was my idea, I really don't. mind."

Heather turned around and said.

"No let's both share Amber"

Amber Gets A Phone Call Before Her Afternoon Run

Amber's flat was a small two bedroom and was a mess with clothes strewn around the place.

Vintage dance music played in the background as she was just getting ready for a run when her phone went off, Amber hopped into the living room still threading her ankle into her tiny lycra shorts and picked up her phone with her left hand while the other worked her shorts over her muscular buttocks. As she pulled the front of her shorts up she was ecstatic to see that it was the number that those two girls had given her, she knew they were an item but she was always looking for a no strings hook up. She had no time for a serious relationship and she'd picked up lots of cute guys at work.

She'd mastered the art of surreptitiously flirting to husbands she could tell were frustrated and had found names and numbers on those tiresome forms before. Never a girl though.

Amber told her home system to lower the music and answered.

"Hello you I thought you'd never call" her voice oozing sex."

Heather was instantly aroused and jumped straight to the point.

"Me and my girlfriend would love to take you out one night and maybe afterwards we could fuck?"

Amber replied.

"Oh fuck yes please but it'd have to be your place as I've got an annoyingly nosey neighbor who's always moaning about me."

Heather was relieved and immediately agreed arranging to get together the next night that she and Lucy were both off.

Amber jotted down Heather and Lucy's names and address on her pad then put on her sports bra and went out into the afternoon sunshine for her run leaving the door unlocked as usual.

As she started to elegantly stride down her street Amber noticed a familiar face as a guy on a bicycle went past making her look back. Strange how she couldn't place him but was sure she recognized him. No matter probably just a one night stand from the past. She chuckled to herself as she told herself she'd probably be more likely to recognize his cock then settled into a rhythmic stride for her run. Amber ran through the empty streets and felt as she always did during a run fantastic. Her red hair in a ponytail flowed behind her baseball cap and it echoed her perfect running form.

She turned into one of the many parks that were scattered all around the Murcan City States, real estate wasn't fought over by corporations and with the rest of the country being wilderness the States could afford the space.

She ran through the park skirting the edge until she got to the rose garden where she crisscrossed the maze of footpaths around the aromatic and beautiful rose beds.

Amber slipped off her hat as she ran under an arch that housed a cooling station and refreshing cold mist engulfed her as she glided through, many of these had been recently put into parks in Floricare for runners and cyclists but everyone loved them in the hot climate.

The park was encircled by a stone wall and adjacent gritty footpath with benches one of which was occupied by homeless Harry, as amber ran past the local celebrity she shouted.

"Hi Harry, I'm working later if you want to come around?"

Homeless Harry was a local conundrum and the authorities had about given up on him as he never stayed in the flats that were put at his disposal. It was accepted that although non compliant he was totally harmless and at no risk. Sleeping out on benches in Floricare with it's climate was almost a nice prospect but nevertheless an official was allocated to Harry and she ensured he had regular washes and fresh clothes through her nagging although he blatantly refused the bedding she offered preferring newspapers.

"Hello beautiful girl."

Came the reply prompting Amber to promise.

"I'll get chef to do you his special."

And then she was passed him just like that but she made a mental note to remember to ask the chef to fry up his bacon, sausages and eggs and of course a fried slice of bread that would be saturated in oil. Disgusting by her restaurant's standard but Harry loved it.

Soon Amber was on the seafront and as always the athletic girl stopped by the kiosk to grab a bottle of water that the beautiful server always had ready to grab.

Before long Amber was back on her street and stopping outside her local Starbucks, as she went into the refreshing air-conditioning she noticed the TV on in the corner and sat down to watch the news while the barista got Amber's usual post run drink ready.

"Here you go gorgeous, one iced latte to cool you off."

He announced gingerly putting the drink in front of her and looking to the TV screen which was showing the news about the unsolved murder in the Engineering State. The barista sighed and looked at Amber before saying.

"You be careful my girl, there are still monsters in this world."

But she just shrugged off the older man's concern dismissing it as a long way away.

"No monsters here mate this is paradise my friend."

He just grimaced before trying to impress his concerns on his favorite customer but Amber just dismissed his overprotectiveness as an old guy thing. As she sipped her drink and watched the TV another customer required the barista who hurried back to the counter. Amber didn't notice the guy at the other end of the coffee shop who watched the girl over a magazine.

Anna's Meeting Went Just As Expected

Anna was always striving for perfection in every aspect of society from the production statistics to the happiness of her people but that was often her downfall.

In this meeting room with her government representatives Anna felt trapped as most of them were against her on the subject she dreaded every month.

She was sat at the head of the long oval table with twenty seven seats, one for each state representative present, one for her and one for Paul her advisor. Anna had to approve all matters put in the monthly meeting for that section of the country that could last several days and all morning they'd been attacking her to put in the death penalty. Every subject is debated and a vote is taken on any action proposed but first Anna had to approve it.

The still young lady for a person in her position of power looked around the room and as she often did took in her surroundings. The large room had an oblong shape to accommodate mostly the oval table but at the far end to her there was a coffee machine and refrigerator for refreshments. The walls were adorned with modestly framed pictures of the different States and as always Anna's gaze fell on the one of Alascation her favorite place by far.

Anna listened to her assistant Paul arguing against the death penalty but she knew the speech already and her mind wandered to her daughter and their last vacation too long ago.

Paul would argue his point but Anna would veto the argument insisting the capital crime would still carry the ultimate punishment. The safeguard was that a vote of no confidence could remove Anna however it had only been proposed twice dying both times with poor support. The young dictator looked towards her advisor who was predictably using his go to argument.

"You can't just eradicate those that don't fit into your perfect society Anna. The point is that sometimes people need care not just putting out the way. The unaffiliated districts are an abomination and executing people was never what we stood for."

Anna knew he was right but some thing's were unable to be resolved with ideals and love. She replied.

"Paul you know that I agree with you but life's just not that simple and no matter how much the system works some people can't comply."

The rest of the council were quiet as usual but Anna knew most of them agreed with Paul. The problem with this brave new world they'd created was that the successes only served to highlight the failures. The contrast was huge with the majority more content than humanity had ever achieved. Yes they'd created a beautiful utopia but always in the shadows was the ugly side of human nature. Anna felt her shoulders tensing at this point and found herself lashing out.

"Well if you've got all the fucking answers why the fuck don't you share them with us?"

Immediately Anna held her hands up in form of apology saying.

"I'm really sorry Paul let's break for lunch shall we, come on everyone let's get a pizza."

Anna winked and made an old joke the council knew was coming.

"It's on me."

loyally they all laughed and filed out after her to go to their local Pizza Hut. As the group walked out the meeting room Charlie stepped into line alongside her boss and wondered if they'd broached the subject of Denmark and Freya yet?

The substantial group of what passes for VIPs in this country left the administration building in good spirits as most of them hated the subject of the death penalty.

Politicians in Murca didn't resemble the thick skinned ones of the past and they were happy to move onto more amicable subjects.

As the group waited to cross the street the traffic which consisted of two cars automatically slowed to a stop as the lead vehicle sensed the obstruction, in this country people were always given priority over mechanized transport. In the lead car a young couple recognized Anna and opened the window to speak to the country's leader.

"Thank you Anna."

They both said in harmony and Anna just smiled a reply.

When the group arrived at Pizza Hut the staff were all pleased to see them and had thanks to a tip off from Charlie prepared a table which comprised of lots of tables pushed together. As the customers sat down Charlie as usual flirted with a young attractive waitress but unusually for the bodyguard there was a new emotion in her mind, guilt. The waitress never noticed though and to Charlie's joy she gave the older tattooed lady a card.

Paul and Anna chatted about their families and both had adult children in various states. Anna's Heather was happy in the care state and Paul had two son's both in the military which was based nearby and Anna envied him the chance to see them whenever they wanted.

The military wasn't a fraction of the size it had been before the evolution and nowadays without the desire to influence in other parts of the world it was a domestic force. That said they still had nuclear deterrents but over the years they were never needed as Murca had been simply set aside by the rest of the world who'd decided to ignore the rogue country as it's social success posed no threat to their status quo.

In the restaurant the mood was more relaxed and in the background the TV showed a familiar public information program in-between light entertainment with a familiar and attractive black haired presenter selling the attributes of the country. Anna just looked at the TV in open disgust as it was no secret that she hated these propaganda programs but then turned towards her old friend.

Paul an older man in his mid fifties always loved this lunch, having divorced years ago he'd struggled to build friendships for himself. Anna had always suspected Paul had Asperger's but him and Anna were the only exceptions to the rule that nobody was allowed to stay in their position on the council more than five years. Paul put his slice of Hawaiian pizza down and meticulously wiped his hands on the napkin from the pile he needed before looking his only friend in the eyes.

"You know Anna maybe it's time for us to stand down and let others take the strain."

She reached out to take his hands in hers and asked.

"Are we becoming dictators?"

That was Anna's worst nightmare and she'd deliberately set up the council to avoid the opportunity for it. Paul laughed uncontrollably and cracked his favorite joke.

"Heil Anna mein Fuhrer." They both enjoyed their personal joke but this time it was overheard by Lisbeth who was sat near them. She was transfixed on them and said simply. "Never"

The Wolf Needs To Hunt

Jake was getting edgy and needed something badly. He'd been checking out the redhead for a week now and knew that she lived alone so was probably single so definitely a prime target. But something niggled at him and he couldn't bring himself to commit even though it appeared totally safe. He wondered if it was the chance that he'd face execution if caught, yes that was it he was losing his nerve, but he knew he'd have to do something about it soon.

It's a fact that once a predator has been born it must hunt and Jake needed that feeling of mind blowing adrenaline pumping through his brain. Jake was in need of a fix more potent than anything felt by any junkie and no fear could assuage it. He had been working with the cripple for almost a month now and he'd had to follow the cute young punk girl around for the first week which had been a revelation to Jake as he'd grown to like her. Having a platonic relationship with anyone was a completely new experience for him and Jake wasn't sure how to deal with it.

He sat back and relaxed taking in his surroundings. It was a pleasant spot on the promenade and Heather had taken him there suggesting it was a good place for John to relax while training. Jake had his own reason to be here as it gave him a good place to watch the promenade hoping to get a glimpse at his favorite running redhead.

Jake looked at the sea beyond the sunbathers who were lying on sun loungers on the beach, almost all of them Jake knew would be completely naked which had taken a lot of getting used to. Jakes old home in the engineering state was a much colder climate and it reflected in clothing. In-between the sunbathers walked waiters and waitresses from the restaurants carrying trays of refreshing drinks which always amused Jake and as always he wondered where they looked when darting between all that nudity.

Beyond the beach were the thousands of wind turbines that supplied the much needed energy that powered everything. All over the country fossil fuels had been discarded as the ugly unviable energy source it is and since the lobbyists lost their grip on power renewable energy systems took over. He listened to the gentle humming coming from turbines that seemed to join in with the sound of the waves and the aggressive squawks of the gulls to create a symphony. Jake thought about how he'd dreamt of seeing the seaside when he was a child never expecting to actually realize the fantasy.

He looked across to John who was sleeping gently in the embrace of his tailor made wheelchair. As he watched his charge Jake considered how his life had changed so much and in many ways the self diagnosed sociopath was desperately struggling to keep up. Was Jake feeling love for the first time in his life, not just a desire like that he felt for the redhead that currently occupied another part of Jakes mind. But love for another human being that was reliant on Jake for his very life depended on him. Jake fumbled the silver dollar in his hand as he daydreamed about an existence that up till now had been totally alien to him.

"Hi John sweetie."

Jakes daydream was disturbed by a dark haired girl in a tight pink crop top that showed an impressive physique. Her left arm was sleeved with tattoos but unlike many these were all grey and totally devoid of color but somehow seemed more meaningful.

She handed Jake a take away cup of coffee that she'd picked up from a kiosk which he automatically took.

"Don't mind me babe I'm a friend of this one's."

She said as she bent over to kiss the now awake John on the cheek. Jake mentally cringed as he found himself saying.

"Lucky guy, my name's Jake I'm knew here but I've been lucky enough to get a job working with John."

Tanya was transparently interested and said.

"Have you been out much? I know a nice place if you want to get together one night."

Jake was shocked by the boldness of this beautiful girl and began to falter.

"Um I've not had a chance to get out at all, but I'd love to meet up one night, that'd be beautiful."

He immediately regretted the stupid line but now was nervous which Tanya picked up on and in a gentle tone said.

"Relax fella I don't bite you know."

She took a card from her bag and handed it to Jake as she kissed John on the forehead. As she took back her coffee and went to walk away Tanya winked at Jake and using her hand indicated to "call me" leaving Jake to look at the card in his hand which introduced Tanya as athletic, adventurous and bisexual as well as having her phone number.

John's imagination was wandering as he thought about Tanya and Jake and then inevitably he drifted off into one of his fantasies.

John found himself back in the zoo and watching a scene that could belong in the mind of Lewis Carroll. Tanya was a cat with an elegant Lycra outfit and her face made up beautifully with whiskers extending from her cheeks, Tanya's long black hair matched her tight outfit and pointed furry ears protruded finishing the look perfectly. By contrast Jake was in a loose dog outfit that looked like a cartoon figure, bedraggled strand's of fur covered his body and hood with floppy ears dangling and framing his face finishing the hilarious look a black nose. John watched as the couple walked through the meadow where there were normally lots of domestic cats but today there were only Jake and Tanya. They eventually sat at a table set with a candle in the middle and started to eat. In a flash the table was gone and cat Tanya and dog Jake were dancing holding each other closely but as Jake looked at John over Tanya's shoulder he smiled what would be a malicious smile were it not for the ridiculous doggy outfit. Then John noticed Jake held a knife behind Tanya's back. The haunting sound of Dance Macabre played on a scratchy old gramophone on an ornate table as Jake positioned the knife pointing to the center of Tanya's back. John braced himself for the inevitable horror his imagination was inflicting on him but before the knife could be thrust a gunshot pierced the sound of the music and Jake's smile turned to a grimace as he slumped in Tanya's arms revealing a pistol in her hand.

"Repent repent."

The voice pierced John's daydream as the zoo scene slowly faded away to reveal one of Floricare's more colorful residents. John never knew his name but the figure dressed as a clergyman with a massive cross hanging around his neck was harassing the sunbathers who were doing their best to ignore him.

"God sees all and he will smite you sinners if you don't change your ways."

John could just make out the figure all dressed in black as he moved around the beach cross in hand. Jake was laughing now and got up to leave the crazy scene, as John's wheelchair fell in line alongside the less doggy like carer John heard sounds of a struggle as inevitably the crazy priest was being apprehended.

For the rest of his shift Jake kept thinking about the beautiful girl he'd met and was feeling emotions he didn't recognize, for confident women had never been a part of his life. Jake was confused as this just didn't follow the script, one thing was for sure this was a new kind of attraction to him and he liked it. As Jake cycled home through the streets that evening he decided to call Tanya and five minutes after getting in he did just that on his flat system.

"Hello gorgeous."

Tanya taunted him.

"So you've decided to risk a night with me then but I've got to confess I can bite sometimes."

Jake was feeling out of his depth as he opened his fridge and took out an ice cold beer but arranged to meet Tanya at a bar near the town precinct at the weekend.

Jake sat on his plain couch in his plain flat with a bottle of beer and turned on the TV to a familiar voice saying.

"Cell better for you, better for me and better for everyone."

Jake slumped back and wondered just what the future held for him.

Three's Company

Amber was off work for a few days and was getting ready for her liaison with Heather and Lucy, they were taking her out for dinner so at least that was one thing off her mind. Amber rarely cooked and instead enjoyed either eating at work or getting take outs as her rigorous exercise regime always ensured her physical status quo.

While she had a short session on weights toning her upper body that already had a muscular appearance Amber thought about homeless Harry and how he'd wolfed down his plate of greasy food at her work. Amber felt a level of concern for the man that she didn't understand but nevertheless her colleagues never minded their coworker sitting with him while he ate. Harry was well into his sixties which didn't help to alleviate the concerns many people felt for him but still he insisted on being the only homeless person in Floricare or possibly even Murca.

That evening Harry told her about his military service and she'd been shocked at hearing about the action he'd seen in a place called Afghanistan.

Amber had looked the country up and was amazed to see that it was on the other side of the world making her wonder what Murcan soldiers were doing there.

There was a banging on the wall which broke her daydream and ruined her weights session but she just said despondently.

"Okay Mrs Weinstein I'll turn it down."

Then impishly she instructed the house system to.

"Set music to miserable old bitch."

Her music immediately lowered to a setting that Amber knew Mrs Weinstein couldn't hear next door, although Amber also knew she'd try her utmost to find any excuse to complain.

She went through and stripping off on the way the girl threw her workout clothes in the direction of her laundry basket then showered. Amber dried off then went through to her bedroom to plan what to wear laying clothes out on the bed. The trick was to be seductive but not slutty she thought, it was so much easier with men where the sexier you dressed the more they liked it. But she knew these girls were different and subtlety would be everything. Jazz music was just about loud enough to hear but way too quiet to enjoy as Amber settled on a summer dress that showed the outline of he breasts well and was perfect length to draw the eye to her stunning legs. Black ankle boots finished the outfit off perfectly but her hair would be a tricky one as it was getting late and she needed to get going. Fuck it ponytail would do, anyway it showed off her neck and shoulders which were among her many sexy attributes. Amber put on a matching white lace bra and thong that showed off her impressive bronze tan that thanks to sunbeds showed no white parts on her slender body. She slipped into her dress and tied up her hair before looking in her full length mirror and telling herself that she's fucking gorgeous and those girls are in for the best fuck they've ever had.

As Amber hurriedly shut her door and started to walk to the bus stop she suddenly felt a chill down her spine and turned to look back but no one was there. Stupid girl she thought just being a prat.

The moment she entered the bar where they'd agreed to meet Amber knew she was going to have a great time and the three girls kissed hello whilst a vintage soccer match played on the massive TV that was mounted to the wall. The TV was sheet thin and showed off the advances in technology that baffled most people.

To Amber's delight there was a table football game and a pool table as well as a darts board but the three of them sat down to drink beers that a waiter bought to them.

"We weren't too sure if you'd like it here but we can always move on after this."

Lucy said gesturing to the beers on the table but Amber reassured her that the sports bar was perfect. Heather looked nervous and was unusually quiet but as Amber sat next to her with Lucy on the other side she started to relax a little. They were in one of several booth's and the lighting was low but that didn't bother either of them as they talked about all sorts of things as the sounds of the football match echoed through the bar. Amber noticed that Heather dressed much more casually in dungarees than her partner who had a pair of tan trousers and a smart shirt, the only admission to Lucy's femininity was the fact that Lucy's shirt was open to an extent that showed off her breasts.

They ate burgers and Lucy and Amber played pool while Heather watched but there was a sexual tension between them that ensured an early departure.

The walk back to Heather's flat had been quite nonchalant, as in the bar they could have been just three friends strolling along with each other perhaps talking about husbands, jobs or any amount of trivial subjects.

Once in the flat Lucy went to the kitchen to get a bottle of wine and some glasses while Amber and Heather made themselves comfortable on the sofa.

By the time Lucy got back they were kissing passionately and Heather's hand was caressing Amber's large breasts through her dress. Lucy just sat down in the free armchair and casually poured herself a glass of wine then settled in to watch her lover enjoying the gift.

Amber wasn't surprised when Heather pounced on her forcing her tongue into her mouth and was expecting the attention on her breasts as Heather had been eyeing them all night. After what seemed an age of petting with Lucy obviously enjoying the show. Amber stood up and slipped her dress off revealing her white lace thong and bra which showed her beautiful and physically perfect body. Heather pulled her around so her legs were trapped by Heather's and started gently kissing Amber's firm perfect abdomen which sent shivers through her body. It wasn't long before Heather pulled the lace aside and to Amber's joy started to work her tongue around her. Amber held her new friends head in her hands and had a rush of pleasure as Heather's tongue explored gently while her dainty hands held her buttocks firmly. Suddenly Amber was aware that Lucy had stripped from the waist down and with one leg on the chair arm was pleasuring herself.

Amber had had plenty of men perform oral sex on her before but this was a whole new experience and the gentleness up till now was exquisite and amazing. But what Amber needed as she approached her first climax was something less gentle so amber found her hands holding her lover's head slowly more and more firmly against her body, Heather knowing what was required from her obliged willingly and soon Amber felt her self let go as she violently climaxed.

The three girls went without saying a word to the bedroom where they played out several fantasies that had lay dormant in three minds, that had developed unencumbered by guilt in pleasure.

Eventually they were collapsed on the bed totally satiated and Heather lay on one side with Lucy in the middle and Amber on the other side. They dozed for a while until the guest found herself being drawn to her own flat and bed, the new experience tonight had been exhilarating but Amber craved normality now.

She lifted Lucy's arm from her waist and gingerly eased out of bed then tiptoed across the flat to retrieve her clothes.

Outside dawn was just breaking and the familiar sound of gulls invaded the scene as Lucy entered the living room just as Amber was lowering her summer dress over her body.

"Thanks for a wonderful evening Amber but why are you going?"

Lucy queried. Amber explained that the experience was amazing but she felt a bit overwhelmed and needed to get home which Lucy had seen before in someone who'd experienced same sex passion with her before. Dismissing protests from Amber Lucy insisted on driving her home.

Lucy and Amber both sat in the front of the car and Amber set the destination. On the short journey through abandoned streets they chatted about running and various races they'd both participated in as the automatic car dispersed scavenging gulls. The streets were empty apart from the birds and evidently Floricare was sleeping nevertheless when they arrived at Amber's flat she was tense. The two girls sat quietly with Amber glancing over to her neighbors flat to see if the familiar curtain twitch would announce that Mrs Weinstein was alert as ever, but she had obviously missed this opportunity to interfere in Amber's life.

Eventually Amber realized that she was being stupid and leaned over to kiss Lucy goodnight. Amber realized that Lucy had her hand on her neck as she felt what she'd intended to be a gentle kiss become hot and passionate their tongues lingering on each other's for what seemed an age after which Amber whispered in Lucy's ear.

"Next time I'm going to be yours to play with."

Then kissed Lucy on her cheek and left her feeling aroused yet again. At the door Amber blew a kiss to her new girlfriend and went in.

The wolf had been waiting in Amber's flat all night and at several points had considered giving up but the greatest attribute for a predator is patience and Jake had learned to be patient well.

When he eventually saw the car pull up through the blinds in the living room window he hurriedly got into position so when she came in he'd be behind the door, he looked at the syringe in his hand and made sure it was ready to administer as he waited for what seemed an age. The morning was just starting with the incessant screaming of seagulls which was so annoying here but would hopefully help drown out any noise soon. So soon now.

Amber had lingered on that kiss for longer than she'd planned and it had given her that tingle of excitement, so much so that she'd considered asking Lucy to take her back but she'd decided that's stupid and didn't want to appear as dithering.

As she opened the front door she saw the car drive off and shrugged at an opportunity lost but a good sleep would be best now anyway. She stopped for a moment to look at the gulls making their insane loud complaints about whatever then wondered about Mrs Weinstein, deciding to call on the nosey old bitch later just to be safe.

Amber walked into her home.

As the door shut the first thing she felt was a strong grip on her neck and instinctively she went to call out but as she did her mouth was invaded by a cylindrical object. Amber gagged on the syrupy liquid and struggled to push away strong hands holding her tightly but soon the room started to spin and a feeling of relaxation overwhelmed her body although her mind screamed to fight. Then she lost control of her body totally as the strong drug that was developed to stop an epileptic fit with all it's potential violence took Amber away from the world of danger and strangers invading her home. Amber felt the strong arms now supporting her as she stumbled towards the couch but it wasn't right and felt as if she was watching the motions from outside as a third person witnessing the scene.

All the while the seagulls kept up their cries as if trying to call attention to a terrible injustice taking place below their rooftop perches but nobody was listening and help wasn't likely to come. Amber felt herself giggling as her summer dress was removed almost compassionately, the Amber that was somehow detached from this scene physically was horrified as she saw her near naked body pushed onto the sofa face down.

Physically she was still giggling though and even the application of cable ties to bind her wrists behind her back didn't abate the childlike laughter which seemed to be annoying her tormenter.

All the while the gulls screamed in desperation.

Amber watched the man who she recognized now as the guy on the bike undress and was amazed at how attractive he was in the naked flesh, in reality she'd definitely have accepted an invitation from him for intimacy but that wasn't happening here.

He's put a condom on somewhat awkwardly given that he was wearing surgical gloves and slowly he climbed on the sofa behind the prone body of Amber as it shook with giggling hysterics all the while the conscious mind of Amber heard the prominent cry of the seagulls from outside getting louder and louder. As the unknown assailant ripped her thong so easily with strength that in another situation might have aroused her Amber could only hear the gulls screaming, so loudly now that she was sure the man would have to hear their appeals on her behalf but he stayed focused on his task. Amber physically felt him applying lubricant to an area so intimate it had always been unacceptable to her sexually although many men had tried. Detached but somehow aware of the horrific violation that was about to happen Amber found herself screaming.

"No please God don't do this."

But her pleas were lost in the cacophony of noise from the gulls. He was in position now and Amber desperately willed her body to fight back but still all she could manage was the insane laughter which was clearly angering him then suddenly it happened, as he thrust his body inside hers the gulls fell quiet leaving only the sound of the detached mind of Amber sobbing.

Homeless Harry was indeed a local celebrity and was always being accosted by well-wishers but he really didn't mind at all. He usually slept in the park and had really tried to live under a roof but the nightmares were always worse then, so as much as possible he would be out in the open under the stars.

This particular morning Harry knew that he'd inevitably be pestered on his bench as he sat alongside his rucksack that had all his worldly belongings inside but he wanted to see Amber. Harry liked the red haired beautiful server but purely platonically as his interests in sex had gone after his military service had left him with severe post traumatic stress disorder. But the opportunity to sit and chat to the lovely girl was always a highlight in Harry's life.

So as the veteran sat watching the squirrels frolicking in the trees his vague concept of time was disturbing him, she'd normally have been gliding past in her shorts and sports bra by now he was sure. And the fact that his favorite person wouldn't invite him to dinner wasn't the biggest concern for Harry who felt a paternal commitment for the girl as well as the fact that he could eat anywhere he liked.

He made a decision there and then and got up unusually early. The girl was probably just not well so a visit from Harry might just be in order, besides those annoying seagulls had descended on the park which always upset Harry.

He knew something was wrong instantly as Harry knocked on Amber's door then opened it just a crack to see.

Harry had seen death before and instantly sensed that death was here. As Harry automatically entered he recognized the sweet metallic odor of blood and had to steady himself.

As Harry walked through into the messy flat everything changed and suddenly the younger man in desert camouflage was entering a much more modest dwelling with no glass windows just square openings and dust on the floor. Harry had this flashback often and it was the reason he would never be able to live indoors again but this was somehow worse and the sounds of automatic rifle fire accompanied the scene. As he walked inside instinctively covering the danger zones with his weapon as his training demanded Harry's eyes became accustomed to the gloom and as had happened a thousand times before the horror was there. The hardened warrior had never been prepared for what he saw that day but how could you prepare anyone for such a nightmare. The first decapitated body he saw was the father then the mother but by far the thing that destroyed his life was seeing the two little boys all headless. Later a thorough search wouldn't find the heads but the Taliban who'd committed the atrocity was proud to put the images of them on the internet and although his superior officers had banned the sites from their soldiers he'd seen them around camp leatherneck.

Harry concentrated immensely hard squeezing his eyes tight shut and when they opened again he was back to reality but the new horror was no relief. Harry felt tears welling up at the monstrous sight of the lifeless Amber lying face down on her sofa and immediately ran to the girl who'd seen through his homelessness and appreciated him as a human being. With strong arms and oblivious to the abundance of blood Harry lifted the body of his one friend and held her close while his tears ran freely. He stood for what seemed like an age before carrying her through and gently laying Amber's body on her bed, he needed to get her out of the room first. Next then fetched a pair of scissors from the kitchen and cut the cable ties so he could put her arms in a more natural position. Finally Harry covered her body with a blanket he found and leaning over gently kissed her forehead before leaving the flat.

Mrs Weinstein returning after staying with her sister was caustic as ever as she saw the man leaving the girls flat and went to make a comment about her sexual habits but she stopped just in time. This one was different and then she realized it was homeless Harry which triggered her inquisitive nosey nature.

"What are you doing in there now Harry?"

She asked then.

"What's that all over you?"

Harry looked down at his hands and clothes and realized for the first time that he was covered in blood, Amber's blood. The last thing Harry noticed as he collapsed was the sound of the seagulls.

They're crying he thought.

Lucy's Introduced To A Wolf

Lucy looked across her bed at her holographic clock which told her it was early, fucking too early. She'd been at her flat since the night with Amber and had spent yesterday catching up with various bits of record keeping for work, reports had to be written by each department with accounts for criminal trends so resources can be adjusted. Every department leader hated it Lucy included but she'd got home yesterday after dropping Amber off and got on with it eventually grabbing a bite to eat and collapsing in bed early and exhausted.

The result was her being awake at this ungodly hour of five fifteen but she decided to get up anyway. The grumpy copper slipped her slender legs out of bed and felt the kind of ache athletes get after a long time of inactivity as she took herself to the kitchenette to put coffee on. Sipping her coffee she thought about Amber.

The night with Amber had been absolutely exhilarating and the thought of her being able to spend more time with her next time was mesmerizing but now she had to get back into the drudgery of life and that meant the always entertaining fucking Wendy. Well that would require several more cups of coffee and a good run to stretch out rebellious muscles to prepare for, so as Lucy finished her coffee she decided to attack a run next so she headed back to the bedroom. She stretched her lycra shorts over her slender firm hips and wrestled into a sports bra.

As she walked outside she sucked the contents of a sachet of energy gel then holding her bottle she started her warm up. It was early and still cool as Lucy just let her legs carry her on this run, she wasn't going to worry about pace or times, she just enjoyed the freedom to run and it was a good release of tension.

Lucy's flat was in the office district and not the best area for running but she'd carved a fairly pleasant path that took in a reasonable amount of greenery in one of the many parks that were a requirement in every part of the country. On her final stretch she sprinted to the familiar newsagent on the corner of her street the morning papers on the stand were slowly enlarging in her vision as Lucy's slender legs effortlessly carried her body along at top speed. But something was wrong in this scenario. As the gorgeous picture on the paper focused in her vision with the headline YOUNG WAITRESS BRUTALLY MURDERED Lucy felt her legs weaken under her.

Mr. Patel who knew everyone in the area came running out of his store to help Lucy up.

"Poor girl what happened? Are you ok Lucy?"

Lucy felt her body retching and bent over to vomit nothing solid almost as if her body had to purge itself of something but didn't know what. She gingerly stood up with the help of her friendly hero and said.

"It's ok Mr. Patel I think I just pushed a bit too hard on my run."

The much loved man smiled at her and in a soft caring voice chastised her for running too fast, which was just asking for trouble. Mr. Patel was one of the exceptions, in a society that encouraged people not to overwork some special circumstances were respected. He had owned the newsagent before the change and it had been in his family for several generations. Nobody would ever take his sanctuary away from him and he ran it solely arriving early and leaving late every day.

The neighborhood loved him dearly and it was returned with interest. Lucy had no choice but to sit in the shop and sip a cup of tea that the elderly shopkeeper had hurriedly made for her as he busied himself mopping up the pavement where Lucy had vomited.

Lucy sat and looked around for the first time taking in the shop that she used almost every day, suddenly she realized that it was almost nest like in it's clever use of every inch of free space to accommodate stock. In this age there was no financial incentive but it seemed that Mr Patel habitually had to have as much stock as was physically possible. She finished her tea and thanked the attentive newsagent then hurried to her second floor flat running up the stairs. Lucy was aware that more than ever she needed to be on time almost as if she was clinging to her routine like a comfort blanket.

Lucy was in her flat now and stripped off to shower yes that's what she needs a good shower then she'd phone Heather. Oh god poor Heather she'll be devastated and Lucy knew she'd need her but she couldn't afford that sentimentality now as only one thing filled her mind and that was that she needed to catch the fucker who did this. She'd go around after work but only after she'd started the investigation. First though she showered for a long time before she dried as she walked through to her kitchen dropping the towel on a chair she sat on the other one at her breakfast bar and phoned Heather who answered immediately in her usual joyful way.

Lucy immediately burst into tears.

John's Anguish

Heather was devastated finding out about Amber, at first she was worried when the normally rational Lucy broke down crying on the phone actually making Heather think she was breaking up with her. When she finally calmed down enough to tell Heather that Amber had been murdered the young carer was so shocked that she had to sit down.

She'd gone to work yesterday oblivious of what was happening to someone she'd enjoyed intimacy with just hours earlier.

Heather was on shift again today and decided to go in, moping around at home would be just too depressing so she got on with her routine.

It was another sunny day as Heather got out of the bus at central support but her mood was dark, still she grabbed her coffee at Starbucks and as she walked in to the coffee shop the TV was running the story about the beautiful waitress who'd been so cruelly murdered. The picture of Amber looking as beautiful as she had just two days ago disappeared and suddenly changed catching Heather's attention, she instantly recognized homeless Harry and wondered where he fitted into the story? She took her coffee and went through her usual routine scan then shower all the while sipping her strong coffee as if it's smooth reassuringly familiar taste would comfort her.

In the shower a conversation was in full flow and everyone was listening to the carer who Heather recognized as one of the emergency response department.

"Anyway he was in a mess when they bought him to the house."

Heather knew the house he referred to was the emergency support residence which housed people who suddenly needed caring for and had a stand by staff ready to respond to an emergency. Heather interjected in the conversation to get up to speed.

"Is that homeless Harry?"

Her enquiry was answered by a girl who'd been attentively staring at the speaker.

"Yes he found that poor waitress."

The guy just looked solemn then carried on with his account.

"Well we all know Harry from when he stays with us occasionally like when there's a storm or something but this time he was a mess. He was covered in blood so bad that we had to destroy his clothes." A voice from the back said.

"About time he's been wearing them for years."

The interrupter was stared down by a few people around him and the speaker continued but Heather wasn't interested in gossip anymore so she just washed and left the speaker to his audience as she walked through towards the lockers and her coffee. She'd find out what happened soon enough from Lucy, although Heather had pleaded with her to refuse the case her girlfriend had been adamant. Heather made a mental note to not push the issue tonight when her lover comes around but was sure she'd never stick to it. She put on her scrubs and desperately hoped she'd get through the day with normality.

John knew something was wrong the moment Heather entered his bungalow, her mood was palpable no matter how much she tried to hide it behind smiles.

She gave John his bath as she so often did when the night staff let him sleep in and he enjoyed the sensation of the warm water on his body enhanced by soft lighting and gentle music.

But the mood was wrong and John discovered the cause while Heather was feeding him his breakfast, the TV on the wall was showing a picture of a familiar redheaded athletic girl. John's heart sank when he heard the reporter saying.

"Her body was discovered by a concerned friend. Police believe that the killer attacked her as she returned home from a night out with friends."

Then the next words made the inevitable link in John's mind.

"We believe that she was sexually assaulted but police are unwilling to say at this point"

Suddenly John remembered her, the girl that the wolf had been so greedily looking at on the waterfront. He felt dizzy and thought he'd be sick but then realized that Heather had stopped feeding him, the almost subconscious link between feeder and recipient had broken. As John's eyes took in Heather to see what had happened he realized that she was crying and to John's horror he instinctively knew that this kind loving angel had a connection to the poor victim.

The day seemed to pass in a dream and after a swim in the public pool they met Tanya and Katie for lunch. Heather appeared to have got her emotions into check now but John knew that she was a mess underneath as they talked inevitably about the beautiful victim.

"Oh my god you knew her."

Tanya exclaimed loudly over her pizza. Katie as usual didn't seem to notice and just carried on eating in her own world. Heather dismissed her friend by saying.

"Barely really but me and Lucy had a night out with her the same night she was murdered. I can't believe that the bastard must have been there when Lucy dropped her off."

Tanya showed her usual lack of tact and glared at her friend mouthing the words silently.

"You fucked her?"

Heather shrugged and mouthed back.

"She fucked me actually."

In the silent secret language that they used around John and Katie. Pointless as it was as John had learned to infiltrate their clandestine conversations long ago and Katie didn't really care. Music played in the background and the busy restaurant bustled with activity as John drifted into a daydream,

Amber was running along the waterfront and being chased as she looked around to see her pursuer but it wasn't sinister in any way, Heather was also out running in her lycra shorts and top and was gaining ground on Amber who was smiling at the prospect of losing the race. John noticed in his dream that there was no one else around and the beach was empty of it's usual sunbeds, Amber seemed to capitalize on this as she swerved off the path onto the soft sand still with Heather in pursuit like a lioness chasing down a gazelle. As they neared the ocean with it's breakers crashing on the beach Amber kicked off her shoes and started to pull off her top then her shorts before she ran into the cool refreshing sea with the first wave crashing into her naked body. Heather was laughing behind and had followed her prey's example to strip off being encumbered as she struggled to get out of her shorts. Amber now had an advantage that she used to start swimming out further until eventually she stopped treading water and allowing the pursuit to end as Heather caught up. They both embraced and kissed passionately with Heather's arms wrapped around Amber's neck as the sound of the waves crashing on the nearby shore finished off the romantic scene perfectly.

Then it suddenly darkened and the sea became choppy as both girls continued their loving embrace oblivious to their surroundings until as if taken by some sea creature that was acting instinctively Amber disappeared into the ocean Heather found herself holding nothing but water and air as she struggled to understand what had happened. She started panicking and thrashing at the water screaming Amber's name but John knew she'd gone forever.

John was awakened from his dream as he heard the next turn the conversation took now audible as supposedly it was acceptable for him.

"Well on a lighter note I've got a date."

Said Tanya.

"And you know him."

She teased. John knew now that Tanya was going to meet the wolf, oh god. John had been amused at the prospect before but that was then and now it was different. The wolf had killed.

"So does he know about your situation?"

Said Heather winking at her friend conspiratorially.

"You know my view on that Hev. When he's got to know my lovely personality that won't matter, anyway who doesn't like a bit of cock?"

Tanya mouthed the last word keeping up their secretive pact to keep the innocence of their charges intact. John laughed inside his cocoon which turned into hysteria when he heard Heather say.

"Sorry beautiful but not for me."

The reply was predictable.

"You don't know what you're missing."

After lunch without realizing the relevance Heather took John to the waterfront and actually they went to the part where he'd seen Amber so full of energy and life. Hard to imagine that that was gone now just like that, one day a beautiful girl with a whole world at her feet the next just a memory. Then he instinctively realized they were being watched as a familiar voice said.

"Hello you two fancy bumping into you here on my day off."

John's blood ran cold at the sound of that voice and he flashed back to seeing his eyes undressing Amber.

"Oh hi mister how are you? Have you heard about that poor girl?"

Heather said making conversation.

"God yes the poor thing. Who could do something like that?"

As Jake said the words he actually winked at John. It was transparently obvious that the wolf realized John knew his secret, fucking hell what next?

"My girlfriend is the investigating officer on the case."

"That would do it"

John thought as he heard Heather's words Jake said he was going to get a coffee from the nearby kiosk and Heather accepted his invitation to take John along. The two carer's chatted as John's wheelchair automatically kept him at a safe distance from Heather. John was shocked at how this monster could play the role of shocked friend as Heather confessed that she'd spent the evening with Amber. Soon they were entering the kiosk area with it's trees walling it off away from view.

They sat in the shade and as always Heather made sure John could see as much as possible and as Jake went for the coffee's John took in the scene. To the left there were a couple of women probably in their forties and definitely an item as they chatted and stared at each other over a pot of tea and pastries. As his eyes scanned around John saw two guys waiting patiently behind Jake at the counter one was in a G string and a crop top and his friend had a short skirt on that clung to his muscular buttocks. Both guys were openly checking out Jake who was dressed unusually conservatively for Floricare.

Jake oblivious to this was sharing a joke with the barista, she was just a teenager by the looks of it but had unnaturally large breasts on a petite body. Jake was laughing with her as she made their coffees taking the time to thicken John's to safeguard him from choking.

Horrifically John understood that the wolf was stalking now as the young girl unwittingly laughed at his joke. As Jake walked back he looked John in the eye and raised his eyebrows conspiratorially as if sharing a thought with the distraught man.

After their coffees Heather said goodbye and took John back towards the bus station.

As they walked off Jake took a piece of scrap paper out of his pocket and looked at Amber's poor handwriting spelling an address and the name Heather. Well he thought that's interesting before putting the paper safely back and walking up to the young girl with the enormous breasts to order another coffee.

A First Date And A First Experience

Jake wasn't nervous he told himself but deep down he knew he was. There was something about Tanya that had captivated him, probably her confidence but whatever it was it had him in a state of anxiety he wasn't accustomed to. He knew he couldn't take her the way he had with that other girl a few nights ago and that wasn't a problem as that beast had been appeased for now although it hadn't exactly gone to plan.

The flat had been okay and eventually when she got home he'd sedated her with the drug from John's stash which was easy to acquire but the giggling was infuriating. That was where the thing had gone off the rails as the attraction was control for the beast that took over and that was lacking. Jake remembered back to the messy flat where he'd undressed the wobbly Amber but instead of fear she'd just laughed her way through the horror and those bloody gulls. He'd fucked her but it hadn't satisfied him in the way it should, however he eventually did get the buzz that he'd craved and after the drug had worn off the panic was at last there.

Jake ignored the TV that was showing another program about the Mars mission and let his mind go back to Amber's last minutes of life, she'd slept off the drug and woken up gagged and cable tied into an immediate fit of panic as her predicament sank in. Jake was behind her and she couldn't see as he admired her stunningly athletic body and especially her firm buttocks that had infatuated him. He waited patiently for her to stop struggling and once again climbed up over her on the sofa which started her desperately trying to break free but Jake knew that was impossible. The only sounds were the muffled pleading cries under the gag that had been ripped from her dress as the seagulls had obviously moved on in search of food and the scene was silent. He was still naked and was wary of the inevitable mess to come and Jake's clothes were in another room for practical reasons but in his excitement his penis was fully erect. Amber reached a new level of panic as she felt his naked body on her back probably expecting a repetition of the earlier violation but she had no idea of the new level of horror to come. Jake now was perched on her back using his body to stop Amber's throes and as she saw the knife pass in front of her face the struggling that had abated came back with enthusiasm but then her head was pulled back and the blade ate into her throat. There was no effect at first but Jake persisted slicing the knife back and forth until he managed to sever her throat causing desperate gasps for air, then suddenly the blood happened spraying out in front of the gasping girl in deep black pulsing spurts. Jake felt himself ejaculating into the cursed condom a necessary pain in the arse in a moment more joyously erotic than the earlier rape, this was the ultimate pleasure of power over life. Jake had then hurriedly dressed and checked and double checked his tidying up, one mistake now would be catastrophic.

The killer left the flat carefully removing gloves once outside surreptitiously and he was walking down the street when he saw homeless Harry on the other side walking towards Amber's flat but that meant nothing to him. Yes he had certainly been in control but the whole effect of the drug although it had subdued his girl wasn't acceptable. As Jake had walked away he'd started to formulate his next plan and he felt confident he wouldn't need drugs nor those fucking condoms come to that. Jake had turned the corner and only just missed the drama that unfolded outside Amber's flat as Harry staggered out only to be confronted by the indomitable Mrs Weinstein.

Now however back in the present there was a new challenge for Jake and he was amazed at his nervousness, sure Tanya was attractive and sexy but for a man who had control over life and death he certainly shouldn't be in this state. But he was and as the familiar presenter repeated, Jake thought for the millionth time on TV.

"Cell good for you, good for me and good for everyone."

He started to get ready.

Finding the pub where Tanya had arranged to meet him was easy and it's façade echoed Irish pubs all around the world except of course Ireland. Still the authentic folk music made Jake feel at least a little more at ease.

As he walked through the open door Jake's senses were bombarded with green as he noticed the music was being played live on a small stage set in the corner where a clearing had been crudely created. The bar was busy with people drinking and chatting while some were focused on the music but not many Jake thought. He was pleased to see the Murcans attempt to replicate Guinness being drunk by several patrons and decided that would help steady his nerves. As Jake scanned further he noticed Tanya sat up on a bar stool chatting to an authentically dressed Irish barman complete with green waistcoat and hilariously a green bowler hat, as Jake walked up to her.

Tanya slipped off the stool to kiss his cheek in greeting introduced Jake to the barman who was actually called Mick and she ordered two Guinness's on Jake's request before they went to a table. As he followed her Jake noticed that his date was wearing loose jeans and a pink sweater but Jake mostly noticed the stylish rip in the jeans that showed Tanya's impressively muscular buttock.

Tanya had got there early so had been chatting to Mick the barman in-between his work but she kept one eye on the doorway to catch her date as if he might try to escape. She was pleasantly surprised to see him walk in in a smart but casual outfit of denim shorts and t-shirt under an open lumberjack shirt rolled up at the sleeves showing off strong forearms.

Tanya noticed that several of the bars customers eyed her date up as he entered causing her to quietly mutter.

"Fuck of you guys this one's all mine."

When he approached her she had to kiss him in greeting to send a message to anyone who had ideas about this beautiful man but she noticed his aftershave which triggered a memory long suppressed.

They took a seat and talked completely openly. Jake found himself telling her about his abusive father and the day he'd been taken into care and how scary it was for him. Then something suddenly struck Jake as he saw that tears were starting to appear in the corner of Tanya's eyes, feeling guilty he reached into his pocket taking out a handkerchief. As Jake wiped away the tears he apologized saying.

"I knew I'd mess it up I'm so sorry Tanya. I've ruined your night and I guess you'll be glad to get away from me."

Tanya, composed now looked straight into his eyes and in her husky voice said.

"No lover you've not. You've just triggered a memory that I've buried for years."

She leaned over the table and taking his chin in her hand Tanya kissed her wolf passionately. Then Tanya broke away and said.

"Let's get pissed then go back to my place and fuck."

The rest of the night was light-hearted and they drank and listened to the music while talking about anything and everything. There were looks from people who knew Tanya as a regular in this pub and more than a few wondered if this handsome guy understood her sexuality but they all hoped she'd be happy, to know Tanya is to love her.

Eventually the band of musicians played their last song of the night, a classic folksong made famous years ago called 'whiskey in the jar' and Mick the barman rang the last orders. As Tanya and Jake got up to leave the smoke filled pub arm in arm they were watched by the regulars.

Mick the barman who'd once dated Tanya and still carried guilt at finding her mixed gender uncomfortable causing him to break it off watched them go. He quietly said.

"Look after that girl, she's fragile."

As they left singing in a rather dodgy harmony.

"Waiting for my daddyo, waiting for my daddyo, there's whiskey in the jarro."

Mick just smiled and went back to his task of tidying up after a great night as slowly the singing faded away.

Sat on Tanya's sofa Jake felt nervous again and it showed, the effects of the beer had worn off on the walk back. He noticed that Tanya's flat was very ordered and was tidy almost to the level of obsessive compulsiveness but that made him feel more at ease.

Outside there were other revelers obviously walking home after a night out and their voices had that air of poorly controlled volume that comes after excessive drinking. Tanya who was still feeling the effects of far too much Guinness just laughed and got up to offer Jake a marijuana cigarette. Jake drew deeply on his cigarette and went to carry on the conversation from earlier by asking Tanya what memory he'd triggered in her? She took the cigarette off him and drew on it as if preparing herself but she wasn't ready to share anything yet about her past.

Her father was an old fashioned man who'd never accepted her sexuality to the point of refusing to call her Tanya, until she'd been approved for gender reassignment that is. Then all hell had broken loose and the man who was a hardened ex serviceman snapped, by this time Tanya or Tim as he insisted on calling her was fourteen and already showing the athleticism that now had become honed into a champion so she wasn't scared. But his drinking was becoming increasingly disturbing, every night she'd be woken by his staggering in late at night and he'd scare the then effeminate boy but he always controlled his temper enough not to hurt her.

As the sound suddenly echoed into the flat of the noisy drunks outside now having sex Tanya and Jake burst out laughing. Tanya put the cigarette in the ash tray and they ran to the window to see what was going on outside and even Tanya was shocked at the view.

The couple were across the street and the young man stood rigidly still with his skirt up at the front to allow his girlfriend to perform oral sex on him as she kneeled on the stone pavement.

"Her poor knees."

Tanya said making Jake snigger like a boy as he replied.

"That's not the worst."

Tanya followed Jake's gaze away from the happy couple and realized that several windows were open with people looking out at the two who were too engulfed in their task to notice.

Tanya held back her laughter to not upset the couple but as his moaning reached a crescendo indicating an end to their escapade, across the street someone started to cheer. The cheer triggered mischief in others and before long the other voyeurs were enthusiastically cheering the surprised couple as she got up onto her feet to stand next to her lover.

Jake and Tanya couldn't join in as they were laughing too much, their laughter was fueled further as the happy couple far from embarrassed stood side by side holding hands and took a bow then turned to face the other side of the street and repeated the show of appreciation for their audience.

The whole street erupted as people who had opened windows in other flats to find out what the fuss was about joined in.

Jake and Tanya went back to the sofa chuckling and Jake started to ask her about her past but Tanya just reached over to pull him towards her and instigated a passionate kiss.

There was no sound coming from outside to disturb them now as the evening entertainment being over, everyone had left the young couple to go home.

Jake felt fingers slowly undoing his trousers and he felt the urge to reciprocate but when Jake went to reach for Tanya's intimate area Tanya firmly moved his hand onto her breast then went back to her task. His now firm penis sprung out his trousers and Tanya gasped at it's thickness. Jake felt her mouth disengage his as she slipped off the sofa and kneeled in front of him.

Tanya loved the sensation of having a penis in her mouth and having been male most of her life knew just how to excite it with her lips and tongue. She looked up at Jake as she licked around the tip of his erection then slowly slipped her full red lips around first his end then taking the shaft into her mouth all the while she explored the tip with her tongue tasting it's saltines.

Tanya kept Jake on the verge of ejaculation for a while then when she felt he couldn't hold on any longer she started sucking the tip again with one hand caressing his testicles while the other expertly massaged his shaft until she heard Jake moan as his semen flooded her mouth. Tanya was shocked at the amount of semen he pumped into her mouth and greedily gulped it down until finally the pulses ended. Tanya had one last swallow then slowly allowed his penis to slip out from her lips. Knowingly she squeezed the last remnants of semen out with her hand and licked it off with her tongue.

In bed later Jake lay awake reflecting on life's new complication while Tanya slept peacefully beside him. How different that nights experience had been from that of Amber. The fear in Amber's eyes had been so exciting to him and gave him an exquisite sense of power but now suddenly Jake had been introduced to another sensation entirely. One of surrendering not control as although Tanya had given him unrequited pleasure it had been clear that she'd had absolute power over him from the outset to even dictating when he was allowed to ejaculate.

Jake felt his penis stiffen at the thought and he thought of awaking Tanya for a chance to repay her the pleasure she'd given him but decided to wait for the morning, then he'd get back in control.

The Shepherdess Needs To Avenge Her Sheep

Lucy also lay awake in bed that night and pondered the events of the day. To persuade her superior that she was right for Amber's case was easy enough as there was little precedent for murder. Since in this world murder was almost unheard of apart from the occasional domestic incident. It was unsurprising as there was no longer the major contributor towards the capital crime and any domestic incidents were easily resolved normally with an outright confession. This was going to test their resolve to the full and regardless of Lucy's involvement she was still the best qualified to find this killer.

Lucy thought about the moment her and Wendy had entered Amber's which had seemed strange after she'd left her there only a few days ago. They were both surprised to see the place showed no signs of a struggle indicating Amber either knew her murderer or she'd been completely subdued from the moment she'd got in.

Lucy's blood had run cold at the thought that he'd been there when she'd intimately wished Amber good night. One thing she was confident of was that the killer was male, a fact confirmed when forensics found lubricant used on condoms around her anus. The thought of what he'd done to that beautiful girl made her nauseous and she immediately pushed it out her mind instead focussing on the pictures the forensics officers had taken of the scene.

Amber had been restrained using cable ties and gagged when Harry had found her. The forensics team had been livid at the fact that the last hobo had moved her body but Lucy fully understood and when she'd read the report by Cortez who'd attended she wondered if she'd done the same. It was obvious from the blood that Amber had died on the couch and equally so that her throat had been cut from behind probably to save the murderer getting covered in her precious life giving blood.

Lucy wondered if the murderer couldn't cope with her looking at him as he slowly watched her life ebb away as she bled out onto her soft cushion. He'd sat on her back and held her down as she'd struggled which was obvious from bruising. Lucy wondered if she'd just thought maybe he was going to perform another sexual act on her and did she still have hope that he'd let her live. The bruising indicated that Amber had put up a good struggle and the last thing Lucy thought of before drifting into a restless sleep was Amber trying desperately to save herself as she saw the knife.

Bleep bleep bleep.

"Oh fuck off."

Came a muffled groan through a pillow as Lucy lay face down on her bed, the covers had somehow slid to the other side of the bed probably a direct result of the terrible sleep she'd had.

Lucy slept naked and quietly wished she was able to feel Heather's soft hands caressing her buttocks but the only sensation was that fucking alarm that she instructed to stop.

"Good morning Lucy I hope you slept well."

Her house system announced in a rather sexy Irish accent.

"You've got one message from fucking Wendy. Message reads….."

Lucy just said.

"Stop please."

To halt the automated system. Then she mumbled to herself.

"No Wendy before fucking coffee.

And slipped on a t-shirt to walk through to her kitchen.

Lucy sat on her kitchen stool feeling the PVC sticking to her bare buttocks she sipped her strong coffee and just sat there for a while thinking. She knew as a well trained police officer that she was overthinking this case and obsessing which undoubtedly Wendy will point out later. Wendy oh for fucks sake the message she remembered as she adjusted her posture, bare flesh and PVC were a bad combination. Lucy decided to call Heather first just to hear her voice more than anything and after checking the time she told her home system to call her. Lucy gritted her teeth as the call rang for what seemed an age but eventually Heather answered sounding a bit flustered. Lucy immediately started to fuss which would anger her girlfriend but couldn't be helped.

"Are you ok babe? What took you so long?"

Heather loved this character trait in Lucy but she'd never admit it and countered with.

"I just had to unwrap my legs from my lovers neck, why? Are you jealous?"

Then Heather sympathetically confessed.

"I was just in the shower actually."

Lucy just realized she'd been baited and laughed as she unstuck her bum from the stool to walk towards the window.

"Well I worry about you ok but maybe that's because I love you so much."

Lucy said as she looked out at Mr Patel going through his usual routine of putting out baskets of produce, it was frowned upon by the authorities as cluttering the footpath but they'd made an exception for the ageing greengrocer.

Heather then spent longer than was necessary reassuring Lucy that the love was reciprocated as Lucy returned Mr Patel's wave through her living area window. Lucy felt the need to apologize as she watched the reassuringly familiar sight of a legend in her community doing what he does everyday.

"I'm sorry Hev but I guess I'm just strung out about this murderer situation. We've never had this before and I'm worried I'm out of my depth and especially worried about you."

The last sentence hung in the air between them before Heather reassured her.

"Don't worry babe we're putting new protocols in place and Jake has offered to walk me to work if I want."

The name stirred a memory in Lucy who felt a pang of relief at the fact that Jake was working with Heather.

"That's good of him babe but I don't want you to take any chances anyway. This monster is clever and I feel shit that I can't look after you."

Then Lucy adjusted the subject.

"How is our hero from the zoo anyway?"

Heather laughed and saw the opportunity to lighten up the conversation.

"He's fine and really got used to John well but the best bit though is that he's actually had a date with Tanya."

Lucy choked on her coffee on hearing the romantic news.

"Does he know? Please tell me he has no idea. Fucking hell that's precious."

Heather chastised her.

"Don't be a bitch you. You know Tanya's lovely and a real catch for anyone."

Lucy just smiled and lamented.

"There's certainly more to Tanya than meets the eye."

They both laughed but Heather conspiratorially said.

"You know Tanya's always suggesting we get together. Maybe a bit of cock might be good for us."

Lucy gave her usual opinion on male genitalia.

"I don't want it any where near me honey you know that. I love Tanya but why the hell she's kept that piece of disgusting flesh is beyond me."

Heather just laughed and excused herself reassuring Lucy that she'd be really careful and after blowing kisses they hung up.

Lucy instructed the home system to give her the message from fucking Wendy and poured herself another strong coffee to bolster her for what's to come. Wendy's gruff voice came on and as usual she didn't mince her words.

"Okay you lazy fucker get your arse out of bed, we've actually got a killer to catch for once."

Lucy wondered if her partner who was a veteran from the pre evolution police and always talked about those bad days was just a bit excited? But fucking Wendy continued in a more grounded tone.

"We've got to interview homeless Harry this morning and I'm expecting the toxicology report in today, oh and the autopsy is after lunch thank fuck so I thought we should go."

There was a pause as Lucy's partner was obviously looking for something then she continued.

"The pathologist is a Dr Avery, sounds like a fucking bitch on the phone but I figured fuck it let's go along. Anyway we're meeting her at two thirty."

Lucy sighed at the thought of seeing Amber being cut open but as she started to sink into a gloom again Wendy lifted her spirits in her usual way.

"So get your cute little arse moving and get me a Murcano with my usual bacon roll on your way in. Chop chop you soppy twat."

Lucy chuckled all through her shower at the prospect of a day with fucking Wendy and skipping her normal run just got ready for work.

As she walked into Mr Patel's shop she had a new air of confidence and the ageing shopkeeper could sense it straight away.

"Good morning officer Lucy."

He said in a tone that reciprocated her confidence while handing over her daily paper.

"Are you going to catch any baddies today?"

Their usual favorite banter seemed to have a macabre edge to it today after Amber's murder. Lucy felt this but with her new found confidence pointed at the picture in the paper of Amber out running in her shorts and vest, she had a number pinned to her vest indicating a race and her stride was so elegant that Lucy thought she could almost pounce out of the page. Lucy simply said.

"Yes Mr Patel, yes."

Jake Makes A Discovery

Jake woke up feeling more relaxed than he had in years which he immediately attributed to Tanya who was sleeping peacefully with her back to him, her beautiful hair was flowing back showing off her perfect neck and amazingly attractive profile. Those lips were invitingly seductive and Jake remembered the ability she had to absolutely captivate him with them last night.

He had not felt his normal need to control her last night but instead surrendered to her dominance as she had him in her power. Jake didn't recognize this completely alien sensation of being the puppet to someone else's mastery but he knew that he liked it. There was a pressure that had been lifted off him which had held him down for so long.

Only now Jake took in his surroundings in Tanya's bedroom and he noticed something for the first time, for the bedroom of such an effeminate girl it was surprisingly lacking in color. Fashionable greyish blue walls showed off subtle artwork except for one picture that drew his eye in it's Colorful splendor. It showed a stylish poolside scene in animation and all the characters lounging and swimming were ducks except one crocodile relaxing on a sun lounger. The picture was entitled "a stranger in paradise" and Jake frowned at the thought that it applied to him so well here in this beautiful state.

Jake was disturbed from his reverie by Tanya stirring in her sleep still with her back to him but now one breast was revealed from under her satin sheet, it's perfect round shape and firm pertness aroused Jake and he decided there and then that he wanted to wake up to this perfect vision every day forever. Now as Jakes eyes sent images to his brain of what could only be described as a perfect sensual picture he decided that he'd pleasure Tanya this morning. Something in the way she'd denied his hands access to her intimate area last night made him curious and the way she'd turned out the light last night before undressing made him wonder if she maybe had some disfigurement.

No matter though as Jake decided there and then that he'd accept any flaw that this beautiful girl could have as his body slipped in behind hers and his hand started to caress her visible breast. Tanya stirred in her sleep and moaned sensually then Jakes hand started to run down her ribs and onto her firm abdomen. Tanya was starting to wake now and her breathing was getting increasingly labored as she was becoming aroused.

What Jake felt next gave him a moment of disbelief as his hand touched the tip of a penis as hard as rock. Jake's hand recoiled as if it had touched a dangerous predator and settled on Tanya's hip but her hand gently but firmly gripped his wrist and pulled his hand back to her erection. Jake almost subconsciously gripped the cause of his shock and Tanya put her fingers around his and gently guided his hand into a pulsing motion.

Tanya was moaning loudly now and her body was starting to quiver then suddenly Jake realized that her penis was throbbing and pumping semen onto her stomach. At this point Tanya released his hand and turned her body to look at Jake with eyes that seemed almost pleading with him then as Tanya snapped out of her thought he leaned forward and kissed her passionately on the mouth. As there tongues entwined Jake suddenly had a revelation, he'd surrender to Tanya fully and give her whatever she wanted.

They kissed and held each other for what seemed like an age then when they were both aroused again Tanya slowly worked her way down Jakes muscular body until she once again had him in her mouth but this time Jake felt a guilt grip him at the fact that he wasn't ready to reciprocate this loving action. The beautiful lady however expected nothing in return and seemed only intent on giving him pleasure.

The couple just lay in bed for another thirty minutes or so holding each other in total silence and Jake was as confused as ever but one thing was undeniable. He'd fallen in love with this complex and beautiful girl. As Tanya turned around to face him he held her close and they kissed passionately, as he tasted her tongue he felt her penis begin to grow but before he could begin to feel anxious at what was expected of him she broke off.

"I've got to get ready for work lover but you can stay here as long as you want. There's food in the fridge if you're hungry."

Jake told her he wasn't hungry and lay in bed while Tanya went through to shower until he realized that he really had to get moving too. He slipped out of bed and gathered his clothes pulling on tight boxer shorts and as he could hear the girl showering and for a moment wanted to join her but stopped himself. As the shower cut out Jake pulled on his jeans and felt for the familiar coin that was always the first thing he checked, but to Jakes horror it wasn't there. He felt his blood run cold as the only thing that his dad had ever given him was suddenly absent.

Tanya had felt good in the shower and had wanted to call Jake to join her but knew from bitter experience that to push someone who'd just learned her sexuality was foolish.

She dried off and wrapped her towel around herself, as she walked through to her bedroom she sensed something wrong. Jake was desperately searching the carpet under the chair he'd put his clothes on last night.

"What's the matter babe?"

As he turned around she was shocked to see the muscular physique of his upper body, then her heart sank when she saw that he was crying.

"It's missing Tanya, I've lost it."

Tanya took his hand and sat him down on the bed then kneeled down in front and holding both his hands calmly asked.

"What is it? Whatever it is we'll sort it together."

Jake explained about the coin and it's significance which just made her feelings for him even more strong. Tanya as calm as ever just said.

"Let's check the living room. You actually took your trousers off there last night remember."

In the living room there was the shining coin on the carpet right where Tanya had knelt down and pleasured him. The calamity was over and the two lovers kissed and went their separate ways.

The Investigation Draws A Blank

Lucy and Wendy were having an early start to a busy day and after a quick bacon roll and coffee they hit the road. As the car automatically drove them into the care district the mood was becoming solemn with Lucy sat in the front facing backwards to Wendy.

The screen played an information piece about the advances in driverless technology, ironically considering they were in a driverless car. But the enthusiastic presenter was boasting that this tech could even be applied to airlines dispensing with the need for pilots. Lucy with her back to the dashboard and TV screen wondered if the guy who obviously loved his subject was actually young or just sounded that way. Wendy who was reading homeless Harry's file interrupted Lucy's imaginings.

"Fuck me he's got a purple fucking heart."

Then she realized by Lucy's look of incredulity that the younger detective simply had no idea what she's talking about.

"It's a military medal Luce and absolutely not common. Our Harry's a freaking war hero."

She thumbed further into the file and showed Lucy a picture of the man she knew as homeless Harry, he was in military desert camouflage and only recognizable by his face.

Harry in his military days was obviously the peak of physical perfection and had a muscular build that normally appeared in magazines. He is holding a purple ribbon with a gold heart dangling in the middle of which is a profile of a man. Lucy pointed at the figure and asked.

"Who's that Wendy?"

Wendy sat upright and proudly announced.

"That man my dear Lucy is the founder of our great nation general George fucking Washington."

Eventually the car pulled up outside a large brick house, it's imposing façade only softened by a carefully tended garden with flowerbeds full of beautiful color and a large lawn. In the corner of the lawn could be seen a small tent next to a bench which was covered in newspapers, both detectives found themselves staring at the strange sight on such a pristine garden.

"Well I'll be fucked."

Said Wendy before they turned and walked up the drive. Inside the staff member who met them was a young girl probably still in her teens which seemed odd to Lucy in such a demanding setting.

"Hi guys you must be here to see Harry."

She said in an annoyingly high pitched voice. They introduced themselves then were led through to a living room with staff in familiar scrubs playing various games with 'guests' There was a pool table and two coffee tables, the pool table had two guys playing on it and several people were doing jigsaws at the coffee tables. But as their guide walked them through they suddenly saw Harry sat in the corner in a wooden chair he looked even more disheveled than normal with his head in his hands. The staff member stopped well short so she could explain.

"He's been like that since they bought him in, he won't sleep inside either so we've had to put a tent on the lawn so there's staff near him and he sleeps on the bench."

Wendy asked.

"What about his clothes?"

The girl explained that they were beyond saving so much to Harry's protests he was kitted out in staff scrubs until they could get some suitable gear sent from the administration state.

Lucy thought he looked somehow wrong out of his old camouflage clothes like a lion without his mane.

Two chairs were bought up and the detectives sat down quietly next to him then the young carers shrill voice cut through the air.

"Harry those detectives are here to see you my lovely."

Far from being angry at the disturbance he looked up at her in a loving way and in his croaky voice said.

"Thank you Floss, could we have a drink please?"

Floss looked across to Lucy and Wendy and they both asked for coffee's. As Floss went off to get drinks Harry leaned conspiratorially and said.

"She's my favorite."

Lucy went from smiling to concern as she explained the purpose of their visit.

"What we need is to hear your account of events when you found Amber."

She frowned and said.

"Anything that you can give us that'll fill in gaps might help us catch the killer."

Harry smiled and said.

"Once they're gone they're gone. I've cried for the beautiful girl but because I'll miss her and it's such a waste for one so young but she's gone and hopefully to a better place."

He sat upright now and focused before starting to speak again as Floss handed out the drinks.

"You see there are different types of humans in this world and I know the type your killer is only too well. In the army you get people who kill because it's required and the job."

He looked straight at Lucy before saying.

"Then there's the others the type that need to kill. You see once they've had that sensation of complete control it's like a drug and this is the type you're hunting."

Harry told them everything he could and went through every movement after he'd decided to go and check on his favorite waitress including the almost ritualistic way he'd untied her and laid her out in her bedroom covering her dignity. Harry apologized for interfering with a crime scene but before Wendy could say anything typical of herself Lucy insisted that it was absolutely ok and forensics had drawn a complete blank anyway.

Harry hadn't been surprised and told them how he'd experienced murderers in Afghanistan who were amazingly adept at covering their tracks.

One positive lead that came out of the interview however was the discovery that Amber had a nosy neighbor which Wendy noted down amongst all the other information he shared, Lucy noticed her underline it in her pad approving the possible break they'd been given.

"I'll be back on my bench soon ladies so if you'll want to talk to me that's where you'll find me."

As they left the bright airy room they noticed that the pool game had descended into an argument over a possible foul which drew Floss's attention. Lucy felt a smile breaking through at the thought of their next port of call.

Nosey neighbors were the copper's best friends.

In the busy restaurant Lucy and Wendy were having a welcome break. Lucy was frustrated and for once was the one who was angry in the partnership and fucking Wendy found herself calming her partner and friend down.

"Luce sweety it's not like we're just sitting on our fucking arses. We've done door to door inquiries and done our best, if only that nosey fucking neighbor hadn't been staying away that night with her fucking sister….."

The thought of such an unlucky break so early on in the investigation hung in the air and Lucy broke the pause.

"I'm just really stressed out at the moment, you know that this is close to home for me. And I keep remembering that the bastard must have been there when I was just outside. I practically gave him Amber to kill."

At this admission the guilt that she'd kept bottled up since the realization caught up with Lucy and a tear slowly slipped down her cheek. Wendy saw the waiter heading to take their order and glared at the poor boy until he held a hand up in acknowledgement and diverted to another table.

"You just fucking put that shit away right now, you and I both know that that's no place to go now or ever come to that. We're just going to put our big girls panties on and have lunch then get back to catching this asshole."

Wendy turned towards the waiter who was just finishing with the other table and in her classy style said "Jump to it garcon we're a couple of fucking starving souls here need feeding" he was shocked but placated with a wink from the world's least tactful copper.

After lunch they went back to Amber's flat to see if it might have suddenly sprouted evidence and as if to mock them, the neighbor now known to them as Mrs Weinstein was peeking through her old fashioned curtains at them.

Once inside Wendy went about the task of looking around and using her years of experience and Lucy called Heather to check in with her.

"Hi sugar tits how are you doing?"

Lucy broke her mood by joking with her girlfriend.

"And you just love them you slut."

Came the reply. Heather then lowered the tone asking.

"How's everything? Any closer to catching the bastard?"

Lucy's voice took a different tone as she confided.

"Not a fucking clue darling and it's driving me mad."

Heather immediately changed her tone and said.

"Babe you'll get there don't let it get you down."

Then Heather opened a taboo topic by asking.

"Are you sure that you're ok on this case? I mean you are a bit emotionally involved Luce."

Lucy felt her adrenaline pumping but pulled herself back.

"I've got to do this Heather. I can't explain why but I just have to find him."

At this point Wendy was gesturing for Lucy's attention so Lucy just said.

"I'll come around tonight and we can go out if you want! I could do with a chance to get my mind off this."

Heather put on her seductive voice that she knew Lucy loved and said.

"I'll see you after work then and we can bring our new toy so you can play with me."

"Fuck yeah babe. Gotta go though something's up."

They blew customary kisses and Lucy turned her attention to Wendy who was waving a pair of very worn running shoes.

John's Reluctantly Taken Out Stalking

John had had an unusual morning which was always a godsend and was out with Jake who was very upbeat which wasn't unusual but more so somehow. John hadn't known what was behind this until lunch when he'd been parked in the waterfront seafood restaurant outside under a canopy to protect from the fierce sun.

They'd only been there ten minutes when a familiar voice moaning and complaining about the tables being in the way caught John's attention. To John's surprise Jake leapt up to greet Tanya with a kiss. Well I guess that answers a question that's been on my mind for a while thought John.

Tanya opened up the conversation.

"I'm so sorry I didn't tell you Jake."

Jake took her hand and in a gentle voice replied.

"Honestly it was a bit of a shock but I think I'm ok, I mean I've never thought about my sexuality that way before."

There was a pause in the conversation then they both spoke at once but Tanya said.

"You first"

Jake just shrugged and confessed.

"I just never realized I was gay babe."

Tanya laughed which drew unwanted attention around the dining area so she stopped and leaned into Jake then said so quietly that John could barely hear.

"My cock doesn't make me a man Jake and you accepting it doesn't make you gay, just open minded."

Then Tanya gave Jake a warm smile as if she was making a sacrifice for him.

"Listen hun I really like you and want us to work. I've been hating myself for not telling you but really you can't know what it's like for a girl who normally has a bigger dick than her dates."

Jake laughed and went to say something but was gestured to silence by Tanya who was getting into full swing and wouldn't be stopped.

"What I'm getting at Jake is that I like you but if my sexuality is going to be an issue then say now cause I can't put myself through the pain. But if you want to move on I'll be very good to you. I'm loyal as anyone and a very giving lover."

Jake held his hand up to stop her and said.

"I'd really like to get to know you more and I'm willing to learn if you're gentle"

Jake winked and said "not sure about that thing in my arse though."

They both smiled and Tanya leaned into him and whispered so quietly that John strained to hear.

"I'm going to fuck you senseless honey."

At this point an octopus came to take their order much to everyone's amusement, except Kate of course. As the cephalopod stood by their table eight arms dangled down two of which managed to win a battle and came up with a pen and notepad. Tanya just looked at the reluctant sea creature and smiled.

"You're new here aren't you fella?"

The octopus added a surprised look to his features now and Tanya felt the need to give him a break.

"The octopus thing is just a bit of a prank they play on everyone new."

As she saw his face drop into a frown she said.

"Just go with it buddy and before you know it you'll be a pirate or a fisherman."

The prospect of a different personification put a smile back on his face and he just said.

"Thanks miss, just as long as I'm out this soon."

To emphasize this the poor man shook himself setting fake tentacles into a frenzy. Then he took their order.

As they ate lunch Jake chatted to Tanya but remained attentive to his charge and sensitively fed John as the TV played a series of awards being given for hard work. Tanya chatted freely as Kate needed minimal attention over food and John and Jake listened respectfully. As the octopus now more lightheartedly served the tables John slipped into one of his daydreams.

In John's mind Jake was swimming in the sea gently gliding through the waves as if he could keep this up forever. Suddenly something caught Jake's eye and he started treading water as if focusing on something too intently to put in the effort to swim. John could make out the body of the kiosk girl floating about thirty feet away as she bobbed up and down and duck dived showing her pert buttocks around a very revealing swimsuit. As she popped up through the waves the material could be seen to be stretching over her huge breasts. Jake saw this too and was starting to swim towards the young girl now with an ominous intent. She was oblivious to the approaching threat as she continued playing following the flowing motion of the waves. It was incredulous that the beautiful girl didn't notice as Jake was really close now but she somehow didn't and soon he was almost able to grab her.

Then suddenly Jake was tugged back by some unknown force and he flailed desperately as he was being pulled away from his prey face first. As Jake scythed through the waves now it became clear what was happening as a fishing line was attached to his cheek with a hook.

As John followed the line to it's source he saw a small boat with two occupants sat at the back, Tanya was sat in a chair that was purpose built for game fishing with her long black hair flowing in the wind and wearing only a pair of dungarees. Her excitement was obvious as her strong arms winched at the fishing rod but the most amazing thing to John was Tanya's companion. The waiter octopus was behind Tanya and holding her shoulders to give her moral support.

The scene instantly changed and now they were on the waterfront and a crowd was gathered to see Jake hanging from heavy duty weighing scales attached to a beam. In front of her catch stood Tanya beaming with pride in her dungaree shorts showing a bulging erection, to Tanya's left is her octopus guy and to her right is the kiosk girl in her straining swimsuit.

The TV broke John's daydream as someone turned the volume up to catch the current award and John was awestruck as the kiosk girl filled the screen beaming with pride. The presenter introduced her as Dawn and handed her the trophy. John just went over the name in his mind Dawn Dawn Dawn.

After lunch Jake and Tanya arranged to meet tomorrow night at hers then kissed goodbye. As Jake walked off towards the kiosk he could hear Katie grumbling and Tanya jokingly dismissing her. Once out of earshot Jake stopped and leaned into John saying.

"Come on buddy let's go and get a coffee."

Jake winked at John and John knew they were somehow both aware of the others thoughts. John just thought.

"Please God not Dawn."

A Movie To Forget

Lucy had come around straight after work and had a change of clothes indicating that she was taking her girlfriend out that night which gave Heather a buzz. Lucy had showered and put on her t-shirt that she always lounged around in at Heather's, it had a picture of an old cartoon mouse on it and stretched down to Lucy's thighs.

Now Heather relaxed on the sofa while Lucy looked for something to eat.

"Is salmon okay babe and boiled potatoes?"

Heather gave her the approval but was engulfed in the TV where the characters in her favorite soap opera 'Alascation nights' were enacting some drama or other, frankly Lucy found it dull so was happy with the deal.

She busied herself in the kitchenette putting the salmon fillets in the air fryer and drizzling garlic infused olive oil on them. The potatoes were ready to microwave in sealed bags with butter so soon Lucy was passing Heather the tray then sitting down with her own dinner. Heather respectfully changed the TV to a political channel which was advertising the coming representative selections for the agricultural state which was always a popular prospect and most of Murca would be sure to tune in.

The outgoing politicians were on screen being interviewed and their relief at ending their term was evident as they explained about the privalege they'd felt to be serving their nation.

"Imagine if one of us was ever selected babe?"

Heather asked in-between eating and the question hung in the air as Lucy considered her answer.

"I'd definitely be willing to serve a term but I think I'd hate it."

Heather just nodded agreement and hoped they would never be selected in the lottery to choose leaders. She knew that they were most likely to avoid the choice and as thirty was the maximum age for selection Lucy only had one draw left in Floricare that was due in two years then she'd be exempt. They both watched the rest of the program before tidying up then going to the bedroom.

In the bedroom the mood became more serious as the anticipation of a night out sank in and Lucy pushed Heather onto the bed to sit and watch her dress. Heather watched excitedly as Lucy slowly removed the t-shirt and dressed herself tantalizingly in lace underwear and stockings and a suspender belt, when she was finished Lucy sat down on the bed and kissed Heather before motioning her partner to find something to wear.

Heather got up still tasting Lucy on her lips and went to her wardrobe and took out her leather effect shorts that she knew always got a desirable reaction. Heather held up the garment but to her surprise Lucy shook her head and waggled a finger in disapproval then pointed to a yellow mini dress. Lucy walked over to her drawers and tossed her a pair of pink cotton panties that were a perfect opposite of the seductive luxurious underwear Lucy had slipped on. Lucy then handed her partner a pair of thick hold up stockings and said.

"I need you to be my innocent little girl tonight."

She smiled and confided.

"For now anyway."

Before long both girls found themselves on the bus to the entertainment district and Heather leaned in to kiss her girlfriend on the lips. The bus was quiet at this time in the evening as it went through the empty streets but on the other side of the bus was a more mature man who was reading a book but obviously interested in the passion that was being played out nearby.

As the bus pulled up at their stop and the girls got up Lucy's knee length thin coat opened to reveal her body in all it's beauty enhanced with black lingerie. The man blew the girls a kiss as they walked past but knowingly never offered his card respectful that they surely didn't need his participation in their passion.

The short walk to the cinema was uneventful and Lucy had wisely buttoned up her coat, as they walked in they scanned and went over to select a movie choosing a thriller which they both knew wasn't the main event tonight.

They both sat at the back and waited for the lights to dim which was Lucy's cue to lean in to her lover and force her tongue into Heather's inviting mouth. As they kissed passionately Heather felt a soft hand slip under her top and round her bare breasts. Petite as they were it was easy for even Lucy's feminine hands to hold a whole firm breast until she turned her attention to the nipples. Heather had small nipples but they soon hardened under the skilled control of Lucy's forefinger which twirled around it's edge. Heather felt a shudder of arousal go through her body like a wave and Lucy who had been kissing Heather's ear breathed more than said.

"not yet."

Her hand Slipped away and undid her own coat buttons to reveal the full splendor of that sensuous lingerie framing those large firm breasts and the black lace covering Lucy's clean shaven vagina and up over her hips. Lucy's hand now guided Heather's to where she needed it and Lucy shuddered as Heather felt under that lacy texture to satisfy her lovers need. Heather absorbed the sound track to the movie that neither girl cared about and found that her fingers were subconsciously keeping time as she slowly manipulated. Heather heard a stifled gasp which confirmed that she was doing right by her mistress then she felt Lucy's hand gently guide her head down to her breasts which were freed from their lacy frame but still round and firm and inviting. Heather used her tongue to tease the nipple much bigger than hers and erect before firmly suckling onto it. All the while her fingers slipped in and out of Lucy in time with the soundtrack which was picking up pace now as obviously building to a dramatic scene that would be ignored by these two patrons. Now Lucy held Heather's wrist as if to ensure her hand can't escape until it's finished it's important task and still the tempo increased. Then suddenly Lucy's body tensed as the excitement finally took over her and Heather felt a tightening of the grip on her wrist then suddenly after a spasm of tenseness her arm was released. Heather gently placed Lucy's breasts into her bra cups and did up her coat buttons before they kissed again tongues entwined as Lucy satisfied Heather in the same way but less gently as was Heather's need for firmness.

Back To Work

Lucy woke up the next morning and tried desperately not to disturb Heather who looked beautiful as ever lying on the bed. The thin sheets they slept under were god knows where probably at the foot of the bed, but the effect was a stunning sight of Heather naked adorned with her tattoos and piercings. But Lucy as always fixated on the serpent. She looked at it's amazing artwork on heather's thigh and stuck her tongue out in an act of aggression towards the piece of art that would be with Heather for ever.

Now out of bed Lucy looked at herself in the mirror and smiled before taking off her stockings and lingerie which had captivated her partner last night. They'd had a few drinks after the movie and on returning home the passion erupted again in a frenzy on the bed the result of which was Lucy falling asleep in her provocative garments. She unrolled her stockings one after the other and noticed the rarity of the sound of rain against the window which gave her another smile at the thought of a good run later in the fresh air. Totally undressed now she went through to the bathroom for a shower as Heather stirred and turned over onto her front causing Lucy to stop and stare at the pure beauty she had to leave so early.

As Lucy finished her shower and dried off she heard the coffee machine gurgling at it's task. When she had dressed into her officious black shorts and jacket and white shirt she walked through to the living room to see Heather in the kitchenette making them coffee and the smell of toast was strong in the air awakening Lucy's hunger.

Heather was in her knickers and crop top and Lucy couldn't resist squeezing her buttock as she picked up the mug of steaming hot coffee with her free hand. Still she halfheartedly chastised her partner for getting up so early which was quickly dismissed over the sound of the rain against their windows.

On the odd occasion it rained in Floricare it rained torrentially and Lucy was pleased she had her coat with her. They discussed their day and Lucy just shrugged at the prospect of mundane police work but she knew Heather wouldn't accept how boring her job could actually be. As Lucy was about to leave she gave Heather the normal hug but something was different and the younger girl seemed to hang on tighter than normal with her arms gripping as if unable to let go.

"It's okay darling, I'll be fine."

Lucy said then went out into the rain.

So today was a plodding day showing photos to people who may have seen Amber running in her area, they'd have to look for service providers who were there day after day and would remember the red haired and beautiful Amber possibly.

But first there was a stop on the way as Channing had got into a fight yet again, so pick up a "posh wankers coffee" then a trip to his district which was always an experience with it's litter and graffiti.

When they got to the offender's flat the smell was offensive but both officers were too polite to show it and as they took in the living room scene. Clothes were strewn everywhere and it was obvious the place hadn't been cleaned in a long time. On the coffee table the ashtray was full of cigarette butt's and empty beer cans covered the rest of the space. He was obviously hungover and was as brash and arrogant as usual and Lucy despaired as he recounted how the other guy now in hospital had asked for it.

Lucy and Channing both sipped their coffees and Lucy wondered if he could be useful in the investigation with his simplistic mind that seemed to see only threat in every gesture and saw the world through violent eyes.

"Ian I really don't want you to be in prison mate but you're going to be reviewed soon and it's not looking good I'm afraid."

Out of the corner of her eye Lucy could see Wendy looking on and knew her cynicism towards Channing but she kept quiet as always. Wendy refused to let Lucy be alone with this violent and feral man but compromisingly always stayed in the doorway.

Lucy just listened to the usual diatribe about how the other guy deserved it which faded into a background noise as she thought about enlisting a violent man to catch a violent man.

Lucy broke the line of conversation by holding up a hand and said.

"Look Ian I'm just wondering if you could help us with a case we're investigating?"

Channing suddenly was attentive.

"You're talking about the wanker who cut up that poor fucker on your side aren't you?"

Lucy caught Wendy straightening out and preparing to intervene but stared her down.

"I'm just thinking that you might be more able to understand the guy with your experience mate. Please don't read into it I'm not implying anything."

Channing shocked bother women when he said.

"Just give me the nod and I'll help you find the fucker. Shouldn't cut women not ever"

In the community car on their way to Amber's flat there was a frosty silence until Lucy broke it.

"Look I know it's desperate but we need to find him and soon. We both know he'll be looking for his next girl as we fanny about."

Wendy just slumped in resignation and accepted defeat.

"He should be locked up but I guess if we can make a use for the animal it'll be something."

They were heading towards Amber's area and the automated vehicle asked for further instructions. They both looked at each other and Lucy said.

"The waterfront first that's where I'd run and anyway Amber was beautiful and liked to show it off. She'd run there for sure."

Lucy gave the car instructions to take them to the waterfront and knew that it'd automatically go to a charging point by the café's and stores. Well that's as good a place to start as anywhere.

Meanwhile not far away Heather and John were just about to leave John's house and his wheelchair wasn't set on automatic for a change as Heather felt in need of exercise in the refreshing aftermath of the torrential downpour.

Heather had a sports bra and Lycra shorts on and John had been fighting his natural urges all morning. There was no prudence attached to clothing or as in this case the sexual nature of it anymore as society nowadays accepted the human body as a beautiful thing. The stigma attached to sexuality in the past was taught at in school nowadays and most children found it hard to believe. People dressed how they wanted whenever and it wasn't unusual to see men in shorts that revealed their bodies proudly and girls in bikinis anywhere.

It tested John regularly.

They set off at a good pace along the wide pavement which was also a result of the evolution as car ownership was irrelevant now and just one model of fully automated electric car was available to all who needed it. You could walk to a charging point nearby and there they were free and open to anyone. Heather pushed John along using her strong carers legs to power walk.

John loved this and the motion soon sent him into a state of dozing as his mind caught up on valuable sleep. John drifted into a dream in which he saw Amber in front of him and looking as beautiful as she did the day he'd seen her with the wolf. Amber slowly walked towards John still sat in his tomb of inanimate flesh and stepped out of her running shorts to reveal a perfectly trimmed flame red pubic patch. Next Amber used her nimble fingers to take John's now rigid penis out of his pants. Then she was slowly lowering herself onto him and he sensed her moist and tight body begin to squeeze his penis.

John was in more or less a permanent state of arousal because his disability rendered him unable to relieve any sexual tension, he instead relied on moments like this when his imagination took over. John felt himself ejaculate deep down knowing he'd embarrassed himself back in the waking world but not caring and in his dream John closed his eyes and allowed the sensation to take him.

When in his dream he opened his eyes again he looked straight into big beautiful blue eyes looking down at him from a loving face. Suddenly the smile dropped and eyes filled with sorrow then to John's horror she started to look upwards as her head tilted back to reveal a viciously coarse cut across her throat which slowly dripped blood like incessant tears for a life stolen.

The shear horror of that mutilation woke John, as he opened his eyes he remembered the embarrassment of his ejaculation in public which turned horror to self pity. A gentle caring voice said.

"it's alright fella no one saw and we're almost at a comfort station Hev will look after you."

At this John realized that she'd seen what was happening and had covered his groin with a blanket. What an angel.

After the comfort station where Heather had kindly turned the lights low to award John some dignity they went to the waterfront area and to John's joy he saw the beautiful façade of the swimming pools. The building had been knew built as most of this area was and the council had approved the bold young architect's submission to build using a Victorian influence with ornate brickwork and a dome of steel and glass that would look in place in London or Paris.

As they entered John could just see the elite pool with those athletes and their beautiful firm bodies showing off muscles that would befit gods in Athenian temples.

It wasn't long before they were getting changed in one of the specialist rooms and Heather was expertly hoisting John to strip him and put on his swimming shorts that were designed to keep any incontinence inside a set of seals on the legs and waist were sympathetically covered by material and they looked normal. Then when John was safely strapped into the simpler wheelchair supplied for poolside purposes with his sling positioned Heather slipped out of her shorts and sports bra. John always marveled at her beauty and occasionally had seen her clean shaven intimate area but he always got a buzz from a glimpse at her round breasts with pierced nipples, today just studs but still sexy.

He wondered if he ever got his life back would he be courageous enough to get a piercing. The answer was a resounding yes as he'd grasp life fully if he was given a pardon from his prison sentence. Heather wore a one piece swimsuit that was in her mind very conservative and intended to be less provocative but to John she'd look amazing in a potato sack.

The lifeguards hoisted John over the pool and as John lowered he felt the water envelope him and the strong safe arms of Heather firmly holding him . She slipped the harness off and the hoist silently retreated. Heather gave customary thanks to the lifeguard who said.

"Enjoy your swim guys, it's always lovely to see John."

Everyone knows John.

As John floated in his fitted life vest and Heather gently guided him he noticed a muscular female swimming in the lane near them. Her front crawl was perfect and her body slid through the water with the ease you'd attribute to a dolphin or another marine creature that evolution had chosen for this purpose. As the girl got to the end of the pool John realized it was Tanya and as she took her goggles away from her eyes she saw Heather and waved in her usual confident way. Then Tanya ducked under the rope that separates the pool and swam underwater expertly emerging smoothly just the other side of John to Heather. John felt the ripple slowly bob his body then Tanya leaned forward to kiss Heather as was normal and John was pecked on his cheek.

The two girls both started the usual small talk and John phased out slowly sinking into his thoughts. Until he heard that name "Jake" Heather was engulfed in her friends description of the night that Tanya had spent with the wolf and the sensual details but John was utterly confused now. He knew in his heart that the wolf was a monster but this guy that Tanya described was different somehow and according to Tanya he was loving and caring.

Tanya said that she was enchanted by Jakes boyish reaction to finding out her sexuality and was so relieved that he was obviously open-minded to a relationship with a transgender woman. Heather was engulfed in the description of a man she had once distrusted.

"We're still taking it easy Hev and I really don't want to scare him off, but I think he might be my guy."

Tanya confided.

"I'm so pleased for you Tanya and he's a looker too. You've nailed it babe. He's good with John too."

At this both girls looked at John and smiled benevolently. Breaking the mood Tanya then lowered the tone and told Heather about Jakes gorgeous cock. Heather just winked and said.

"Well you'd fucking know"

After the girls had had a good gossip to John's delight Tanya offered to help Heather change him which added a nice opportunity for the girls to continue their conversation. The lifeguard soon started the operation of hoisting John out while Tanya using muscles that were toned to perfection pushed herself up onto the side of the pool and stood by his wheelchair ready to help him in. After that the three of them retrieved their clothes and after John was attended the girls dried and dressed chatting about allsorts of twaddle but John wasn't paying attention to the conversation.

Before lunch Heather took John along the waterfront for some fresh air and they passed the coffee kiosk with it's usual young attractive barista serving drinks to customers. To John she looked so sweet and innocent and his heart sank at the thought that she could well be the wolf's next prey, if only he could tell someone.

Then a familiar and friendly sight greeted both of them and before John could blink Heather had hit the monitor button on John's chair that paused it where it was and kept an eye on him through sensors.

Heather's head turned to wink at John then she ran up to the officious Lucy who was wearing her shorts suit and tight t shirt with her badge around her neck. The fact that Lucy was obviously working didn't stop Heather from jumping up wrapping her legs around the taller girls waist and arms around her neck. The two kissed and after a few moments a voice behind Lucy said.

"Let go of her for fucks sake the girl's working, can't you see?"

Heather detached reluctantly and stuck her studded tongue out at Wendy while putting on her sad face.

"Spoilsport."

Wendy just smiled and said.

"Well fuck it I guess the world's soppiest copper deserves a coffee break. Fuck off you two and I'll carry on for a bit then catch you at the car pool in an hour."

Heather literally jumped for joy and to Wendy's embarrassment planted a kiss on her cheek and whispered.

"You're not so tough are you Wendy?"

Then the two of them walked back to John before walking hand in hand to the kiosk John's chair gently propelling him alongside.

The kiosk girl was indeed as her appearance suggested young at seventeen and was doing a years work before deciding what to go into for a career which she felt would be teaching.

Dawn loved life and was openly sociable with most people which caused her to be the focus of many young men and women but she'd held off relationships which she felt would complicate life at this point. If there was one thing that Dawn felt uncomfortable about it was her very large breasts but for sometime she'd been looking into a reduction.

When the police officer had asked her about that poor lady who'd been murdered she'd had felt a sadness as she did recognize the beautiful red haired girl and explained that she ran past most days.

The cop took down her details and quizzed Dawn about timings and when she'd last seen Amber then moved on.

Later on the barista was surprised to see the officer come back with that sexy girl who's often with the crippled guy but then saw them kiss which cleared up the question of their relationship.

Heather went up to get three latte's and the girl thickened John's on request, Dawn made polite conversation and then said.

"Who's the guy that comes out with your friend? He seems nice."

"Oh Jake you mean yeah he's a good guy but I'm afraid he's in a relationship."

Heather felt she had been a bit mean but was so pleased for Tanya that she didn't want it ruined. Let's face it who could resist those gorgeous tits.

"sorry babe."

Heather lied frowning and walked away with the coffees.

Lucy and Heather enjoyed their coffees in the setting and especially enjoyed the refreshing coolness that always followed rain here. But soon the conversation turned to the murder investigation. It was obvious Lucy was becoming fixated but felt she hadn't any choice and was driven by guilt after that night.

"I don't know Hev, we've been through everything we can and it feels like we're racing against the clock."

Her girlfriend leaned in and kissed Lucy on the lips then said softly.

"It's not your fault that Amber died babe, there's an evil bastard out there and you'll catch him."

Then changing the subject Heather filled her partner in about Jake and Tanya.

"Apparently he tugged her off but she'd given him a blowjob already so he was probably still recovering from that."

She told her.

"Fucking hell Hev just come out with it why don't you? Still I'd never have had him down as open minded."

Lucy then added.

"You know if you fancy Tanya I really don't mind, in fact it'd be quite nice to try out."

Then she quickly added.

"but I don't want that cock in me if it's all that you say."

Lucy gave Heather a horrified look which made her laugh. Heather just held her hands out to indicate largeness but said.

"I don't think I could again after Amber hun it's all just still a bit painful. You're all I need at the moment."

On hearing this Lucy gently touched Heather's cheek and whispered.

"I fucking love you."

Then winked and looked towards the kiosk where the barista was busy serving customers.

"But I'd love to get my lips onto those tits one day."

Heather just looked shocked and said.

"You fucking pervert she's only a little girl."

They both laughed and then kissed passionately before Lucy had to go leaving Heather to help John with his coffee that was now cooled. As Lucy walked off she couldn't help but notice the kiosk girls breasts that were resting on the counter.

"Oh for fucks sake."

She thought then went to meet Wendy.

Meanwhile whilst instinctively swallowing coffee John was screaming in his mind and never felt so hopeless in his life. He desperately wanted to shout to Lucy and one word kept forming in his mind.

"Wolf, wolf, wolf......"

The Wolf Has A New Plan

Jake took his time planning his next conquest and was meticulous in his preparations all inside his mind, like an actor learning his lines he just kept going over it again and again.

It's a known fact that serial killers like anyone learn their vocation through a process of trial and error and the engineering state mistakes had been eradicated but also Amber had been a lesson.

Jake sat at the kiosk clearing surrounded by thick trees most days he was working with John and on his days off he went in the evening to read his book and built a rapport with the girl now known as Dawn. He noticed that towards the end of the day there were practically no customers and once the hatch was closed at eight o'clock no one ever showed up. Perfect. He certainly wasn't going to use drugs again but had another option that was just as effective and as the kiosk was out of view from the footpath it really didn't matter.

That evening Jake had a shoulder bag with all he needed and as he'd hoped the area was deserted when he waited in the shadows near the kiosk.

As she lowered the hatch turning the kiosk into a shed Jake began his plan, he ran up to the door at the back making himself out of breath and urgently banged on it. Soon the familiar pretty face appeared and was full of concern as Jake told Dawn he'd been attacked and could he come in and sit down.

So that evening she through an act of compassion sealed her fate.

It all happened so fast and the small young girl was powerless to resist his strength. Suddenly she found herself being held by the neck with one hand and the other over her mouth while a now emotionless voice told her not to scream or he'd cut her.

Dawn fought back sobs as he cable tied her hands behind her back and placed duct tape over her mouth, she was helpless as strong hands ripped her top open to reveal her chest. Then her eyes looked down in horror as he produced a knife and cut her bra releasing her breasts. She was still standing up but as he looked down towards the young girl's groin her knees gave way.

He strongly lifted her back to upright and tutted as he flashed the knife in front of her face then raised a finger to his lips. Dawn was sobbing and muffled moans escaped her as he took her shorts and knickers down and lifted her onto the counter. Before she knew it his penis was forcing it's way into her, painfully destroying her virginity, this monster was thrusting like an animal for ages.

Then suddenly she sensed him pull away and his penis slid out of her before those hands lifted her off the counter then that voice ordered her to kneel. He said she'd done well and one more thing then he'd let her go.

Dawn felt a pang of hope as he ripped the tape away from her mouth. She'd sucked off boys before to placate advances and hoped that it would be her final torment.

But this was different. With her back to the counter there was no way to back off as he forced his penis so far into her throat that she couldn't breathe. The monster had one hand around her neck but the other hand was cruelly pinching her nose to deprive her of much needed air. She gagged for breath when he eventually withdrew but before she could get the lungful of air she desperately needed his penis was once again thrusting into her throat.

Dawn's body desperately tried to back away and struggled helplessly and her hands strained against strong cable ties. But the one action that could stop her torment was impossible as her mouth opened wide on instructions from her brain screaming for the essential air her body screamed out for. But still he kept one hand firmly around her neck and the other pinched her nose while she struggled to no avail.

As the teenager's world began to spin and her struggling slowly dissipated the last thing she felt was that of semen invading her now still throat.

Jake lifted the now limp body and delicately kissed her on the forehead then lay her gently onto the floor. He looked down to her and frowned as one might paying respects to a recently deceased partner, the sick irony passed him by as he continued about his task completely guilt free.

Then suddenly a problem as he heard staggering footsteps approaching and voices. Jake held still too afraid to even breath it seemed and looked down at the lifeless body of Dawn.

"Dawn honey come out with us."

Came the first voice quickly followed by the other.

"We're having a barbeque on the beach."

Then there was knocking on the door that seemed to shake the wooden kiosk making Jake worry that the door wouldn't take the aggression but it did and soon the knocking stopped. The first voice still slurred came back again but resigned now to failure.

"Your loss Dawn it's going to be awesome."

Then to Jake's relief the footsteps started again slowly getting fainter until Jake felt courageous enough to sneak a look only to see they were gone. He looked at the limp body lying sadly on the floor and then got on with his task as he reached into his bag and pulled out a small can of petrol. Jake took a moment to take in the body of Dawn once more the girl who'd befriended him so openly then he coldly splashed petrol all over the kiosk but mostly on the body. It was getting dark inside the kiosk now and Jake knew the sun would be going down outside.

The killer stepped gingerly through the flimsy door and struck a match as he glanced towards Dawn lovingly but as the flame flared in the dimming light Jake never hesitated even slightly and flicked the match onto Dawn's still body.

As he strolled down the path Jake heard the flames erupt behind him and didn't even spare a thought for the young life he'd stolen.

In the kiosk tomb the flames started to take hold and we're now attacking the walls and rolled along the ceiling as if trying to escape this scene of horror.

As the petrol fueled fire heated her bare flesh to a point that caused it to disintegrate Dawn's eyes snapped open, awoken from the effects of severe oxygen starvation by the intense human drive for survival consciousness cruelly returned. Her muscles failed her due to the shock her body was under and as she tried to scream her raw damaged throat wouldn't allow the action. Instead a coarse pathetic groan marked the final plea for mercy from the poor young girl.

A New Turn In The Investigation

The fire had been featured on various news outlets and firefighters had been interviewed at the scene but it was of no immediate concern to Lucy and Wendy. Until the fire investigation revealed that it was a petrol fire and after a quick call to the manager responsible for these kiosks, it was confirmed to be arson as he'd assured them that no petrol was allowed in those premises.

The manager was clearly already shocked and hearing that his young charge had probably been murdered he broke down on the phone needing soothing from the fire investigator.

So inevitably the case fell onto the desk of Lucy who buried her head into her arms, she only raised her head when Wendy looking over her shoulder said tactlessly.

"Don't tell me you fucked this one too?"

Lucy got up and ran out of the office drawing attention from other officers until Wendy who'd followed glared around the area and shouted simply to everyone.

"Fuck off"

In the hall Wendy approached with her hands up and said.

"I'm really sorry Lucy, what can I say? I'm a cunt."

Lucy just looked at her partner through reddened eyes and said.

"We've got to catch him.

"Wendy drew her attention to the possibility that it may not be him but they both knew instinctively it was.

Back in the office they both looked at the case file and Wendy skimmed through.

"Young, attractive, and inside so relatively safe environment for our guy to take his time."

Lucy looked at her partner and asked the question they were both thinking.

"Why the fire?"

"I mean it's not like he's trying to hide anything."

Wendy just said.

"What do we know fire does? Destroys evidence. So I'm guessing he wanted to get more intimate with this one.

"Lucy sat upright suddenly buzzing."

I bet he was sick of using a condom and gloves. This time he wanted to feel his victims body."

Wendy stared at Lucy.

"So he's getting confident and reckless. We're going to get him Lucy, sooner or later."

Lucy just said.

"Sooner not later, it's got to be sooner. I'm not losing any more Wendy I can't."

Their moment of thought was broken by Lucy's phone ringing.

"Yes we'll be right down."

She said and looked at Wendy.

"The hospital is going to do the post mortem.

"They both picked up their things and rushed off."

At the hospital they were surprised when doctor Avery probably in her late fifties met them at the entrance personally this time. It's very unusual for professionals in such a position to be so senior as there are so many young people to replace them, normally by their fifties people take a less demanding role. She was very confident in her manner, she'd obviously been waiting and introduced herself.

"I'm doctor Avery I'm in charge of post mortems and unexplained deaths. I'm here to liase with you and I'll help as much as possible but if I'm honest such severe burn victims don't often reveal much."

Lucy took in the older lady's appearance and noticed that she was in scrubs that were well used and frayed in places. She was obviously not a desk jockey.

"Are you carrying out the autopsy yourself this time Dr Avery?"

Lucy asked rather more toxically than was necessary and wasn't surprised at the answer.

"Yes definitely I tend to deal with unusual cases myself as I've had more experience than any of my team."

Dr Avery quickly added.

"But a member of my team will assist for the experience. We rarely get burn cases and it'd be a good study."

Lucy felt her anger rising at the way she was describing a young person but kept it to herself, only Wendy noticed and touched her partners back to offer support.

They passed a Starbucks and Lucy excused herself to get a coffee then when back with two cups said to the doctor.

"We're ready when you are, please lead on."

The autopsy room was as expected clinical and meticulous and a younger man also in scrubs was waiting for the start of what presumably was an exciting part of a normally dull job. The two professionals got themselves ready and soon the investigation into the poor girl began.

Lucy and Wendy stood well back and let the two doctors go about their work and it quickly became apparent that Dr Avery hadn't just been pessimistic in her negativity. There really was little left to reveal but the police officers listened intently as the junior doctor used a cruel looking tool to cut through Dawn's ribcage, the relief when the whirring sound ended didn't last long as the doctor a young man in his twenties inserted a clamp and started to open the ribs using a ratchet motion.

Lucy thought she would be sick at the cracking sound as charred ribs surrendered to stainless steel. Wendy reached across and squeezed her partners hand to offer support, but both detectives were bought back into focus as Dr Avery announced that she'd died of smoke inhalation explaining that the lungs were charred inside. The discovery of the cause of death was dire and shook Lucy who'd assumed the young soul had been dead before the fire, but evidently she'd endured further torture before her end.

Once finished with the front they turned her over rather more clumsily than one would expect. Then Dr Avery confirmed what everyone thought saying that her hands had been secured behind her back as her arms were locked in that unnatural position. Dr Avery broke their thoughts saying in the officers direction.

"In my opinion this poor girl was definitely murdered."

It was the first bit of emotion the medical professional had shown but was quickly turned back to cold professionalism as she said.

"The victim is probably young as her bones indicate, I would guess at teens but definitely no older than twenty five.

The rest of the autopsy was unhelpful for the investigation and Dr Avery left her subordinate to tidy up and walked towards Lucy and Wendy shaking her head. She lowered her mask and said.

"This poor girl would have died in agony officers. I'm really sorry we couldn't give you any more help."

Lucy was more comfortable now as Dr Avery was obviously showing more emotion and shook her hand saying.

"That's ok doctor we weren't expecting much but you've confirmed some things which always helps."

As they turned to leave suddenly an unexpected sound jolted them in their steps. The junior doctor was calling Dr Avery back.

"Maria I think she's clutching something in her hand but I just can't get it."

Everyone was around the table in an instant and Dr Avery reached for a small electric saw. A grim wining sound filled the room as she skillfully cut the clenching black hand until the junior doctor was able to snap each digit at the base.

Then something slipped out of the dead girls grip falling onto the table and slowly spiraling until noisily settling on the cold steel. The room was silent until Wendy broke the spell in her usual way.

"Fuck me I haven't seen one of those in fucking years."

Dr Avery stared at Wendy but said nothing then Lucy just reached into her pocket to get an evidence bag and after putting on gloves she gingerly picked up the disc and bagged it. Now Dr Avery found her voice.

"How on earth did she get a dollar coin? I mean they've been gone for decades."

Lucy just smiled at the realization that at last they had a break in this investigation.

An Interesting Night

Tanya had persuaded Jake that it would be fun to go on a double date but Jake being normally very socially awkward hadn't been looking forward to it. In truth Heather true to form lightened up the whole mood with her childlike charm and even had Jake laughing at her jokes.

The dinner had been pleasant and they'd all had fun in the rather over the top (as usual) Mexican restaurant. But eventually while they were choosing dessert Jake finally asked the question he'd been eager to all night.

"So Lucy are you any closer to catching that killer then?"

Lucy just sighed and admitted.

"I'm sorry to say we're not really. We thought we had something but it didn't work out."

Her mind drifted to the expert at the museum informing her that dollar coins were actually quite common. It seemed a lot of people hung on to them as mementos after they were called in to be recycled.

Then Heather broke the thought snapping.

"No work tonight you promised."

Lucy just leaned over and kissed her girlfriend's sulking face saying nothing until Tanya glared at Jake causing him to apologize.

The rest of the evening was fun and the restaurant staff encouraged their customers to get up dancing to a mariachi band who played their hearts out. Tanya and Heather took the opportunity but Jake and Lucy declined and having had several drinks too many found themselves talking about the incident at the zoo. Lucy embarrassed Jake somewhat with her praises but soon to Jakes relief it was time to go home. The foursome made a big fuss of thanking the staff and they walked outside into the dark night.

It was a short walk to the car pool where a rather bored looking night attendant jumped out of his comfortable chair as the group entered the office.

"Hi folks I've got a real treat for you guys if you want."

The foursome looked surprised at the change to the normally mundane part of the evening and as they showed their surprise the attendant beamed a huge smile. As they walked through the many cars that all looked identical except for color suddenly something different appeared. Heather broke the silence.

"It's got no roof."

Lucy noticed that her lover's eyes were wide in fascination and felt the need to ground the moment.

"Is it safe?"

The attendant explained how these new 'convertibles' are strengthened specially and perfectly fine. He said that several were being trialed in Floricare and this one has just arrived. Heather was her usual self now pleading with the others insisting that it would be fun. And soon they were heading off into the night leaving the satisfied attendant behind. Tanya and Jake in the back and their friends in the front facing around in their seats to chat to the back passengers. Heather was feeling impish and emboldened by drink she looked into Jakes eyes and said as the wind blew her hair.

"So buddy have you paid Tanya back that blowjob yet?"

Tanya glared at her friend and said.

"Fucking bitch you know I'm not that shallow."

Then looked at Jake saying in her sexy voice.

"No pressure lover you just take all the time you need."

Jake just looked at Tanya then towards the front of the car where Lucy was transfixed by her lover's conversation bomb.

"I have to admit I was shocked when I first found out and it's taken a bit of getting used to but I think I'm ok now.

"He looked into Tanya's big round eyes and said.

"I'm falling for Tanya in every aspect and she's perfect just the way she is."

Lucy started to say something but before she could Tanya had grabbed Jake and was passionately kissing him with her black hair freely getting blown about. Lucy just turned to Heather and kissed her on the lips saying softly.

"I love you bitch."

The moment passed as the car automatically pulled up outside Tanya's flat with a soft voice announcing.

"You have arrived at destination one."

Tanya offered to continue the evening at her home but Heather and Lucy both knew she only wanted Jake there now and after Lucy and Heather sat in the back to get the full effect of the openness of the new convertible. As the car drove off Lucy winked at Heather and whispered.

"We know what Tanya's getting tonight."

Changing the subject Heather remembered something that had been niggling her since it's mention.

"So what's the news about the murder case then? Are you keeping secrets now bitch?"

Lucy just laughed as the car automatically conveyed the two lovers home.

"It was really nothing but at the time felt like it meant everything. That last girl you know the one from the kiosk, well it turned out she was clutching an old coin which we thought was significant."

Lucy looked sad now and sighed.

"Apparently there are loads of them that people kept as mementos so it's nothing that'll help." Heather sensed her girlfriends dismay and pulled herself into Lucy's side of the car which initiated another passionate kiss as the car conveyed them through the deserted streets.

Meanwhile at Tanya's flat they'd settled down on the sofa with a glass of wine and talked about the evening until Tanya broached the topic that was on her mind.

"I really don't want to rush you Jake and I'm not just saying that. You're nice and I don't want you to do anything that makes you uncomfortable."

Jake took both her hands into his and looked her in her eyes.

"I'm not uncomfortable with you Tanya and I really want to be the man you want me to be."

Tanya braced herself for a "but" yet instead Jake leaned in and kissed her then he took her wineglass and put it alongside his on the coffee table. He kissed her again but this time his free hand felt down to her crotch and started to caress the phallic shape under her jeans. It was easy to undo her flies and as if it was a clockwork toy all of ten inches of penis sprung up making Jake gasp.

He was stroking it now with his man's hand barely reaching around the shaft but Tanya he knew desired more from him than this. As her hand reached up and gently pushed on the back of his neck Jake realized that now nothing was beyond what he'd do for this beautiful girl. Jake felt her circumcised penis at his lips as he shut his eyes through passion not embarrassment. Jake allowed his lips to part and as the enormous penis slipped into his willing mouth he realized that Tanya had a firm grip on his head with strong hands. Far from putting him off this tantalized Jake and he was actually getting excited by the submissive element as she worked his head up and down.

Then suddenly he was released and found her kissing him again before Tanya stood up and pushed Jake onto his back, in no time Tanya was naked from the waist down and climbing onto him while masturbating herself. Jake willingly surrendered when his head was held up to receive the penis again but only for a few minutes then she withdrew to start masturbating over him. Now Jake knew what was required and looked Tanya in the eyes as the semen started to cover his face in small spurts, the warm sensation was exiting him and he couldn't stop himself leaning in and taking her penis in his mouth as her hand pumped every drop of semen out.

Afterwards Tanya pleasured Jake in her talented way then they both went to bed ignoring the wine glasses still full. Jake went to sleep with Tanya's arms around him and feeling her breasts in his back and her flaccid penis against his buttock and slept better than he had in years.

John And The Wolf Go Swimming

John had seen the news on the TV about the beautiful kiosk girl and her untimely demise and it had sunk him into a deep depression, although nobody would ever know. As always John's emotions were trapped in his prison of the human body that stubbornly refused to serve him.

He had been put to bed that night as usual but things inside John's mind were different even if physically nothing had changed. The unwilling confidant to a murderer had in the night when left alone with his thoughts come to a decision. While John waited for dreams to release him he made a vow that he would somehow stop the wolf from killing again, and as the infuriating whale song played gently in the background and lights set to dim green failed to relax him John acknowledged the only way he could possibly save anyone from Jake.

He'd have to somehow get his body to work again, at least his vocal chords that had been sleeping so long.

As John slipped off into his dream world where he was free of his broken body he found himself somehow walking into the living room where it was daylight. Heather was sat on the sofa and brilliant sunshine was pouring through the windows acting as another indicator that he was in fact dreaming. John sat next to his angelic carer and she cuddled up to him as she fixated on her favorite soap again 'Alascation nights' The scene was in a lodge in the frosty vacation state and several characters were acting especially badly and over dramatizing their lines making John wince and say to Heather.

"I've got no idea why you watch this crap."

Heather just looked up at him and winked which seemed conspiratorial but John looked closer at the TV now and realized that the actors were all too familiar. Suddenly he found himself alone and watching Heather, Lucy and Tanya on the TV dressed in jeans and lumberjack shirts and Lucy actually had a thick fur hat with side panels dangling over her ears. Heather was telling Lucy that she had to go and fetch some wood for the huge open fire and as Lucy and Tanya looked on she started to put on a heavy coat.

As the three of them painfully overacted the scene John saw outside the window the face of Jake but different somehow and looking greedily at Heather. John still in his living room found himself shouting at the TV.

"Don't go out there Hev for God's sake."

But to no avail as Heather now dressed for the snowy scene picked up a coal bucket and left the other two chatting.

As she stepped outside John had a different view from outside and could see Jake by the window now looking towards the closing door as Heather slammed it shut, then she walked towards him greeting him warmly.

What had been different about Jake before was obvious now and he had dark hair but apart from his face all his body was covered in brown fur, Jake had the body of a wolf with pointed ears and strong hind legs but standing upright as he fell inline to walk with Heather who was skipping along and swinging her bucket.

John felt panic rise in him as Jake looked straight into the camera seemingly at him in his living room and smiled as his big wolf ears seemed to twist back and forth.

Heather was at the wood shed now and fumbled with the door latch through thick mittens, she looked at Jake and said.

"Can you get the door mate?"

Jake just held up his front paws big as anything and with fur barely covering menacing claws and said.

"Err I don't think so Heather."

On cue the sound of fake canned laughter came out of the TV but John just looked at the scene horrified. Eventually Heather managed the latch and they both disappeared into the wooden outbuilding leaving John just looking at the outside view. The building suddenly emanated a horrendous noise somewhere between a wolf growling and a human cry and sounds of a fight were filling the otherwise idyllic winter scene making John feel sick.

To John's surprise the sound gave way to a repetitive metallic clanging over and over again until it slowed then silence for a few seconds, then with great comedic timing one last almighty clang before Heather emerged through the doorway carrying a battered dented coal bucket. Heather looked back through the door and shouted into the darkness.

"And if you try that again you'll get the bucket again."

Before she started skipping towards the lodge and as the titles started and the laughter sounded again.

John had been pleased to wake up from a restless night during which he'd had several more lucid dreams but reassuringly they'd all ended in the wolf failing to harm anyone.

As he lay in bed waiting for his morning routine to kick in John concentrated all his efforts on his hand and particularly one finger. His logic was that any movement he achieved would activate areas of his brain into life again hopefully leading to speech.

John stared at the stubborn digit as sunlight sneaked in through his bedroom blinds distracting him, he screamed in his head at the mental effort and all the time he was aware that soon the opportunity would be lost. John was in the middle of this struggle when suddenly his day started with the entrance of Jeff who he mentally cursed until ashamedly telling himself it wasn't Jeff's fault. All the while relaxing music started and soft lighting gently increased in intensity. And another day was beginning.

After an invigorating bath John ended up in his bedroom on his bed, classical music played in the background and now the bright Floricare sunshine was lighting up the bedroom in defiance of the blinds.

It was going to be a day with Jake he knew as he was well aware of the staff rotation and it was easy to work out what activity was in store today. John could smell the cream being applied to his areas at risk from sores and it was the waterproof one. As a magnificent orchestra played what John thought was Beethoven he was being expertly rolled from side to side on the bed to slowly slide his pants up. A similar maneuver achieved his t-shirt slowly sliding down his back as they were accompanied by an aggressive sound of drumming from the system. Then when ordered the hoist silently drifted into position and the sling's hoops were hooked on for him to be elevated in a sitting position then delicately lowered into his chair.

Later as Jeff was busying himself in the kitchen John sat in front of the TV and watched the bleak news about Dawn the kiosk girl. His heart sank as a quite sensitive clip was paying tribute to the once vibrant young girl who had had her future stolen away and as the film of Dawn played out showing her with friends of her own age group, John became even more determined to stop Jake striking again.

"Good morning guys."

Came the greeting from a familiar voice then as the murderer saw his latest victim on TV his face visibly changed.

"Oh God not another murder surely."

Jeff frowned and confirmed.

"Yes I'm afraid so. It was the girl from the coffee kiosk on the waterfront. You know the one."

Jake feigned surprise and said.

"But she was so ysaid."

John could feel the anger bubbling up inside him as he heard the words both at Jake for the murder and at himself for his pathetic inability to prevent it.

Once out of the house Jake told John that they were going swimming not realizing John knew already. As they walked the short but pleasant journey John noticed Jake looking elated as if he'd had some kind of an epiphany. In fact Jake was positively radiant which in normal circumstances would definitely radiate outwardly but instead it was having the opposite effect on John. The good mood was taken as a disturbing harbinger by the impotent man and his mind ran away with the dark thoughts that the wolf could already be thinking about a next victim. But surely not so soon after Dawn.

As the sun beat down on the paralyzed John he worried that the time he'd assumed he had may not be available. He snapped out of the dark negative thought and decided that a time limit might be just what he needed to challenge his useless body to activity.

Jake brightly said good morning to an elderly lady they passed and when he was confident she was out of earshot he looked around before leaning down to say.

"She struggled like crazy."

The wolf winked and smiled saying.

"Her tits were lovely and she was cute as hell, I think I was her first."

Then Jake straightened up and seeing the pool with it's beautiful architecture said.

"Let's find me a nice sexy lifeguard to play with shall we?"

The routine had gone as normal with John was despairing throughout as he was changed into swimming gear.

T they went through to the poolside past several patrons who were in the changing rooms in various states of dress men and women together as normal. Jake didn't pay attention to them in their varying degrees of nudity as it was obvious to John they weren't for some reason a source of any interest to the wolf who was just looking for a specific prey.

As they got through to the poolside John tried to take in every lifeguard hoping beyond hope that none would catch Jakes eye. As he was hoisted into the nice warm water John only saw male lifeguards and as he floated enveloped in the warmth John realized that no women were on duty.

Jake was getting frustrated and his previously good mood was dissipating but to John's surprise he was still caring and gentle as John floated in the lovely warm water.

At one point he noticed a sexy young girl with blond hair and in a G string bikini but he wasn't interested. Even when she was obviously flirting with Jake by making a show of pushing herself out the pool obviously so that Jake had full view of her stunning bare buttocks her body drew not so much as a glance.

After going through the exercises that were essential to keep John's body healthy and mobile eventually Jake gave up and gestured to the lifeguard that it was time to get out.

John was elated that the wolf hadn't found his prey, he knew it wouldn't stop him but he just didn't want to witness it.

As they wheeled through the changing rooms John was laughing hysterically inside his silent tomb. He was laughing all the way up to hearing those fateful words.

"Can I help you guys?"

Jake had become despondent and was pushing the pools wheelchair through the now empty changing rooms when suddenly a voice called out from a corner.

"Can I help you guys?"

The sweet young voice came from a girl in the corner that both of them hadn't noticed. She had a beautiful figure and was half way through slipping a red lifeguards swimsuit on having got to her waist. John noticed a pair of perfectly formed petite breasts before she finished dressing.

"Fucking hell not her please."

John recognized her as a friendly lifeguard who always had time to chat to Heather. John cursed that beautiful person's helpful nature as she walked up to assist them with their task.

The lifeguards strong arms worked expertly on the harness and hoist as she and the wolf talked about various topics but mainly about John. She was a kind soul John could tell as she always included him when talking about him which he found was a good indicator.

As John was in the special changing room there were just the three of them and Jake surprisingly was protective of John's dignity expressing thanks for the help before undressing John. The girl nodded approval and said she'd wait outside until John was dressed. As she walked towards the door both men noticed her swimming costume that barely covered her strong athletic body. Her blonde straight hair reached halfway down her back in a plait and the image was one of pure beauty.

Jake looked at John once the door closed and just smiled.

After dressing John and himself the wolf called the unsuspecting lifeguard back in and John was hoisted into his chair, as he was lowered he despaired at a surge of arousal at the sight of her body stunningly covered by her one piece costume. What John used to accept as an essential part of life somehow felt dirty and shameful, he knew if he was honest it was nothing but perversion all along but had managed to suppress that fact due to his disability. To John's horror as they parted company and Jake thanked the lifeguard she reached into her bag and handed the wolf a card as she winked at him.

"Oh fuck"

The wolf was a different person as they left the pool into the beautiful sunshine and had a strong sense of purpose in his stride which just lowered John's mood even more.

An Investigation Stalled

Lucy and Wendy were getting more desperate and the proposition from Lucy to get Channing to look at the case files surprisingly was greeted by Wendy as a good idea.

Wendy hated Channing and didn't hide it but the view of a violent man may just make the difference. As they had passed through the border into his unkempt district both detectives hadn't said a word as if anticipating an unspeakable disaster to come. They had agreed to pick the known rowdy drunk up outside his flat which pleased Wendy who hated going into that messy dirty abode but both doubted he'd remember. As they pulled up to their surprise he was stood there ready.

"Fuck me it's clean as a fucking whistle around here!"

Remarked Channing as they drove through the residential district towards Amber's flat. As a crime scene the flat was sealed and for want of another option had been considered a good starting point by the officers but surprisingly their miscreant consultant was reluctant to go there. It was only when Lucy had softly asked him what was bothering him that Channing had opened up with the revelation.

The man to Wendy's shock burst into uncontrollable sobs as the car slowly traversed the area and eventually confessed that he'd been terrified since the last murder. Amber it turned out fitted the description of Channing's daughter who'd left his district years ago to start what was called a productive life.

Naturally father and daughter had once had a strong loving relationship but the man had disowned his only child for moving out of the place he'd called home. There and then as the quiet electric community car drove on past people going about their business oblivious to the emotional outpouring inside Channing let it all out. The car suddenly had an awkward atmosphere inside until in an attempt to lift the mood Wendy said "We'll have a look at the flat Ian then go to the waterfront for lunch mate. To show our gratitude."

Ian Channing visibly brightened up at the prospect. There weren't the tasteful restaurants in his districts just the somewhat seedy café's and rough bars. As they chose not to contribute to society therefore it was decided they'd have to live without the benefits but some exceptions had to be allowed so the café's and bars were accepted.

The society that Ian was experiencing now had well and truly given up on those who refused to adapt.

"Thai."

The word came out of the blue and surprised Lucy and Wendy then Ian elaborated.

"I've always wanted to try Thai food if that's okay?"

"Sure Ian that's all good. It's the least we can do."

Wendy shocked Lucy with her submission to Lucy's sensitive approach.

Then the car announced their arrival at Amber's modest flat breaking the moment. The car was officially commandeered so they knew it would be there when their grim task was finished, a privalege only certain departments had.

So the trio alighted and Channing having accepted all else that day expressed his surprise at the lack of security in his special way.

"They thing would be wrecked in no fucking time in the dumping ground."

He was pointing at the car. Lucy wondered if he'd ever understand that that's exactly what made it safe here but said nothing as Wendy opened the security lock that had been attached to the door. As the door opened the metallic odor of stale blood hit the three of them, only Channing spoke saying.

"Now that's a fucking familiar stink, she bled good and proper by the stench. Poor kid."

Wendy gripped his arm before he went in and looking him in the eyes said "You don't have to do this fella no one will think less of you."

Then added.

"Thinking of your daughter mate."

Channing removed her hand and said.

"You don't realize Its for her I'm doing this."

Then the two detectives looked at each other until Lucy spoke next.

"Well let's do this then Ian."

Ian smiled and returned to form.

"Fucking hell you bitches got me all soppy then. Let's see if I can help you catch the cunt shall we?"

Inside the flat was just as before as both police officers knew it would be and Lucy was saddened and felt guilty at her lack of attention to Amber lately favoring the new victim Dawn. Lucy could almost sense the fear she must have felt at being grabbed as she walked in after her night out and had to mentally pull herself together. Channing just said.

"I'd have grabbed her as she walked in if it was me."

But somehow there was remorse in his voice as if experiencing this violent scene reflected on his poor choice of lifestyle. He continued though.

"I'd want her to feel there's a hope as it'd make her do what I want. If she realized that she's going to die she'd struggle too much."

Then Channing looked towards the blood stained sofa and carpet nodding.

"Cut her from behind then just after he finished fucking her I reckon. Blokes don't go in for lingering after and this guy wanted to get it over I reckon."

Then he added.

"Have you girls thought about the fact that he did her in from behind? I reckon he's not a born monster but has had a bad past."

Lucy who had been scribbling notes looked up and said.

"Do you think abusive parents Ian? We could work with that but what makes you think so?"

The streetwise man just smiled and said.

"You girls are really too nice for this shit aren't you?"

Then Channing stared into Lucy's eyes until Lucy looked away. Channing smiled and said.

"It's all in the eyes my lovely. Only a born monster can look into the eyes as he kills, I'd only do that if I hated the cunt. No this guy is a predator that needs to kill not one that wants to."

Wendy muttered something causing the others to look at her.

"Like a hunter, like a wolf."

Wendy repeated.

"Fuck yeah"

Said Channing.

"The wolf doesn't hate but hunts because nature made it that way. It's learned from seeing it's parents hunt."

At this point Wendy broke the mood saying.

"Fuck this let's go for lunch."

Two Wolves Meet

After their swim Jake had as normal gone with John in tow to the waterfront and as normal it was a sunny day so equally as normal the sunbathers were out en masse. Jake had become accustomed to the nudity now and didn't spare a glance towards those bodies but John being older had never got used to it and couldn't help looking.

As the waiter's strolled around with trays of iced drinks and sunscreen in small containers a body suddenly popped up among the loungers. John recognized the serpent tattoo on Heather's thigh first but then it became mostly covered by a pair of loose shorts as a matter of decorum. Heather made a beeline to intercept her friends and seemed to be her usual bubbly self, John noticed a waiter hand her a card as she went by and in true form Heather took it and tiptoeing to gain height kissed his cheek before turning back to her task putting the card safely in her pocket. The waiter was visibly watching her bottom but John had a view of her breasts adorned with nipple rings as she closed the distance. Jake had stopped causing John's wheelchair to follow suit and soon they were exchanging kisses and Jake just looked at his friend's bare breasts saying judgmentally.

"Heather?"

Which she just shrugged off and changing the subject she asked about an upcoming event.

"So mate it's her big fight tomorrow night."

He picked up at the prospect of watching Tanya fight and smiled at his colleague.

"It's going to be a great night Hev but I keep wondering how I'm going to cope with seeing her in that ring?"

His smile slipped as he thought about the violence of his lover's chosen sport. Heather sensed his concern and put her arms around her colleague giving him a hug and saying.

"You fucking big softie don't worry you get used to it. I hated watching at first but it's ok now."

Then she laughed and added.

"Besides Tanya's unbeatable."

Jake asked Heather to join them for lunch but she declined explaining that Lucy was working here today and unusually wanted to avoid her partner siting professionalism, Heather however had sensed overprotectiveness in her girlfriend and had decided to comply. As she walked back to her lounger Jake now noticed the waiter paying attention to his friend and frowned then snapped out of it and looked down to notice John was asleep.

In John's dream he was in the arena in the unusual attire of a referee and introducing the fighters with great enthusiasm. As John walked to the blue corner he grabbed the dangling microphone with one hand and with the other he held up Tanya's bandaged hand.

"In the blue cornerrrrrrrr."

John shouted into the mic and extending the last word for effect.

"Is Tanyaaaaaaa."

At the mention of her name an invisible crowd erupted into cheers and applause as Tanya punched the air with both hands. She looked stunning in loose silk shorts and a sports bra both jet black with gold linings. As the crowd's applause subsided John paid attention to the opposite corner that was covered in red padding and sat on her stool in her perfect fitting swimsuit was Cheryl.

As John approached she jumped to her feet and started to warm up by jogging on the spot lifting her knees up high as her breasts bounced up and down barely being contained by her inappropriate swimsuit. John gave Cheryl a similar introduction and she had the same rapturous applause until she turned back to her corner. John noticed that unlike Tanya Cheryl's hair was plaited and ran down to her buttocks that were being barely covered by the lifeguard's red swimsuit.

As both girls got up again and came into the center of the ring to shake hands the traditional way John woke up to see Tanya approaching him in real life by the restaurant. She gave John her customary kiss then turned to Jake who wrapped his arms around her in a loving embrace then they went in.

In the restaurant they were shown to an ornately decorated table with a silk table cloth and a thick purple candle burning in the middle. As the aroma of jasmine hit John's senses he noticed Tanya was on her own so she must have the day off.

An attractive oriental but not Thai John was sure waitress in a kimono took their order. The inappropriate clothing was not lost to John but went unnoticed by Tanya and Jake who were checking the menu and John doubted would have noticed anyway.

Soon the order was placed and John was looking forward to his taste buds being treated to flavors of delicious spices expertly put together.

After a delicious meal Tanya looked at Jake and said.

"So are you coming to mine tonight lover?"

Jake smiled and said."

I thought you'd never ask, what shall I bring? Wine?"

They agreed on a bottle of wine and that they'd order burgers from McDonald's then got ready to go.

As Jake maneuvered John Tanya smiled towards him and said.

"Watch out lover it's the police."

Jake startled and looked up at the three people entering the restaurant only one of whom he recognized. Recovering his composure quickly Jake said.

"Hi Lucy how are you?"

Lucy introduced Jake and Tanya to Wendy and Channing explaining that Channing was helping them to profile the killer. All the while Channing stared at Jake. Lucy as always leaned in to kiss John on the cheek and excused themselves saying.

"Gotta go as we Really owe this one a good lunch."

At this they separated and the trio of detectives and ruffian were shown to a table. Channing shivered dramatically and said.

"Now that guy is scary."

Lucy thought it was a strange reaction to John but kept it to herself as they ordered.

Cheryl Is Being Hunted

Cheryl is a lifeguard and loves her job but firstly she is a mother of a three year old girl called Chloe. Cheryl's life is a simple one mostly but with a twist that some might find uncomfortable but it's the thing that attracted her husband to her.

Underneath the beautiful clean cut façade of the nice girl is a lioness with a penchant for causing pain.

When little Chloe is eventually in bed asleep the quiet unassuming girl becomes a woman or in fact a dominatrix. That person is currently using her new strap on to inflict exquisite agony in her husband who's lying face down with his face buried in the pink pillow on their marital bed. He's naked but Cheryl is clad in stockings, suspender belt and basque all black lace befitting her alter ego.

He muffles a groan as she thrusts the fake penis deeper into his anus, the sound of him moaning creates a quiver in Cheryl that ends in an orgasm.

Having satisfied herself she pulls the man over onto his somewhat sore backside and after taking off the instrument of his suffering she relieves him orally.

Afterwards they are both lying in each other's arms and talking as if they hadn't just performed what many even today would think was a disgusting act.

"How was Chloe's first day at pre school?"

Cheryl asked.

"She cried just like you said she would darling."

Cheryl kissed him on the forehead and held his face into her now bear chest. Her impressive chest was a source of erotic obsession that he liked to nuzzle to. She said.

"Mummy knows her little girl Dan but it's still for the best. Trust me."

Cheryl gets up and walks across the conservatively decorated bedroom peering through the curtains as she opens the window they'd shut earlier to keep in Dan's moans of ecstasy.

Was that a person across the street or just the shadows playing tricks on her. She goes back to bed turning the light out and cuddling into Dan's back. Unable to resist she bites him on the neck causing an.

"Ouch"

Followed by a more affectionate.

"Love you."

Jake was watching the second floor bedroom and saw the beautiful Cheryl appear to open the windows and was surprised to see she was naked, well as far as he could see anyway and what he did see excited him. Yet still to him her nudity looked inappropriate for this young girl who appears so nice at the pool. To his horror she looked towards him but he ducked into the shadows quickly.

Jake had been jittery since seeing those two coppers at the Thai place but was getting that under control now as a plan formulated in his mind.

Jake And The Gang Cheer On A Savage Tanya

The inter county games were approaching fast and there was a buzz in the air with a big promotional campaign including TV and radio advertising always ending in the phrase "Cell, better for you, better for me and better for everyone"

Currently at the sports center Lucy, Heather and Jake were sat in the front row of an arena anxiously awaiting Tanya's entrance.

It was the final trial for the chance to represent the state and the crowd were desperately waiting to see a contest that promised to be a close and exciting event. Tanya's opponent was an Asian girl from the Philippines who'd been allowed to enter the country as a desirable immigrant. Tanya had been friends with her opponent for some time even intimately once but tonight Gizelle represented an obstacle that the ever competitive Tanya had to get past.

Heather took in the building and was impressed with it's design in a classical Greek style with ornate pillars running up to a ceiling painted with a scene of the ancient Olympics.

There were pictures of naked athletes of both sexes including transgender partaking in sports with a background that resembled the Roman Colosseum.

Then Heather was drawn back to the present as the referee started to introduce tonight's contestants.

"Welcome to the Olympiad sports center and the last of our MMA trials for the honor of representing Floricare."

He looked around the crowd and smiled then said.

"Better for you better for me and better for everyone."

This last sentence warranted a massive applause with the crowd shouting.

"Evolution."

As had become customary. The referee raised his arms to calm them and when able started to say.

"In red and working in care looking after a lovely lady so well is Tanya."

He lingered on the last syllable of her name which charged the crowd many of whom were themselves carer's. Then after Tanya had done a circuit of the ring he introduced Gizelle in the same way and the crowd equally cheered for the waitress who many of them knew from the restaurant where she worked, the same restaurant that had agreed to open after the fight to host a party to celebrate whichever girl won for both were invited along with their friends.

The fight was as expected a close match with Tanya winning by a narrow margin. Both girls hugged afterwards and tears were forming in Tanya's eyes as the referee announced her the winner holding her exhausted arm up for all to see. Gizelle stood in the ring keeping a respectful distance while her friend and opponent had her moment of glory and until called forward by the referee. Before anything could be said they hugged again and Gizelle held Tanya's arm up again to a massive applause from the crowd. The referee just stood and watched as the two friends caused the audience to reach a new crescendo of applause.

In the crowd Jake, Heather and Lucy were excusing themselves as they shimmied past people desperate to see their friend before she got to the changing rooms. When Tanya and Gizelle left the ring people lined the pathway wanting to see the heroes of the night but Tanya immediately made a beeline for Jake as he was ushered under the flimsy barrier by security. Tanya literally jumped into her boyfriend's arms and they kissed passionately until an official respectfully suggested that it was time to get ready for the party. Tanya reluctantly agreed and said loudly to Jake.

"I'll see you at the party."

Soon the group supporting Tanya found themselves at a party awaiting the arrival of the fighters. They were handed champagne by a colleague of Gizelle's as he smiled a bit to familiarly with Jake but to no avail as he was only desperate to see his lover again.

There were a group playing Jazz on a stage and the singer caught Heather's eye as she sung the classic 'summertime' so eloquently it would have made Ella Fitzgerald cry. As the group found a table near the dancefloor the singer in-between songs introduced her fellow musicians one by one prompting solo performances that led to roars from the revelers. Once everyone else had had their moment the stunningly beautiful blonde singer in a figure hugging sparkling mini dress introduced herself as simply Louise and they immediately burst into their rendition of 'Mac the knife' causing an influx of dancers to pour onto the floor. As Louise sang the rather interesting lyrics about everyone's favorite gangster the athletes entered the venue to huge applause and whooping. Gizelle and Tanya entered hand in hand and both looked amazing bar the bruises and Tanya couldn't help but imitate punching Gizelle in the eye that was already showing a colorful bruise causing an escalation of cheers.

They both had dresses on but Gizelle's was by far the most fetching as she had the more effeminate figure however Jake only looked at his bruised battered girlfriend. He ran over and fussed over a split lip that was taped together but Tanya just dismissed his attention and hugged him tightly.

Later that evening after several drinks Lucy, Tanya and Jake were sitting at the table sharing in the kind of conversation people do when drunk and Jake wasn't paying attention. Instead he was transfixed on the dancefloor where Heather and Gizelle had been dancing for several songs. The two couldn't be anymore different with Gizelle in her elegant figure hugging dress and Heather in her faux leather shorts and flimsy open backed top that seemed to hand tantalizingly just over her breasts. As Jake watched them move majestically together he unusually didn't pay any attention to the conversation going on next to him.

On the dancefloor however Heather was in her element and was in awe of the muscular strong dance partner she found herself with. Gizelle didn't drink alcohol so had been happy to dance with the petite sexy Heather instead of sitting with the increasingly inebriated group. But she was starting to feel the strain of having fully committed her energy to the contest earlier and leaned into her dance partner saying.

"Let's go outside for some air."

Heather excitedly agreed and said she'd catch her up. As Gizelle went towards the patio Heather ran towards Lucy excitedly, sitting down beside her she stared into Lucy's blue eyes and put on her best pleading face.

"Can I kiss her pleeeeeease?"

Lucy smiled and said.

"Of course you can but don't go falling for her. You're mine honey."

Heather replied with a kiss on the lips and unable to control her excitement she ran towards the patio catching up with the fighter. Once outside they sat in a comfortable sofa away from the crowd and started to talk, Heather was fascinated by the ability to fight ones friend in a contest of combat and just turn off the rage. Gizelle explained to her the point.

"Oh honey you don't understand it at all."

Confused looks prompted a better explanation so Gizelle continued.

"There's no rage as such just determination to win. You see you're never out of control in the ring."

More confusion emanated from Heather's face as the sound of music from Louise's group battled for dominance with the waves crashing on the beach a little way away. Gizelle went on to try to get the point across.

"Okay take marathon running as an example. If I was setting the pace in a race and I knew an opponent had a strong finish I'd set a fast pace to try to hurt her. That way hopefully she'd fall off before the finish."

She smiled at her well used analogy and explained further.

"You see the marathon runner wants to hurt the opponent but just competitively. They're still friends."

Heather was infatuated by this conversation and when she looked at Gizelle's split lip similar to Tanya's she gently caressed the wound with her finger and said.

"Just a competition."

Then they were kissing to the sound of soothing music accompanied by the sea.

Jake liked Heather and ironically quite liked Lucy but he couldn't understand how they shared their love so freely. He was sure he could never do with Tanya who seemed to be transfixed on the erotically charged couple outside. The music had changed tempo and dancers were enjoying more intimacy on the dancefloor like the girls Tanya watched. Jake caught Tanya's attention by leaning into her and kissing her on her lips, he enjoyed the taste of Tanya's lips as their tongues teased each other. When they finished and looked into each other's eyes Tanya just held Jake in her arms and smiled at Lucy who smiled back. The music soon picked up again and lent a new vitality to the evening which prompted Lucy to say.

"Shots."

As Heather and Gizelle sat back down at their table.

The evening was only just beginning.

Hangover Sex Is The Best

It had been a fantastic night and Lucy woke up in Heather's bed and in a fog of confusion that accompanied her hangover. Lucy started to recap as people do on these mornings after, she lay with her back to Heather and felt her hand reach around and start to caress her breasts as she tracked back.

Yes the party had been great and both groups of supporters had mixed really easily. Lucy remembered feeling aroused as she sat and watched Heather and Gizelle dancing together and holding each other in their arms until inevitably they'd kissed outside.

She paused her train of thought distracted by a finger and thumb gently squeezing her nipple, fuck that's nice and Heather hasn't done that before.

But she still felt the need to remember the night before so Lucy took the invading arm and placed it on her stomach which was immediately misinterpreted and the amorous hand started to move down towards Lucy's groin. At this Lucy gave in to the inevitable and closed her eyes as her body started to quiver with pleasure while Heather's fingers worked magic. Soon Lucy was in a violent orgasm and barely noticed the bedroom door open until her explosive climax was over.

Opening her eyes Lucy looked straight into Heather's face.

"What the fuck?"

As Heather smiled Lucy felt someone kissing her neck and it all came back suddenly.

"Morning Gizelle."

Heather said and leaned in to kiss Lucy passionately.

"I'm cooking breakfast, it'll be ready soon lovelies."

As Lucy started to focus on her partner she noticed she was wearing an apron and as she turned to leave Lucy realized Heather was only wearing an apron that accentuated her perfect buttocks beautifully. Heather was immune to hangovers which was a constant annoyance to Lucy but as she left Lucy turned around to look into the beautiful Philippine face and kissed Gizelle passionately then said.

"Breakfast now gorgeous but we're not finished here."

As Lucy said this she squeezed an amazingly firm arse that didn't give at all.

Gizelle sat on the bed and Lucy searched for her underwear on the floor, she noticed the bruises on the Asian girl.

"She gave you a beating didn't she?"

Gizelle just winked and said.

"It's all about the sport for us."

Then she displayed a devilish smile and said.

"Believe me she's feeling it too."

Meanwhile across town Tanya was indeed feeling it but not enough to curb her arousal spurred on by the excitement of remembering her big win, Tanya could feel her erection grow with every breath. Jake woke up to the now familiar sensation of a hard penis against his buttocks. A strong hand reached around to stroke his now erect member as Tanya whispered into his ear.

"Do you want to try something new?"

He just nodded and Tanya reached behind to the bedside table, Jake heard a drawer open and the unscrewing of a cap. Then knowing what was about to happen Jake gasped as Tanya's huge penis prodded at his body. She leaned in to whisper.

"Just tell me if you want to stop."

Then his world erupted into a level of sensual pleasure he'd never dreamed of before.

In Heather's flat there was something nagging at Lucy's hungover mind as she ate her fried breakfast that Heather had prepared for all three of them. Lucy thought again that her girlfriend had an annoying immunity to hangovers as she sat at the table. Heather was still in just an apron which was arousing Lucy intensely and that along with her hangover clouded her thoughts.

Gizelle had only dressed in a flimsy vest and knickers and her nipple was clearly visible through the side which wasn't helping. Lucy felt overdressed in her silk pajamas and knew that the passion she'd woken to was just the beginning.

But now Lucy concentrated on her breakfast while Gizelle showed Heather her bruises like war medals, Heather looked at a multi colored one on the athlete's beautiful firm buttock as Gizelle held her panties out the way. Lucy leaned in and kissed it better then Gizelle sat back down and pulled Lucy towards her and holding her head kissed her passionately. Lucy gave up on her train of thought and pushing her plate aside joined the other two.

Jake was experiencing a sensation like no other and Tanya's firm hand had coaxed an ejaculation already. To Jakes surprise he became hard again almost immediately and Tanya was euphoric as her hand stroked his rock hard erection. She had been gentle as she eased herself inside him but there was no easy way to accommodate her enormous penis and Jake could tell she was being sensitive as she slowly pushed and withdrew in a gentle motion. Then suddenly she withdrew and Jake sensed her ejaculation on his back which just turned him on to the point of rapture.

Heather had stood up and guided Gizelle to start performing oral sex on her when Lucy had undressed and Lucy knelt behind her girlfriend and started to work with her gifted tongue causing spasms in the small girl. So all three stayed in the kitchen until Heather erupted in orgasm then they returned to the bedroom.

After all had been satisfied the three girls now completely naked collapsed onto the bed and slept in each other's arms Heather in the middle.

Lucy dreamed of the night before and Heather and Gizelle were dancing again only both were dressed as MMA fighters and their silk shorts and tight tops showed off their beautiful bodies. They slowly moved to the music and the dancefloor was empty apart from them watched by a referee in a black and white striped top.

The bell rang and both dancers broke away and went to their prospective corners.

All the while Lucy could hear Tanya and Jake talking in the background as if her subconscious was determined to make her notice something. As the bell went and Heather and Gizelle embraced again to sway to the music Lucy just made out Tanya's words.

"What happened to that coin you had lovely, I haven't seen it in ages."

Jakes masculine voice replied.

"Don't know darling I must have lost it somewhere."

Lucy's eyes snapped open.

Lucy Needs To Protect Her Sheep

Lucy had made feeble excuses at Heather's and was heading into the corrections department to meet Wendy. A frantic phone call had got Wendy out of her bed to the moans of her husband but this was more important than anything, Lucy just told her she knew who the killer was and that was enough to get fucking Wendy moving.

At the office Lucy had left the car in their parking station specially allowed to public servants and stopped off for two coffees on her way into the building.

Once in the office seeing Wendy Lucy said.

"Its Jake Wend I know it is."

Wendy just held her hand up to calm her partner down and calmly said.

"Ok girl let's just take it step by step. So what makes you so sure?"

Lucy filled Wendy in on the discovery that Jake had lost a coin, all the while Wendy just sat on the edge of the desk frowning and occasionally shaking her head until she stated the obvious.

"Not enough Lucy, it's not enough."

Lucy was about to protest but Wendy stopped her with a glare.

"We both fucking know that those coins are everywhere and there's fuck all forensic evidence after the fire. And the Amber murder was meticulous. If you think it's him I'm good with that but it's not enough for a court, you know I'm right."

Lucy slumped and resigned herself that her friend was correct.

"He'll kill again Wendy we both know he will."

Wendy just smiled and said.

"But this time we're ahead of him Lucy. Can't you see we've got him but just need to be patient. If we arrest him now he'll get off and probably never kill again if he's smart."

They both sipped their coffees and sat thinking the same thing with neither prepared to say the obvious solution, until Lucy finally said it.

"Of course if we were to catch him in the act next time there's no way he could get off."

Wendy smiled and said.

"We've got him Lucy. We just have to get him under surveillance then he'll lead us right to his next victim."

Then Lucy suddenly had a realization, looked her partner in the eye and said.

"What about Tanya? It's going to ruin her but she can't know about him. Should we tell her?"

Wendy just halted her partner there and bought them back down to earth.

"We've got to make sure we're definitely right before we move forward so let's check back."

The two of them spent the rest of the morning looking through records and tracing Jake's movements to ascertain that he's definitely capable of the crimes. To their surprise and partly confirming their suspicions they realized that Jake was possibly the engineering district cop killer.

Wendy called their counterpart in that state while Lucy went for more coffee and found out that indeed that case had died at the time Jake moved. The detective said that he was convinced the killer would strike again and actually said he thought the murderer was progressing. He explained that he suspected a link to a rape victim that had come forward but it was an old case and couldn't be pursued. When Lucy got back Wendy filled her in and they started to build a plan to trap a wolf among their sheep.

The Fragility Of Jake's New Life

Oblivious to his previous night's mistake Jake had woken up that morning happier than ever. He never would have thought he'd be in a relationship like this in a million years and the complex situation between dominant and subservient partner was exhilarating. There was no doubt that in the bedroom Tanya was dominant but with a sensitive air and this morning just enhanced his love for her. Jake realized that she could have really hurt him and many would have got a massive thrill from doing just that. The dimensions were scary as Tanya was so huge and his fear had enhanced the experience but she'd been nothing but gentle and caring.

As he had lay on his side with her slowly entering and withdrawing but only just enough to arouse them both Jake realized that he was in love.

He finally finished showering and grabbed the towel off the rack then walked into Tanya's kitchen to find her in her pajamas and cooking breakfast. The smell of bacon really aroused Jakes senses and he realized how hungry he was as he wrapped his arms around Tanya's waist and began to kiss her on the nape of her neck. As she told him to let her cook Jake couldn't resist reaching down to grip her penis while his left hand caressed her breasts.

Lucy got back to her own flat later on that day and immediately regretted not going to Heather's but deep down she knew she'd need to bolster her resolve to tell Heather about her suspicions.

As that evening she walked towards the corner store and the welcome familiarity of the ever happy Mr Patel Lucy realized that it wasn't just suspicion, she knew instinctively that Jake was a killer.

"Hello officer Lucy."

Came the comfortingly normal greeting and Lucy felt herself relaxing.

"Hello Mr Patel how are you today?"

The grocer was the absolute king of small talk a skill handed down from retailer to retailer through generations of his family but today he was serious as he stood behind the counter.

"How are you getting on with catching that awful murderer?"

As Lucy considered her response he unusually cut her off.

"I remembered a story in my family that might help if you'd permit me?"

Lucy who's interest was perked by the man's unusual behavior just nodded approval. Mr Patel visibly excited by the chance to help continued.

"Well you see my family is descended from a high level of nobility and before leaving the old country we were very rich and powerful. That is before the British changed everything."

She knew he was referring to India but wasn't aware of the ruination that the empirical British had created through their withdrawal from that continent. Still he continued.

"Well my family had a big house with many servants and they had a daughter who was due to marry into another powerful family which would secure a future of comfort for her. But there was a problem in that she was being heard to be entertaining a young man in her bedroom in the night."

Mr Patel just looked solemnly at Lucy as if she was the epitome of innocence and this idea would corrupt her. Lucy just thought 'good for her' but nodded seriously as her friend carried on.

"Well her father was furious when he heard talk among the servants about a man in his daughter's room and he acted quickly and strongly. He had locks put on her bedroom windows and assuming that it was one of their neighbors he sent a message to the neighbors family warning them to control their son."

Mr Patel paused for a moment to serve a customer around Lucy and smiled at the gentleman who scanned out a bottle of milk. As the man who Lucy knew from the street left Mr Patel called a farewell greeting but then quickly turned back to Lucy eager to continue.

"Well the father slept well that night but the next morning again he heard the rumors of infidelity so he called to a servant and ordered him to secure the bedroom window properly this time but again the next morning there was more gossip so the father stepped up the level to protect his daughter and inevitably the garden had two armed servants sat to watch the window."

The smiling shopkeeper started to laugh at an internal joke that Lucy hadn't heard yet but soon he explained.

"It took the father two weeks to find out that the intruder was actually one of his young servants getting in through her bedroom door. The handsome young man much to the daughter's misery was dismissed."

Mr Patel's face took a more serious visage now as he said.

"You see officer Lucy sometimes we are so focused on strangers that we miss the people familiar to us."

Lucy appreciated the point especially after her realization about Jake and took Mr Patel's hand in hers. She said.

"You know Mr Patel you're absolutely on the money."

Before heading off to tell Heather the thing that would destroy her.

But Lucy decided to go for a run first to clear her mind then after a refreshing shower she packed her overnight bag and left her flat. As she walked out into the cooler evening she was apprehensive about her girlfriend's reaction to the news but was still adamant that telling Heather was for the best. Lucy knew that she'd have to leave Heather's early the next morning to get to the office in good time but she had to give this news face to face.

On arrival at her flat Heather was surprised to see Lucy back but still ran up and jumped into Lucy's arms wrapping her legs around the stronger partner. Lucy had dressed in her work clothes and that in itself gave the ominous impression of seriousness so she decided to change first.

Walking out of the bedroom in the normal long t-shirt Lucy was relieved to see that Heather had poured them both wine and a song she didn't recognize was playing. Heather handing Lucy the glass explained that after she'd rushed off this morning Gizelle had dragged Heather around to the Bringy where she'd found these CDs to play on her vintage stereo system. Lucy was pleased of the distraction from her task and picked up the CD case that informed her the music was by 'Pink Floyd' meaning nothing but it sounded great.

No this won't do she thought as she took a long sip of the cool crisp refreshing wine then she told Heather everything. She told her about the coin and the coincidence that Jake had lost his. She told Heather about the cop in the engineering state being so shocked that the attacks had suddenly stopped in his state. Most importantly she told her love about the fact that the cease of attacks timed perfectly with Jake's transfer to Floricare.

All the while to Lucy's concern Heather just said nothing and stood still occasionally sipping her wine almost subconsciously as the music played in the flat. Heather was shell-shocked and glared at her lover in disbelief until Lucy had to break the silence.

"You said yourself that you were suspicious of him."

Heather retorted "That was before I knew him for fucks sake. I can't believe that now though."

Heather took Lucy's wine glass and probably to give herself time to digest the information she'd received as much as any other purpose she went to the fridge. Coming back and handing Lucy the replenished glass Heather looked sad in an almost defeated way.

"He's so good with John Lucy, I really can't believe that such a gentle man could do such horrible things to that girl at the kiosk and oh Gods Amber."

Lucy who had let her love get it off her chest then stood up and walked over to comfort her.

"We're sure he's a rapist from the engineering state and he killed a cop too. Sorry to put you through this Heather but we've got to stop the bastard before he kills again."

Heather turned around and Lucy saw something in her eyes that she'd never have expected, anger was Heather's prevalent emotion while she digested the information being given to her.

"You're wrong Luce I'm sorry but the guy I've got to know and who lovingly cares for John isn't a murderer. I mean what type of evidence is there, a coin for fucks sake just a fucking coin."

Lucy took Heather's hands and as softly as she could reminded Heather that the dates all make sense between his old home and here.

"Trust me Heather we're not taking this lightly. You must realize the mess we'd be in if we're wrong and spend our time chasing Jake while someone else kills another poor girl."

Lucy noticed her hand shaking. Lucy knew it'd hit Heather bad but had no idea it'd be this hard for her to accept. All she could do is look on while the woman she loved battled to digest the information. Heather suddenly stopped and looked straight at Lucy.

"What about Tanya?"

Tanya was as happy as she'd ever been, she had won a major fight last night and she was in love with a beautiful, gentle and caring man. She thought for a minute about Gizelle and considered calling her but thought not, she'd let her friend deal with her disappointment the way all true champions did notably by training hard.

Tanya gently stroked Jake's soft blonde hair as he lay on her sofa with his head lying on Tanya's lap. He'd quickly fallen asleep this evening when they'd settled down after dinner and Tanya had let him rest while she watched an old movie. As she'd watched the comedy she'd noticed Jake having a nightmare and as he'd moaned unintelligible words she'd comforted him by caressing his hair softly . In fact she'd carried on the sensitive loving act even though his dreams were peaceful now but she was being distracted by the movie.

How To Trap A Wolf

Lucy got up early the next morning in her own flat and worried about Heather, she had eventually left under a storm cloud and really wasn't sure where their relationship stood with all that had happened. Lucy knew she loved Heather beyond all reason but she just couldn't get the message through that Jake was in her mind a cold hearted killer. She understood why as over the months since he'd first entered Heather's world he'd shown himself to be a loving caring person. To a seasoned police officer like Lucy that was perfectly believable and she'd learned that people could have two completely different persona's but to Heather understandably it made no sense.

Lucy sat in her kitchenette on a stool in just her t shirt and remembered how the atmosphere had been when she'd left, they'd agreed that Lucy should take time to concentrate on her work and for Lucy that meant catching Jake but to Heather undoubtedly it meant Lucy discovering she was wrong. Fuck it's going to be a long week.

Lucy finished her coffee and went to change for her run putting on a sports bra and briefs as it's already hot outside, her running shoes were by the door as always and as she left the building and started to slowly build up pace, her mind was on how to catch a wolf.

Surveillance wasn't going to be easy as in the district that Jake lived in drones were unusual and CCTV had not been installed and as Lucy glided along lightly as was her running style she pondered the problem.

Left at the end of the road and cross over to the other side ready to take a right towards the park, God it's hot already.

How to watch Jake without him knowing?

In the park now and running along the path that goes around the edge, gravel crunching under long swift strides.

When does he find his victims?

Crunch crunch as her pace increases as her muscles are fully warmed up now and her body is functioning perfectly, breathing steady and deep.

When are women likely to let their guard down around a stranger? Why does Heather now trust a man who she once didn't?

Entering the green that serves as a communal area and remembering watching a movie here in the open air with Heather on a picnic blanket, Heather's head resting on Lucy's lap as Lucy stroked her hair. Lucy was more interested in the movie which epitomizes the correctness of many years ago.

"Mummy, mummy I do believe the boat's sinking."

Says a little boy on the big screen. What was the film called? About a disaster long ago.

But suddenly she's bought back to the present as she sees a large group being led through Tai chi by an instructor. Slightly uphill now and Lucy's pace slows accordingly but she still works through the matter in her mind.

What have the two girls got in common with Jakes routine? When's it likely that they crossed paths with him?

Leaving the park now and back on the tarmac.

The waterfront it has to be, Dawn worked there and Amber ran that way almost daily and of course Jake would take John there.

As Lucy approached the little corner store run by lovely Mr Patel she stopped and realized the obvious solution to the problem of surveillance.

Mr Patel was busy sweeping the pavement outside his little store as he did every morning when the lovely girl he called officer Lucy came jogging in and took her usual paper and a can of cola. She looked at the headline on the front page and burst out laughing which surprised Mr. Patel as he knew she was a conscientious police officer. They shared the usual greetings and as she walked away towards her flat Mr Patel looked at her noticing that her running pants had run up in-between her buttocks, he would never get used to these modern ways he thought as he guiltily watched for a bit longer than was appropriate. Then the last dedicated corner shopkeeper looked at the headline in the paper rack that had incurred such a joviality.

"Police are baffled as to the identity of the serial killer"

Wendy wasn't amused at Lucy's suggestion and didn't hide it.

"Fuck right off with that mental fucking idea right now."

Lucy knew it was coming and in a pre prepared response she calmly said.

"Ok then clever, you come up with a better idea!"

they were in their little office and outside the hustle and bustle of the corrections department continued ignorant of the moral debate going on behind a flimsy partition wall. Wendy just slumped into her chair behind her desk which was as ever a mess.

"You know I can't but really Lucy it's too much."

Then she looked at her friend and smiled.

"Do you think we'll get permission to try it? How about the technology I mean bugs are tiny these days and a camera is easy to hide but this is pushing it a bit don't you think?"

Lucy was ready for this and opened a window on her computer that showed surveillance aids that were available to law enforcement. She had found it before Wendy got in and was amazed at what was in it, a Nano audio bug that was in a sticker and most amazingly to her was a camera that was built into a bolt which could be attached to anything where there was a need for a simple bolt.

Like on a wheelchair.

Permission was easy to get from their supervisor as the case had created so much tension in the state that even the government were looking into it which was causing a lot of anxiety all the way up the chain of command.

In fact the two coppers came away thinking that they could have asked for just about anything and would have been entertained. As they left the supervisors office he just said.

"I don't care what you two do just get this bastard off the streets and quickly"

The technical department of the corrections building was a dingy room in the lower floor of the building and there was machinery everywhere. The two detectives knew this as the place that maintained the more overt surveillance equipment like the drones that watched Channing and his district but there was more here.

A rather nerdy technician quickly ran over to intercept them as Wendy picked up a damaged drone with only three rotor blades left.

"That's very fragile miss."

He frantically said like a mother protecting a baby and prompting Wendy to put the machine back down rather clumsily making him wince. Wendy just said.

"Okay Einstein don't get your fucking panties in a twist."

Making Lucy snigger and embarrassing herself, she quickly changed the subject.

"Why's it so cold down here?"

But the technician who was inspecting his baby drone for damage just dismissively said.

"Oh that's for the computers or they overheat."

Satisfied that Wendy had done no harm he put the surveillance equipment down gingerly and walked over to a corner of the room to retrieve two lab coats. Lucy noticed that the guy had a thick jumper on and corduroy pants both of which were rare in Floricare. As they put on their coats that gave more of an allusion of warmth than the reality the two detectives explained their requirements. The still anonymous techie brightened up immediately as his day was suddenly going to be more interesting by far, led them past a cluttered desk covered in all kinds of computer equipment and small sensitive tools and to a cupboard.

He looked around and for the first time smiled as he said.

"Let me show you ladies the toy box."

The technician took his time to explain the amazingly simple equipment which comprised of a book of stickers of literally hundreds of colors so they could blend into any background which was the audio device and a selection of bolts of different sizes which hid an amazingly tiny camera. Then the tech handed them a simple tablet and showed how to synchronize the chosen devices. It really was simple and even the technophobic Wendy grasped what was needed.

So all that was needed was an opportunity to fit the devices which Heather obliged as she had been taken into their confidence and only Heather, such was the importance to avoid Jake's suspicion. Heather was skeptical still but agreed to go along with the idea, in her mind only to prove her friends innocence.

Afterwards when the two officers left John's house there was a cold farewell between Heather and Lucy which disturbed Wendy enough for her to question her partner on the way back. Lucy just shrugged and said that she'd come around but if not some people couldn't handle dating coppers. Wendy was reminded of bad times when the police workload was huge and relationships were always tested but just thought how lucky she was to be married to Dick.

Heather cried herself to sleep that night.

The Wolf Swim's

Jake was in work again but felt tired after being up late discovering pleasures that he hadn't known existed before his new life. He had decided that he'd have the lifeguard then stop his little hobby. He knew he could stop anytime he wanted but like an alcoholic put the commitment off.

Jake got John ready as always and actually had a time schedule in mind as he'd been watching Cheryl in his free time and Jake knew she'd start her shift at twelve o'clock. So he wanted to be walking through the changing rooms at ten to in the hope of her helping them again. Not just a perverse stalking issue though as Jake felt that he needed her to feel safe around him in order to get safely into her house when the time came.

John noticed the sense of a need for punctuality in Jake and realized there must be a malevolent motive. He'd spent the last three days with Heather trying to will his muscles that had once been strong and able to allow him to communicate but nothing, not even a twitch.

John remembered hearing medical staff talking about his injuries and that it was highly unlikely he'd recover any movement but he was for the first time in years desperately trying to prove them wrong. Not today though, definitely not today.

They got to the pool in good time and Jake pushed John through the clinically designed changing rooms scanning for a glimpse at Cheryl's athletic body but nothing. She wasn't there and before long the two guys were going through the motions of hoisting and changing John without her.

Meanwhile several blocks away Lucy sat watching the screen looking for any clue that they'd be given that a predator was hunting. Wendy got back into the car with two burger meals handing one to Lucy, she nodded to the screen and asked.

"Any luck yet?"

Lucy just shook her head and took her lunch.

"They're going swimming now so I guess we've got a break."

In the pool Jake was disappointed to see no beautiful blond in a very provocative swimsuit but nevertheless he got on with his duty to John and helped him stretch long unused muscles. Unfamiliar music played as warm water helped to soften stiff muscles and all the time Jake looked for a glimpse of his prey but nothing. He was convinced she started at twelve and it definitely wasn't one of her days off.

Eventually they got another lifeguards attention and John was hoisted out and into the chair that stayed in the pool area while Jake climbed out. Jake thanked the lifeguard then she kissed John's cheek and wished them a good day. Jake pushed the chair through to their changing room through the communal area in a cloud of disappointment.

As the two men entered the room Lucy and Wendy perked up having enjoyed a peaceful lunch. This was going nowhere Wendy thought as Jake maneuvered John into position and she just sat back and sighed.

"Fuck this is boring."

Lucy just glared at her partner but couldn't argue.

That is until the door burst open and she walked in. The wheelchair was situated in the corner with a great view of the room and the stunning lifeguard grabbed their attention. Wendy leaned in to turn the sound on and said.

"I think we're in business."

Cheryl had been running late but the rare chance to dish out some delicious punishment to her ecstatic husband was worth it, then as she had been getting changed Danny who'd been covering for her informed her that she'd just missed those two guys you know he'd said John is it? And his carer the good looking guy.

Cheryl needed no more information and was in the changing room like a shot, she had the hot's for this guy and was thinking how she'd love to let her toys loose on him.

As she dashed in she noticed that he was almost finished but still offered assistance.

"Let me get the chair ready for you guys."

Cheryl noticed he perked up at her entrance and was emboldened to make conversation.

"How are you guys today? Sorry I missed you but I was running late today."

Her mind flashed to her husband lying face down and tied to the bed with heavy chord (handcuffs were so dull) his buttocks glowing red from the whipping she'd administered.

As they hoisted John into the encompassing comfort of his personal wheelchair John noticed the callouses on her palms and wondered how a lifeguard could cause such damage?

As the banter continued over the now sleeping John the two police officers watched with interest and Lucy broke the silence.

"Look at his eyes, he's definitely into this lifeguard in a weird way."

Undoubtedly Jakes eyes were different to normal and gave off a malevolence that convinced them they'd been right to pursue this line of enquiry. As they both watched,

Jake looked over Cheryl's athletic shoulder and straight at the camera almost straight at the two officers through the technology.

Wendy and Lucy both looked at each other and said nothing but then looked back to the screen as if nothing had happened. The tech support guy had warned them that this type of technology could 'mess with your head' so they attributed the moment to that and got on to the job in hand.

As the two unsuspecting subjects of attention made their farewells Wendy was tracking through the footage for a good picture of Cheryl. Lucy just sat back and said.

"We've got the bastard."

Tanya See's Jakes Other Side

She knew something was wrong with Jake, as if he was fighting a battle inside and Tanya was too scared to confront the issue with him.

Tanya had been through enough pain to know that trying to influence life just led to disaster and she'd been let down by more than her fair share of lovers. So she was unsurprised to get the feeling that it was happening again, disappointed yes, upset yes, but surprised no.

They were going to a bar where there was a live band playing, to Tanya's surprise Jake also liked jazz music and as pretty much every type of entertainment was strongly encouraged by the authorities it was easy to find a jazz club.

Revenue and monetary return had long ago ceased to be the driving force for the entertainment industry and venues could take on any style that the government accepted was necessary for societal requirements.

So these two lovers found themselves walking up to the Blue Note bar on the high street. Live jazz was blasting out of the place as they approached and walked around Al fresco tables bustling with people enjoying the cooler evening air.

The bar itself looked seedy and had been designed to give that impression when built but once inside there was an atmosphere of smoke and chatter of as many people as could be squeezed into a place that if it could be described in one simple word that word would be 'cozy'.

After scanning in they walked past the entrance to the downstairs bar and walked upstairs Tanya first and leading Jake by the hand. Tanya knew this place well and was eager to get Jake into an intimate corner with a beer so they could enjoy their night out. If he was going to break it off with her she was fucking well going to make him regret every time he remembers tonight. As they walked around the bannister at the top of the stairs Jake was shocked to see a young couple probably teenagers kissing in an embrace. It wasn't the kiss that took Jake by surprise it was that by their shoulder and arm movements it was obvious they were masturbating each other. Tanya however took it in her stride and led Jake into a less busy room where on a stage at one end four musicians hammered out jazz amazingly well. Two guys probably in their fifties or at least forties played trombone and trumpet and looked to be almost dueling as another younger man sang along with the melody. But at the back the drummer who was beating her instruments as if her life depended on it was a young girl of twenty something with crew cut blonde hair and her entire body tattooed, she looked amazing in a short leather skirt and string vest that showed off petite bare breasts underneath. Tanya pointed Jake to a table in a dark corner and soon joined him with two beers. As they drank they both watched the band play but before long Jake felt Tanya's hands undoing his flies to release his already erect penis and as her lips slipped around his tip Jake was indeed fighting a battle within.

Who's Watching Who?

Cheryl was oblivious to the surveillance that her little house was being scrutinized with while she bathed her daughter. Regulations stipulated that in order to provide a good home for a child the couple had to agree that one of them would give up work for the first eight years, this being assessed as the most essential period that needed parental influence. Cheryl and Dan had agreed that he was best suited for that role but Cheryl always enjoyed an opportunity to be a typical mother in tasks like cooking and bathing little Chloe and today was just that day.

The bathroom resembled any other family bathroom with toys and toiletries everywhere and the walls had murals of cartoon figures on them which Chloe loved. And currently she was giggling uncontrollably as mum was blowing bubbles off her hand into the air to land on Chloe's head. Dan called from another room.

"Don't get her too excited darling or we'll never get her down."

Chloe and her mother looked into each other's eyes seriously and Cheryl broke the moment with a big smile and said simply.

Simply."

And both girls carried on having fun.

Meanwhile outside in the shadowy darkness a hooded figure waited patiently and listened to the sounds of laughter coming from an upstairs window. It's ok he's patient and can wait to carry out his task so let the family have their fun.

Meanwhile in the sparse empty flat opposite in a darkened room two bored police officers watch the family residence while they ate noodles that they'd bought in with them and heated in the microwave, the only kitchen appliance they could be bothered to use.

They were both as yet unaware of the hooded figure who is hidden to them by a tree. They should have seen him approach but Steve had been using the bathroom and Toby had only looked away for a few minutes to text his wife and so the watcher was undetected by both predator and prey. Both policemen were oblivious to the stalking hooded figure as they enjoyed their dinner just as much as Cheryl who enjoyed bath time.

In another area Heather is working a late shift having stepped in to help out after Tracy was taken sick with a stomach bug. She really didn't mind as she missed Lucy painfully and working took her away from a lonely flat, Heather had enjoyed an evening sitting with John until it was time for him to get to bed.

Besides, now John was in bed asleep and she could relax until Jeff arrived at eleven to start his night shift, that's three hours to watch TV and chill. Heather made a mental note to phone Lucy when she got home, she needed desperately to know the bitch still loved her after their stormy parting the other day which had weighed heavily on the young girl. The thought of Jake being a murderer just couldn't sit in Heather's mind and that was partly due to the good natured character that he'd shown himself to possess but mainly because the two carers had built a strong bond since the incident at the zoo. It's a trait of humanity to build people up into a particular type good or bad, attractive or ugly, intelligent or stupid it's what we all do, to pigeon hole people into a particular slot. So basically to Heather Jake was a caring to John, loving to Tanya and friend to Heather. Murderer just didn't fit into this and no matter how much Lucy reasoned her this mindset could not be broken.

Heather sighed in frustration at the information program that was interrupting her evening watching old soap operas, she especially wanted to catch up on Alascation nights and as the screen showed a familiar well groomed face Heather mumbled quietly.

"Cell better for you better for me and better for everyone."

John in his bed had been asleep for some time and the wind had picked up outside, the angry sound of it had helped John to get to sleep as if help had been needed. John had been exhausted all evening but not from activity, instead John had exhausted himself today by mentally desperately trying to force his body into activity but to no avail. He'd been trying to just move the slightest of muscles now for days and the fact that he knew the clock was counting down for Cheryl that beautiful vibrant girl spurred him on.

In his slumber as usual John was dreaming and his dream as normal took it's usual dark direction. As was often the case John was an invisible third party at the beginning as Cheryl in her lifeguard's costume walked alongside the pool. But something was unusual in this scene and as John took in the panoramic view it became obvious, there was only one person in the pool namely Heather who wore her rather revealing swimsuit as if in competition with Cheryl

Meanwhile in the corrections building a response team led by Lucy with Wendy at her side was being briefed. Since the discovery of Cheryl as the probable next victim their office had been abandoned for a larger operations room which had ample seating for the ever expanding team, as people were being re assigned daily, such was the concern for the young lifeguard and her families safety.

The room was in no way reminiscent of the functional type of accommodations that existed before the evolution. This room had multi colored walls in soft pastels of lilac, green, yellow and orange and all around were pictures of an abstract style, the seating was also very comfortable with sofas and armchairs all different and some even able to recline.

But no one was lounging now, instead they were all transfixed on the screen that Lucy was referring to changing from picture to picture at her command. They had been through those of Jake to freshen the mental image and were showing Cheryl and her husband with Chloe. All the pictures were from the registration department and up to date as was a requirement for public records. Lucy finished up with her plan for the surveillance.

"So guys we're obviously in a code red situation still here and I don't need to emphasize how dangerous this one is. The family have no idea and we need to keep it that way so keep your guard up and let's be inconspicuous entering and leaving the surveillance base. Has everyone got the clothing requirements?"

There were nods all round and groans as they'd heard this every day for a week now.

To allay suspicion there was a full range of clothing to wear that matched so the family and their neighbors wouldn't think that eight different people were entering and leaving. They all matched day by day. The cover was that the house was being occupied by two gay guys as only men were on the surveillance team and they staggered entry and exit so only one man could ever be seen but the two guys were distinctly different in fashion making it easier to accept.

Jokingly the team called them Wilfred and Jeeves for reasons that Lucy never understood. The team were comprised of ten guys pulling six hour shifts roughly and never exactly (nothing said surveillance like coming and going on the hour) Two men were on standby Incase of unforeseen circumstances and Lucy and Wendy were arranging their own shifts around Jakes work schedule so they were likely to be at hand if he made a move.

Steve came back into the bedroom from yet another bathroom visit and quizzed Toby about the situation, Toby just said.

"Boring, fucking boring mate."

Steve looked at the various screens around the room and said.

"Apart from the wierdo in the hoody you mean."

Toby snapped to attention and looked at the figure who'd just stepped out of the shadows for a minute. The person's face was impossible to make out but height and build certainly matched their suspect. Steve was on his phone before Toby had even taken his eyes away from the screen.

"Yes Wendy it's Steve here. I think we've got him boss, we're sending the video over to you now."

In the office Wendy interrupted Lucy as she was closing the meeting saying.

"Sorry Lucy but we need to see this."

As she said that a box appeared on the screen and Wendy instructed the system to open it. There were several sharp intakes of breath as the hooded character was visible watching Cheryl's house. Lucy just said.

"We're on guys."

And then a well planned operation began.

Cheryl had put Chloe to bed and went to their own bedroom while her husband tidied up downstairs, behind closed curtains and completely oblivious to the drama happening across the road she opened her wardrobe and flicked through the hangers as she chose an outfit that would satisfy her passion. She undressed and slipped on black stockings and attached a suspender belt, then she chose a basque that enhanced her already perfectly formed breasts. To finish with she laced up a pair of high heeled boots which were essential for what she had in mind. Cheryl sat down at her dressing table and started to tie up her hair, he was in for a treat tonight.

Cars were positioning themselves in pre programmed places nearby and police officers were checking firearms, none of them had ever had to use them except for standard training that took place every three months. This was the real thing though and firearms had been authorized so every officer had a pistol and holster as that was deemed sufficient.

In a society where weapons were almost impossible to acquire police officers generally felt safe. But now in every car there was an excited atmosphere and Wendy being the only officer old enough to remember a time when this was more common felt the need to reassure her juniors.

She warned everyone not to let their nerves get to them for fucks sake look before firing and make sure they identify the target.

Heather meanwhile was bored of watching her favorite trash TV as the doorbell rang, she was surprised as it was only just gone eight o'clock and she was scheduled till eleven tonight when she would go home to her little flat. John in his bedroom heard the doorbell too and a pang of excitement entered his normally bored mind.

Cheryl's husband entered their bedroom and was dumbstruck to see his wife in her sexiest outfit and only missing her knickers which sent his heart rate soaring. On shutting the door he stripped hurriedly while Cheryl started to tie the ropes onto the bedposts. In their excitement they didn't hear the front door open and as a hooded figure walked in they were too indulged in their fantasy to notice.

Then suddenly the world exploded in an instant as people came barging into the quiet residence guns in their hands.

"Oh God no"

Screamed the intruder as he was bundled face down onto the stairs. Lucy had her knee on his back and her firearm aimed at the back of his head while an unfamiliar voice pleaded for forgiveness. In the background there was the sound of a child crying and then the couple emerged from a bedroom in dressing gowns, hers in particular looked out of place revealing black high heeled boots at the bottom.

Cheryl was shocked and her mouth opened and closed several times unable to frame the words. Her husband was rushing to Chloe's room seemingly oblivious to the circus in his home. Lucy looked up from her crouching position and calmly said.

"Please try not to be alarmed Cheryl. I'll explain everything as soon as we've secured this piece of shit."

But something was obviously wrong to Lucy as she started to get up and release her suspect. He was only slightly built and nowhere near the muscular physique of Jake. Lucy felt her world collapsing as she pulled the hood down to reveal a teenager with crewcut hair and a face covered in acne. He was actually crying now and said pleadingly.

"Please don't tell my mother. Please don't."

Once the child Chloe had been calmed down by her father he walked downstairs and into the kitchen to join Lucy, Wendy and Cheryl as they looked down at the young boy who was now holding a glass of lemonade. The confused husband looked towards Cheryl questioningly but she just shrugged and said.

"I've got no idea darling."

Lucy suggested that they all sit down and while Wendy supervised the other police officers to their stations Lucy looked towards the young boy and said.

"I think you'd best start at the beginning don't you?"

He explained that he'd met someone who claimed to be looking for a young man to join him and his wife for a night. The boy was obviously shaken and said that he was told to just come upstairs after he saw the lights go out and only the one bedroom was lit. The boy was assured that he'd be welcome to join the couple who liked to entertain young men.

Lucy was deflated as she once again was asked for assurance that his mother wouldn't find out but asked him to report to her office at his convenience to fill in a report on the evenings events. Wendy who'd come back in was cursing under her breath and took out her phone to report to the other officers.

"Relax guys it's just a prank by the sounds of it. The kid's harmless."

Then she looked to Lucy who was in the process of taking the juveniles details and yet again assuring him that under no circumstances his mother needs to find out about tonight's episode.

When he'd gone off rather hurriedly Lucy looked at the couple and smiled.

"I think a cup of coffee would be nice and I think then I owe you guys an explanation."

Her smile faded as she said.

"I think you two might need something stronger than coffee though."

Heather was just coming around as the fog in her head started to lift. She remembered answering the door and being shocked to see Jake there then she turned to lead him through then nothing, just blankness. She realized that she was lying face down on the sofa and then felt a bolt of fear spread through her when she couldn't bring her arms around from behind her back to help push herself up.

Then she heard Jakes voice but somehow it wasn't right, somehow there was a different character to it and there was anger and menace. It was definitely Jake though and he paced around as he told her how he'd not wanted this.

"Everything was absolutely fine until your girlfriend started getting too smart and then she goes and fucks everything up for all of us."

He appeared to be fighting some kind of internal battle as if two people were debating in his mind as to the best action. Then Jake saw Heather look towards John's bedroom and suddenly his voice returned to the one she recognized.

"Don't worry Heather I would never harm John but you on the other hand. I really like you but I've got to show that fucking bitch of yours that she's not won. You see she's taken everything away from me now so I've got to take something away from her."

He paused suddenly and stopped walking and appeared to be once again fighting an internal battle inside his mind. Then Jake shook his head and started pacing again as he continued his speech.

"I fucking love Tanya but now that's fucked, all by fucking Lucy. It's over Heather and I'm finished but she's taken my Tanya away from me and I'm going to take away someone she loves."

In the bedroom and inside his prison of flesh and bone John screamed. He heard the commotion and to his horror saw Jake dragging the limp body of Heather past his door, at first John thought she was dead but as soon as he heard Jake talking, to his relief John realized he'd just knocked her out. But now it was apparent that she was in grave danger and John was helpless, he was useless as his internal thoughts screamed out.

John's worse nightmare had come true and like the useless creature he was John had been unable to stop this turn of events. John had spent all his energy lately trying to will his body into functioning on at least a vocal level but now it was clearly too late. He felt more desperate and hopeless than ever.

Lucy was utterly deflated on her way back to the car, the only consolation was how amazingly well they'd taken the news that their lives were in such danger. It was almost as if they were actually excited by the whole situation like it gave them an adrenaline rush.

But that wasn't any comfort and to think that they could have utterly blown it because of a childish prank made Lucy's blood boil.

"He has probably not seen us Luce. We've still got every chance of catching him."

Wendy was trying to pick up her deflated partner but somehow the tiredness that had accumulated over the past week had hit the copper all at once and she was exhausted. Then the fucking last straw was an alert that rang out on Lucy's and Wendy's phones at the same time. It was a standard warning of an emergency in one of the care residences but they occasionally occurred and the police reluctantly attended. It was common for staff to trigger them somehow by accident so they didn't spark a dynamic response. Wendy just said.

"Fuck it we've done our bit tonight. Let someone else pick it up."

But Lucy found herself taking the phone out of her pocket and studying the screen, her facial expression triggered Wendy's interest. Lucy looked up and muttered.

"It's John's house and Heather is working tonight. I don't get it, she'd never accidentally activate this. I've moaned about them before and she's really nervous of the command words."

By now they were both in the car and Wendy had scanned into it's system. Wendy just shouted the command.

"Urgent response."

that only applied to emergency personnel and Lucy read out the address off her phone. They quickly strapped themselves in as the car slowly crept away until it sensed the seatbelts then they were thrust back in their seats as the electric motor without any hindrance accelerated to the fastest safe speed.

They both started to plan their response on arrival as the interlinked system commanded all cars in the route to give their vehicle priority. They would all pull over automatically and stop, any passengers would know that there's an emergency vehicle coming through.

Heather was understandably terrified and murmured under the strip of duct tape over her mouth, she was scared for her life but also aware that Jake was obviously also a rapist and Heather was lying face down tied up and wearing her familiar scrubs shorts and top that were both loose and easily bypassed. Heather realized that her lower buttocks had become visible as she'd been laid face down and felt a fearful tremble take her body.

Somehow Jake read her mind and seemed to enter his familiar sensitive phase. He walked over and sensitively pulled the shorts fabric down to cover her body saying.

"Don't worry Heather I'm not interested in fucking you, you're a friend and I couldn't do that to you."

Then he just looked at the knife in his hand for what seemed an age and said.

"I've just got to show that fucking bitch girlfriend of yours who's in charge then I'm going to."

The last word hung in the air as Jake fought his internal battle, then he continued.

"I can't let them catch me and it's just too fucked up to think of prison. Anyway they'd kill me themselves, it's a life for a life isn't it so I'm fucked either way."

Then he looked at Heather and frowned.

"But I'll make it nice and quick Heather as you've been nice to me."

That latest comment incurred a new bout of frantic struggling from the captive and she strained with all her strength against the cable ties that bound her wrists and ankles.

In these moments so much ran through Heather's mind, things like the fact that she'd not called her mother in too long and especially the argument she'd had with Lucy a week ago. How stupid she felt now in this horrific scene as a man she had defended paced up and down obviously fighting his conscience to let him do something that he didn't want to. If only Heather could talk she felt at least she'd have a chance of pleading for her life, if she could only take the side of whatever semblance of decency still fought on his good side against what was obviously a monster within. She thought of all that gentleness he showed to John but suddenly she thought about the beautiful red headed Amber so full of life and enjoying every minute only to have that vitality stolen. She thought about how Amber had had her throat slit from behind and Heather felt nauseous at the thought. Then Dawn sprung into her thoughts so clearly enjoying Jakes company while he ordered coffees, her beautiful eyes and young complexion framed by her long brown hair. So young and now never to experience life.

Suddenly there was anger instead of terror, how fucking dare this asshole presume to be able to have such monumental power over beautiful people. To be able to just take away not just a life but a future of a human being. There and then Heather decided she wouldn't plead for her life, she'd fucking fight for it.

Heather's train of thought was instantly broken by a voice she recognized even through the tinny microphone. The same microphone gave Lucy's voice authority that wasn't always apparent in their interactions. Lucy had tapped into the houses system on the way as a matter of standard practice and it registered Jake as well as Heather inside, she was frantically scared for her love but had to hold it together as a life so precious to her was relying on her now.

"Jake come out now mate, it's all over, we know it was you and were staking out the lifeguard. But you're smart buddy you worked that out didn't you? You've played us and won so now just come out and we'll talk."

Jake was visibly shaken but recovered well and gave Heather a conspiratorial look as if they were in on a joke that no one else understood.

"You've ruined everything Lucy. Everything good that has ever happened to me like Tanya and John. All because of you so now I'm going to take something from you that you love, because you've taken everything away from me."

Jake was obviously in his dark phase as he shouted a response and Lucy recognized that. It scared her to think what could be happening inside but she had to hold it together. She tried her best option and tried to plant an idea in his head that hopefully would be her best chance to help Heather.

"I understand Jake mate that you've been robbed of your break here and I don't want you to make a mistake. Heather is your friend but it's me you must hate as I'm the fucker who's ruined everything mate. Come out and you can see me and we can resolve our problem without Heather having to die. We both love her so let's leave her out of it."

Lucy was desperate to draw Jake outside and had every hope that his need to have her look Heather in the eyes as he killed her would be his weakness. She never expected him to take up her offer of hostage swap, just get him out of the house where Wendy who had positioned herself perfectly could have a shot.

Wendy had quietly slipped out of the car and placed herself on the side of the house so if Jake came out she'd hopefully have a clear shot at him without endangering his hostage. Wendy was relying on Lucy as the tactful person she is to talk him out.

For what felt like an age there was silence as Lucy stood by the car sweating in the warm evening air, distraught but determined to remain professional for Heather's sake. She had decided to give Jake time to think as she was desperately playing on his anger towards her and he needed freedom to come to a conclusion that would finish him.

Jake broke the reverie and not saying anything had taken Heather through to the front door having cut her legs free but as they walked through Lucy saw he had a knife to her lover's throat pressed so hard that there was a trickle of blood running down her neck. Out of the corner of Lucy's vision she could make out Wendy in her vantage point unlikely to be noticed by the man who had consumed so much of her energy in the preceding weeks.

Through the grey of night she could make out Wendy shaking her head and Lucy realized that her plan was failing, that knife that was obviously very sharp was to firmly against Heather's throat and clearly Wendy knew his physical reaction to being shot would kill Heather.

Lucy was defeated and she accepted it now as she looked her love straight in the eyes. Was this the last time that she'd see that passion for life in those beautiful eyes. Lucy did all she could do now and pleaded.

"Jake I'm begging you please don't kill her. There's got to be another way we can end this."

Tears were streaming down Lucy's eyes now as she threw her pistol into the car. She was no longer a police officer but instead she was a lover who was seeing her life unfolding in front of her.

To Heather's surprise she realized that Jake was crying too and not for the first time in this unfolding nightmare she wished she could talk to him. She could feel the cold blade against her throat and every breath felt like it was going to force the cut that would end her life. She didn't dare to move and was trying desperately to slow her breath to keep the knife from eating into her soft flesh.

Jake was battling more than ever now and his compassionate side was losing to the embittered demon that wanted so much to get back at Lucy and in fact life in general that had given him the chance of love just to take it away again. He knew death was going to be the inevitable outcome of this standoff but was he going to take Heather's life as a final act of defiance.

Then he saw the one sight that could possibly tilt his psyche towards the only honorable choice. The sight of Tanya screaming and desperately trying to get past the two officers who restrained her was just too much for his soul to bear. That pleading in those beautiful eyes and the desperation with which she fought her suppressors was all Jake needed to realize how this could only end.

As Heather felt the blade release it's pressure from her neck, time seemed to slow. Jake heard nothing now and all his mind could sense was Tanya's pleading eyes as she saw the knife retract from Heather only to bite into the throat of her love.

The blade cut deeply and swiftly as the stunned observers looked on in shocked horror and blood sprayed the collapsing Heather as her knees collapsed under her only to be drawn into the arms of Lucy who'd sprinted the distance between them.

Lucy held Heather in a Godlike grip as if to let go would be to let go of life itself as she kissed her over and over all over her face. Tears were flowing between both girls now to merge together as if they were becoming single fused together.

Wendy stood over the convulsing form of Jake gun pointed at him as if he still posed a threat as ridiculous as it was. Then Tanya who'd freed herself from her captors closed the distance and was soon holding her lover up in her arms and sobbing uncontrollably. Mercifully Jakes bleeding had slowed to a trickle as his life drained away in a blackish stream out of his gaping wound. His convulsions had slowed also too as if his body had given up and resigned itself to it's end. He sensed a certain feeling that had been missing in his life for years and just for a moment remembered the sensation of safety as he'd hidden under his bed as a child. With his last bit of strength Jake just managed to look up into Tanya's eyes then it was all over.

Revelation

The coffee kiosk had been rebuilt better than before and a big sign named it. "Dawn's Place."

In honor of the young girl who'd ended her life so tragically there.

The group had agreed to meet there and even Tanya had come out for the first time since that night almost two weeks ago. It was clear that she'd not been sleeping and Lucy imagined her crying at nights but that would heal in time. Heather sat next to Lucy with a scarf around her neck that hid a scar that would also heal and the other side of Heather was her mother Anna.

She'd come straight away to be with her daughter and had been ecstatic to meet Lucy in spite of the circumstances. Wendy sat opposite awkwardly as it wasn't in her character to mix with a famous person like Anna. And at the end was John who it seemed should be invited too.

Lucy was talking and for want of other conversation she explained what her and Wendy had found out about Jake.

"So apparently he used to work on the surveillance devices in his home State so it was no wonder he knew we were onto him."

Lucy explained that Jake had indeed been the serial rapist and murderer from the engineering State but had decided to leave after murdering the cop. Lucy remembered finding out about Mark the cop who'd been Jake's first victim and she felt a tinge of melancholy as she thought about the quiet introverted character she'd read about in the report. Tanya just looked up and said.

"He wasn't a monster to me you know. He really loved me I know he did."

At this Heather reached out and held her friends hand saying nothing. Lucy continued.

"He'd had a violent father it seems and as a kid was subjected to horrors that we'll never be able to imagine. But still to do those things?"

The last words hung in the air for an awkward few moments as everyone thought of Amber and Dawn then Anna broke the spell with a statement.

"Well I've decided to agree to drop the death penalty."

Everyone stared in shock as it was well known how Anna had always stood on the issue. She just smiled and said.

"I know now that he wasn't born a monster but life made him into one. But inside that tormented man there was a person who could love Tanya enough to defeat the monster. That's made me realize there's always hope and love can heal anything."

Anna just looked at Tanya and finally announced.

"We need screening to detect people like Jake and a facility to care for them and I'd like you to help me set it up Tanya."

Tanya lit up at the prospect and quickly accepted, as they talked about it the new barista bought a tray of drinks to their table and gently handed them out. She was a more mature lady than Dawn had been but her uniform showed off a gorgeous figure and as she handed out the coffees Lucy noticed a card with a name and phone number under hers which she secreted away as the barista winked at her. No one had seen but awkwardly Lucy felt the need to cut in with something that had been on her mind since that night but hadn't seemed urgent.

"What I don't understand is if Heather's mouth had tape on it all along and Jake sure as hell didn't, who set the alarm off?"

As a confused group looked at Lucy from the end of the table a strained croaky voice that had only been used once in many years said.

"Help, help, help."

THE END